Hidden

HIDDEN

Catherine McKenzie

New Harvest
Houghton Mifflin Harcourt
BOSTON   NEW YORK

First paperback edition 2015

This edition published by special arrangement with Amazon Publishing

For information about permission to reproduce selections from this book, go to www.apub.com.

www.hmhco.com

First published in Canada by HarperCollins Publishers Ltd

Library of Congress Cataloging-in-Publication Data
McKenzie, Catherine.
Hidden / Catherine McKenzie.
pages cm
ISBN 978-0-544-26497-7 (hardcover)   ISBN 978-0-544-46290-8 (paperback)
I. Title.
PS3613.C5558H53 2014
813'.6 — dc23   2013045634

Book design by Brian Moore

Printed in the United States of America
DOC 10 9 8 7 6 5 4 3 2 1

In memory of Rodrigo Contreras, who always told me to write what was true, rather than what was easy.

Hummingbird

Suppose I say *summer*,
write the word "hummingbird,"
put it in an envelope,
take it down the hill
to the box. When you open
my letter you will recall
those days and how much,
just how much, I love you.

—RAYMOND CARVER

Prologue

The last thing I had to do that day was fire Art Davies.

I hate firing people. Truly. Of all the things I hate about my job — and their number are legion — having to tell someone they can't come to work anymore is the worst.

But the consultants had been called in (again), and the recommendation was right there on page 94 of their 217-page PowerPoint presentation: *The accounting department is overstaffed by 1.2 people.*

1.2 people!

Who talks like that?

When I got the summary of the consultants' report — there's a guy in Reports whose entire job is, you guessed it, summarizing reports — I flipped to the page he'd so helpfully marked with one of those yellow stickies with a red pointing finger on it and my heart sank. Next to the recommendation that I reduce my department by 1.2 people were the words: *Art Davies??*

Art Davies?? I read again, and my heart fell a little further. Because those question marks might've seemed innocent, but they were as uncertain as a bullet to the chest.

Report Summarizing Guy is the direct liaison between management and the consultants. His job is to implement enough of their suggestions to justify the consultants' ridiculous fees, and enable management to make their own PowerPoint presentation for the board claiming that 74 percent of the recommendations had been implemented.

So job well done.

Art Davies. *Fuck*. Art Davies is the guy who hired me six years ago, back when the department was a third the size and there weren't any consultants around to notice that he wasn't really the guy you wanted to entrust hiring and firing to. Truth be told, Art wasn't the guy you wanted to entrust a lot of things to, but he was a great guy. Always in a good mood, quick to forgive your failings, always sending around some hilarious YouTube video right when your day was at the nadir of sucking.

I'd worked hard to help him escape the last two rounds of consultants. But he'd Peter-Principled himself to the head of the department, as guys like Art are wont to do, and when I'd been at the company enough years to satisfy the brass, we switched jobs. A couple years ago, I went up and he went down, and Art, good ole Art, took it so well you almost could've believed he didn't give a shit.

"Couldn't have happened to a better person," he said, slapping me on the back like we were on some sitcom. "Look forward to working for you."

I'd gone home in a deep funk and told my wife I wanted to quit. It took her hours to talk me out of it. Phrases like *great opportunity* and *think what we can do with the extra money* bounced off me, my resolve untouchable.

Until she said, "Art will probably be happier this way, you know. He never struck me as someone who wanted responsibility."

I didn't want to admit it, but she was right. Art probably would be happier if he didn't have to hire and fire people, or report to the board, or implement Report Summarizing Guy's suggestions.

So, I didn't quit. Instead, I traded desks with Art, putting the silver-framed picture of my family in the faint dust outline the picture of his family had left, and went back to work. And now it had come to this.

And I couldn't help wondering, if rising to the level of your own incompetence has a name, does having to fire the guy who hired you have one too?

When I'd phoned Tish to tell her about it, she'd made a small noise of sympathy. She knew how much I hated firing people.

"Why don't you let HR do it?" she asked.

"No, I can't do that."

"Why not? Management does it all the time. Trust me."

"Aren't you always calling them pussies when they do?"

She laughed, a melodious thing. "Yeah, yeah. I wouldn't call *you* that though."

"Sure."

"You know I wouldn't."

I sighed. "Okay, maybe not. But still."

"You have to do it."

"I have to do it."

"Let me know if you want some tips."

"You mean if I want your five-point plan for firing people effectively?"

"How the —" She clucked her tongue. "You little bastard. You read the whole report, didn't you? Unbelievable."

I smiled, even though she couldn't see it. "I like having all the information."

"Uh-huh."

"I have to keep ahead of those guys. You never know when they're going to train their high beams on you."

"You are so *busted*."

"I should get back to work."

"Have fun with your numbers!"

"You know I will!"

I hung up and ran my hand over my face. As much as I liked talking to Tish, it didn't change the fact that Art had to go, and I had to do it.

I spent Friday doing everything I could to put off the inevitable. But there wasn't anything I could do about Art's termination package, which was sitting on my desk. A blue folder full of helpful hints about what he might do with his future, and a single sheet of paper outlining his *non-negotiable* severance package. Fifty-six years old, twenty-two years with the company, not in management — thanks to me — meant he was getting 28.4 weeks of severance pay.

What was it with this company?

Couldn't they ever think in round numbers?

But no, they couldn't, because that would affect the pie chart, and that might end up with an eventual recommendation that *they* be *terminated??*

At four forty-five I gave one last sigh, and checked my email one last time. There was a message from Tish saying simply: *Good luck.*

Thanks, I typed back, *I'll give you the blow-by-blow later.* I hit Send, turned off my computer, put my hands on my desk and pushed myself up.

Inertia's a funny thing; even though it doesn't make any sense scientifically speaking, I swear I had to push harder than usual. My steps down the hall also seemed heavier, thicker, like the feeling you get in a dream when you're trying to run. Treacle air, molasses legs.

Art was sitting at his desk, an Excel spreadsheet open before him. He was squinting at the screen over the rim of his glasses. He never did get those bifocals his ophthalmologist had recommended a few months ago, and as per the package tucked under my arm, he had four weeks to do so or he was shit out of luck.

He glanced up at me. "Hey, Jeff, you think you could help me out on this one? I can't seem to get the columns to balance." He shook his head, half self-mocking, half puzzled.

"Why don't you leave it, Art?"

"I have to get it done today. It's on my goal sheet."

"It's okay. You don't have to do it."

"You're a braver man than—" He stopped abruptly as he caught sight of the folder. "That's not ... I mean ... they couldn't ... not after all this time ..."

"Why don't we go into the conference room?"

He rose to follow me, shocked into silence. If my footfalls seemed heavy before, my feet were cement blocks now. We made it into the conference room, and Art slumped into the nearest chair. I tried not to slump into the one across from him. *Project an air of confident compassion,* Tish had counseled me. But what did that mean, really? I had compassion all right, but confidence?

There was no way I was ever going to be able to look Art in the eye again.

Concentrate on outlining the details of the package. She'd said that too.

I opened the folder and read the text from the one sheet in a monotone. *"We're sorry to inform you that your position has been eliminated. In appreciation for your years of faithful service to the company, we're happy to offer you—"*

I stopped reading because Art was crying. Not sobbing, just a stream of tears flowing from behind his glasses and collecting on his shirt in spreading pools of wet.

Christ. What was I supposed to do now?

Sometimes a reassuring hand on the shoulder is appropriate. Tish's words kept coming. *Sometimes I let them cry, just being there for them.*

I opted for the latter, partly because I couldn't bring myself to move my hand, but also because it seemed like that kind of gesture should come with words, and I had no idea what to say. That it was all going to be okay? That he'd find something else, something better? That he wasn't going to lose his house, or have to raid his kids' college funds to avoid it? I couldn't say any of those things. It wasn't going to be okay, and he wasn't going to find something else.

Guys like Art never do.

Not at fifty-six.

Not when the guy firing you is the guy you hired.

I have to hand it to Art, though. Sixty seconds of silence was all it took to pull himself together.

He lowered his glasses and wiped his eyes with the back of his hand. "I expect you have to finish reading that."

"Yes. I'm sorry. It's—"

"Company policy."

"I'm sorry," I said again.

"It's okay, Jeff. Don't give it another thought."

I hung my head. Art was comforting me for firing him, and for a moment, it actually made me feel better. Was I the worst person ever?

"This will be over soon," I managed to get out.

"Thank you."

After I read through the rest of the miserly conditions of his package, Art had to suffer the final indignity of having me watch while he packed up his stuff. Back when I started here, a guy in Art's situation would've been given a proper send-off. They'd have called it "early retirement," and there would've been a nice lunch, maybe even a nice watch. Art would've gotten slightly drunk, and someone would've made a speech about how much Art had done for the company, told a funny story or two about his time here, and said he would be missed.

But that was a long time ago. Now, I pulled white, flat-packed banker's boxes from the supply closet, folding them together mechanically, wondering how many were required to pack away twenty-plus years.

It ended up being two.

When it came right down to it, Art traveled light.

He finished packing. I pulled a dolly out of the same closet and stacked his boxes on it over his protests that he was perfectly capable of doing it himself.

"I know you are," I said. "I want to do it, okay?"

"You're the boss."

He smiled sheepishly, a silent acknowledgment that none of this would be happening if I wasn't the boss. Or maybe it would. If I'd quit when I wanted to, someone else would've been promoted, or brought in from the outside, and they might not have protected Art from this day as long as I did. Who knows?

Either way, I still felt like an asshole.

Art picked up his light tan coat and slipped his arms into it. By tacit agreement, we left the building by the fire exit, which kept us from having to do the I'm-being-escorted-from-the-building walk past the still half-full office.

I followed him, wheeling the squeaky dolly behind me, hoping his boxes didn't tip over. I'd done my best to look away while he was hastily emptying his desk, remembering a story he was fond of telling about the first person he had to fire. Don Somebody, who was an old-school, three-martini-lunch guy whose lack of productivity in the afternoons had finally reached the notice of the higher-ups without any help from consultants. Art had tried to track the guy down before lunch, but he kept getting pulled into meetings.

He finally caught up with Don around three. He was standing next to a filing cabinet like the leaning tower of Pisa, and he didn't take the news well. After his swearing had been reduced to short, sporadic bursts, he'd agreed to clear out his desk. Don reached for the top drawer, but it was stuck. Art wasn't sure if Don was so drunk he forgot what was in the drawer or if he simply didn't care, but he lifted his foot off the ground and placed it on the desk for leverage, tugging on the drawer's handle for all it was worth. It came unstuck, and Don and the drawer tumbled backward as a stack of porno magazines fanned across the floor.

The way Art tells it, Don was completely unfazed. He collected his magazines and held them against his chest.

"Only thing I wanted to take with me, anyway," he said as he lurched out the front door.

I took the wheelchair ramp down its long, gently sloped diversion from the front doors. Art waited for me at the bottom, his face now expressionless, his posture screaming *Let this be over*. I followed him through the parking lot, past rows of cars backed carefully into their spots. He stopped in front of a silver Pontiac Vibe. The left side mirror was cracked.

"Kids," Art said. "You know how it is."

"Sure," I said, though, thankfully, Seth wasn't old enough to drive yet.

He popped the hatchback and I stacked his boxes inside, closing the trunk lid with a *thud*. We stood there awkwardly for a moment; was this a handshake occasion, or were we going to hug it out? Art solved my dilemma by reaching out his hand.

I took it. "You take care of yourself," I said. "Sorry about all of this."

"I'll be all right. Who knows? I might take up golf."

"Call me if you do."

He folded himself into his car. The engine started neatly and Art was composed enough to look left, then right, then left again before exiting his spot. I watched him drive slowly through the lot, toward the sun's setting orb, shielding my eyes against its glare. I'm not sure why, but I felt responsible for him while he was still on company property. Once he made it off the lot, I felt, he'd be all right.

After his car was absorbed into the end-of-day traffic, I turned back toward the building. The sun was glinting off the large windows, and I couldn't face going back inside. I decided, instead, to walk home. The air was warm, my car would survive the weekend where it was, and I had my phone. I could file my report on Art's firing on Monday.

I tucked my hands into my pockets and took a shortcut through the parking lot to the main road. Home was a mile away, and the sun felt warm on my face. I closed my eyes for a moment to concentrate on the feeling of it, and I guess that's why I never saw it coming.

PART 1

CHAPTER 1

Late for Dinner

Friday's an ordinary day at the daycare, if there is such a thing when you have thirty children between the ages of one and four under your supervision. There are no visits to the emergency room, despite the fact that Carrie Myers gets a penny stuck in her nose. The parents make their usual number of calls, from zero, in the case of the Zen 20 percent, to ten, in the case of Mandy Holden.

It's all because of the video cameras. Standard issue in daycares these days: twelve cameras (six in the baby room, six in the toddler room), all strategically positioned so any concerned parent can watch their child all day long via streaming video if they want to.

I'm glad Seth graduated prior to the invention of the Daycare Cam. I tell myself I'd be in the Zen 20 percent, but I have enough evidence to the contrary to know I would've had the camera feed open on my computer screen eight hours a day.

But since that was never a possibility, I can let myself feel annoyed when I catch a scuffle out of the corner of my eye on a toddler room monitor (they're arrayed around my desk like I'm the head of security, which, I suppose, I am), and I hear LT's wail through the wall moments later. I count down the seconds. Three, two . . .

"Hi, Mandy," I say as I pick up the phone, not bothering to pretend I don't know who's calling. Mandy Holden calls between five and ten times a day with questions ranging from her son LT's caloric intake to any incident she picks up on from the black-and-white video she watches all day long. (He's called LT after his father, Trevor, because he's "Little Trevor" in looks, expression, everything. Around here, when the parents aren't listening, he's referred to by the name he's earned: "Little Terror." Thank God the video plays like a silent movie.)

"Did you see that, Claire? That other kid —"

"His name is Kyle."

"Whatever. He pushed LT over! He needs a serious time out, and if you're not going to talk to his parents, I will."

"You know I can't call a child's parents every time there's an isolated incident."

"Isolated incident! He did the same thing last week."

"Actually, if you'll recall, it was LT who pushed Kyle that day. Kyle pushed back in retaliation."

"Retaliation my ass. I saw the whole thing."

"I'm sorry, Mandy, but I reviewed the video as per your request. LT was definitely the aggressor." In fact, at this very moment, LT's meting out his revenge on Sophie Taylor by stealing her snack. I'm sure I'll be getting a call about that too.

"Are you suggesting my son has anger-management issues?"

"Of course not. I'm simply saying that three-year-olds, particularly three-year-old boys, often get in scuffles. You can't read too much into it, no matter who the instigator is." I glance fondly at the picture of Seth at that age pinned above the monitors. He's smiling with a little-teeth grin, a perfect mixture of mischief and innocence.

"Instigator!"

I pause deliberately and lower my voice. "However, if you'd feel more comfortable removing LT from our care, you're perfectly entitled to do so."

I'm playing my trump card. Every daycare in town is full to the max. Mandy isn't going to give up her slot unless LT's taken out of here on a stretcher.

"I never said anything about taking LT out of Playthings," she huffs.

"Well, I seem to be getting a lot of these calls lately, and we do have an extensive waiting list."

I can hear her grinding her teeth. "I'm expressing *concern* for my *child,* Claire. I don't think that deserves a threat."

"Now, now, calm down. You know we all love LT. We don't want him to leave. I want you to be happy."

"I'm happy," she says. "LT is happy."

"That's great. So we don't have an issue?"

"No. Everything's fine. I have to get to a meeting . . ."

"Talk to you soon."

We hang up and I rest my head in my hands. I love running Playthings, I really do, but sometimes, particularly on the days when the Mandys of the world are in high gear, I wish I were back in the grown-up world, dealing with grown-up problems.

Of course, that world was full of adults complaining about the way their babies were being treated too.

Much to the chagrin of some of the parents, my lunch hour's a sacred thing. I don't accept calls — in fact, I can't be reached at all, and unless you're a fellow student at the music conservatory, it's like I don't exist.

This is a rule I implemented soon after I started Playthings, when I was still being swept by the waves of sadness connected to why I chucked my law career and started the daycare in the first place.

"You need to make time for something purely yours," my doctor told me when I complained about having trouble sleeping, and the general listlessness I still felt. "Something that brings you joy. Did you have anything in your life like that? Before?"

I could've taken the easy road and told him that what I used to do was run frantically between work and child care, that I hadn't had time for anything else. I hadn't had much time for me. Instead I said "Piano" in a small voice, even though I hadn't played in years. I no longer even owned a piano; we'd left it behind when we bought the house because it wasn't worth paying the extra money the movers wanted for something I touched only to wipe away the thin layer of dust that marred its glossy surface. It felt like an easy decision then, but now I wasn't so sure it was the right one.

"Piano it is," Dr. Mayer replied in a voice that brooked no opposition. And something about it, something about how it was connected to me *before,* caught hold in my brain.

I left his office and drove to the conservatory, which was located a few minutes away. I parked my car and looked through the windshield at the brightly painted building. Like Playthings, it was clearly a place for kids. I could see the child-painted mural inside made up of bass clefs and off-proportion guitars, a relic from my own childhood, many hours of which were spent in that very building. They gave adult lessons too, they always had, but the whole thing screamed Suzuki Method, and I almost didn't go in.

But I'd said I would, and so I did.

In a few minutes, I had a lesson scheduled for the next day with Connie. The receptionist had met my tentative request for Mr. Samuels, the kind teacher from my youth, with a blank stare.

Connie was a taciturn Germanic blonde who'd somehow ended up in Springfield. ("How?" I asked early on. "Complicated," she replied in a clipped tone that invited no further questions. "We work on scales today.") When she realized that I knew more than basic chord structures, she started giving me increasingly complicated pieces. And once my muscle/brain memory kicked in, I started to make something of them.

I kind of hated Connie in those early days. (I suspect the feeling was mutual.) I complained to Jeff one night, a few lessons in, that Connie had missed her calling as a drill sergeant.

"So quit," he said as he stripped down to his underwear and climbed under the covers. "If you're not having fun, fuck it."

I slipped in beside him, resting my back against the headboard. I flexed my fingers. They were full of a dull ache, like the early onset of arthritis.

"I kind of feel like it'll be fun eventually. Or maybe that's the wrong word." I paused, not knowing how to talk about looking for joy, and how it sometimes felt like it was just a few notes away.

"Well, she can't be the only game in town, right?"

He was right, but the two younger teachers I tried were so used to the kids-who-were-working-just-hard-enough-to-appease-their-parents that they'd grown soft, their fingers slow. When I sight-read the pieces they'd put in front of me, saying, "Now, this should be a real challenge," they'd get these funny looks on their faces, like *that wasn't supposed to happen*. One of them told me bluntly: "You should be playing with Connie." The other simply "forgot" our lesson one day and never called me to reschedule. Either way, I got the message.

So back I went and here I am, sitting on the hard piano bench in a room with perfect acoustics playing Debussy's *Reverie*. Connie's standing next to me, waiting to turn the page. My right foot's working the damper pedal, my left heel's keeping time. As the haunting melody tumbles out, I lean in, like I'm trying to catch the notes, gather them close. And now there's *un poco crescendo* and the music's flowing through my fingers, into my chest, suffusing my brain. The world is receding, receding, and yet I feel, for lack of a better word, alive.

When I get home around five, Seth's at the dining room table pretending to do his homework. But our in-need-of-replacement TV is still emitting that strange, staticky sound it does for the minute or so after it's been shut off, so I can tell what he's really been up to. Now what I need to decide is whether I'm going to call him on it.

Letting Seth be home alone for the hour or so between when the bus drops him off and when Jeff or I get home is a new thing we're trying since he turned twelve in February. He lobbied hard for the freedom, showing us that he was old enough, responsible. He kept his room clean, his grades went up, and he actually put down his PS-whatever-they've-gotten-to-now when we asked him to. We agreed to it on a trial basis until the end of the school year. If he doesn't screw up, we'll talk about making the arrangement permanent.

It's nice to have the extra money, though I miss the chats Ashley (Seth's long-term after-school babysitter) and I used to have at the end of the day, the updates she'd give me about how Seth acted when Jeff and I weren't around. As Seth gets older, the opportunities to observe him when he isn't aware of it are few and far between. Teacher-parent interviews, reports from his grandparents, my chats with Ashley, that's about it. Now, if I want to know what my son really thinks, I'll have to resort to spying.

Seth raises his head slowly and gives me the smile that melts my heart every time I see it. I've steeled myself against it to a certain extent (I had to), but it's worked on babysitters and women in grocery stores his whole life.

"Hey, Mom."

"Hey, buddy, how was school today?"

"Same."

"You have a lot of homework?"

"The usual. I'll be done soon."

"It needs to be done before dinner," I say in a tone that's way too close to my mother's.

"Mom, jeez, it's Friday."

I raise my hands in surrender and head to the kitchen, thinking about what's in the fridge, wondering whether I should cook or if we should go out for dinner. Jeff mentioned something last night about having to fire someone today, someone he was upset about. Did that mean he'd rather go out or stay in? Out is a distraction; in might mean him drinking too much and brooding about it.

Out it is, then.

I pick up the phone and dial his work number. When he doesn't answer, I try his cell. It rings and rings and then goes to voicemail. I glance at the clock. It's five fifteen, about the time he usually gets home on Fridays. Maybe his meeting went long; firings are never easy. And it's such a nice day out, he might've decided to go to the driving range and hit a few balls first. He doesn't like bringing bad work energy home if there's a way he can leave it behind.

I spend the next hour working on a new piece Connie's given me (Haydn's Sonata in F Minor), working out the fingering, letting the notes linger in my brain as I tap them out silently on the kitchen table, and now it's a quarter after six and Jeff really is late. Another round of calls to his cell and work phone get the same result as before, so I dig my cell out of my purse and text him: *Home soon?* I hold the phone in my hands, waiting for his reply, but none comes. Eventually, it powers down, like it's tired of waiting.

I feel a small trace of annoyance, but I brush it away. He often gets lost in whatever he's doing. His focus is something that astounds me still after all this time. Getting mad about it would mean I was mad at something fundamental about him, which I'm not.

But I *am* hungry. "Seth, do you want to order in?"

Seth comes bounding into the kitchen like an eager dog, lunging for the drawer where we keep the takeout menus. After a small skirmish, we decide on pizza, Seth promising that he'll eat at least one slice of vegetarian so he gets some vegetables today.

Jeff still isn't home by the time the pizza arrives, so we eat at the kitchen table while I gently probe Seth about his week. He dodges my questions like he always does, his mouth full of food, his answers a combination of "Jeez, Mom, honestly," "Dunno," and "All right, I guess."

I try not to take it personally. I try to remember how I was at that age, the secrets I kept.

I let Seth take his last piece of pizza into the living room while he finishes his homework. I bring our dishes to the sink, which sits in front of a window overlooking our front lawn. I'm washing the dinner plates when I notice that it's almost seven thirty, and now maybe I am mad that Jeff hasn't even bothered to check in.

A police cruiser slows to a stop in front of our house. There are two uniformed officers in the car. The one I know, whose name I can't bring to mind though we went to high school together, is sitting behind the wheel. He's gripping it like he's girding himself to do something unpleasant. I watch them, curious, as they slowly exit the car, two burly men. I wonder if the neighbors' teenage daughter is in trouble again, but it isn't their walkway they're lumbering up; it's mine. My mind jumps to Seth. What could he possibly have done that's worthy of police attention?

Then my heart clenches with the sudden knowledge of why they must be here. My hands sit in the sudsy water, turning gently to prunes.

They're at the front door, and still I can't move. They don't look my way, just straight ahead, and push the bell, harder than they should. The chiming gong bounds through the house, a brassy sound I've never liked.

All this happens in real time, not slowed down or speeded up, only the time it takes for them to walk to the front door and ring my bell, but it's enough time.

"Mom!" Seth yells. "You going to get that?"

My brain is screaming *Go to the door! Don't let Seth be the one who answers it!* but I can't bring myself to move. In this, of all moments, I can't bring myself to protect my son.

"Really," I hear him mutter as he clicks off the TV and shuffles toward the front door.

Now my feet are moving, my mouth is open, but I can't get the words out. I don't beat Seth to the door, which is swinging open, revealing the officers. And my son, my beautiful, intelligent son, sees the unpleasant task in their faces, gives me a look of horror, and runs.

CHAPTER 2

How the Promise Gets Broken

"Have I got this right, Tish?" my best friend, Julia, asks in a distracted tone. "You're saying you haven't heard from this guy in a couple of days?"

I'm lying on my dining room floor, the phone receiver cradled under my ear. I can feel the itchy wool rug beneath me, and the hardness of the wood floor it covers. There's a string of old spiderwebs dangling from the plaster cornice on the ceiling. I have no idea how long it's been there. I don't usually lie on my dining room floor. I don't usually have a reason to. But my heart feels like there's a hand holding it, and that hand is squeezing, squeezing, so:

"It isn't the number of days, really, but that he hasn't answered my email—" I stop myself before I add an "s." I have to be careful here.

There's a hint of movement on my leg. It's a small black ant. A line of them is marching across the floor from the kitchen. I don't know where they're going, but I seem to be in their way.

"I still don't get it. What's the big deal?" Julia asks. Her three-year-old calls for her in the background. His father shushes him.

And that's the million-dollar question, because the big deal is what took me four hours to place this call. The big deal is what I'm still not sure I can say out loud, though I've got Julia on the line.

"Tish," she says when I've been silent too long. "This really isn't a good time . . ."

Here's my out. I could let her go, give in to the fact that she doesn't really want to know what I called to tell her. She might even forget we had this conversation. The taste might remain on her brain, but the substance would be gone, like the thought you have right before sleep, the invention, the perfect line, the thing you ought to write down and never do.

I could let her go, but I don't. Because I'm drowning here, on the floor, with the ants marching across me, the phone slick in my hand. If someone doesn't pull me out, I may be lost forever.

"Please. Don't hang up."

"All right. Give me two minutes. Don't go anywhere."

I almost laugh. If I could go somewhere, anywhere, I'd already be there.

I hear the phone click onto the kitchen counter, and the brief negotiation with Ken about taking care of Will for a few minutes.

"Yes, it's important," she says, followed by a mumble of assent.

I listen to Will's wail as his mother leaves the room, and Ken's curse and immediate apology, like his three-year-old son would be mad at him for swearing.

"Okay," Julia says a minute later. I can hear the silence behind her. "I'm in the study with the door closed. What the hell's going on?"

I felt the first flutter of worry Friday night.

After dinner and a movie with Zoey on the couch while Brian worked late, I realized Jeff had never written to say how the firing had gone. He'd been fretting about it so much, I was sure he'd be eager to tell me all about it. But when I checked my email, there was just the message he'd sent earlier in the day.

How'd it go? I typed, and waited a minute for his response. When it didn't come, I put my phone down and gave my attention back to Zoey, who was impatient to tell me the problems she had with *Letters to Juliet*, the movie we'd watched.

Brian got home while Zoey was on point #7.

"And why do the main characters always have to hate each other at the beginning of the movie? Like, hello, red flag. It's so obvious they're going to get together."

She stopped her tirade to run to the door and jump on Brian's back, insisting he take her for a lap around the house even though, at eleven, she knows she's kind of too old for it.

Brian dropped his medical bag and complied. Zoey whooped with delight. I followed them through the kitchen to the dining room, and up the stairs to her bedroom. It was getting late, close to ten, and Brian ended his tour by dumping Zoey on her bed and pointing to the red, glowing numbers on the clock next to it.

"You need your sleep, kid," he said, his voice gravelly from a long day. "Big weekend."

"I know."

He rumpled her hair, and I kissed her cheek. Together we said, "Don't read too late," then we laughed, the three of us, the laughter following us down the hall to our bedroom.

The sight of our soft king-sized bed made me exhausted. I began to undress.

"Late one tonight," I said.

Brian loosened his tie. "Sorry about that. Harry's kids had croup again."

"You must be the last doctor in the world who still makes house calls."

"I hope not."

I gathered my clothes together and dropped them into the hamper. Brian came up behind me and slipped his arm around my waist, placing his lips against my neck. I leaned against him, briefly, trying to summon the energy to return his kiss, finish loosening his tie.

"I'm exhausted," I said.

"I can be quick."

I looped my hands around his neck. He was smiling, but I knew he meant it too.

"Why don't we wait until it doesn't have to be quick?"

"I'm going to hold you to that."

"Good." I kissed him, pressing my lips tightly against his to seal our deal. "You coming to bed?"

"I think I'm going to eat something first, watch the news."

"Don't stay up too late. Big day tomorrow, right, kid?"

He smiled. "It is."

We kissed again briefly and separated, me headed for my nightly ritual in the bathroom, he to the leftovers waiting for him in the fridge. A few minutes later I slipped between the cool sheets and rested my head on my pillow. I didn't even bother reaching for my book. Instead, I curled onto my side, and the last thing I remember thinking is *I hope Jeff is doing okay.*

Saturday morning passed quickly while I made sure Zoey and Brian had everything ready for their overnight trip to the Spoken Word Regionals, a three-hour drive away.

Zoey's dress needed a last-minute ironing, and she's always pretty particular about what she eats on competition days. It was almost eleven by the time they'd packed themselves into the car. Brian was going to have to drive faster than I liked to think about to get there on time. I watched him back out of the driveway, waving at them through the kitchen window. Zoey had that determined look she always gets, her game face I call it. Brian was wearing his game face too, a mixture of nervousness and pride, similar to my own, I expect.

They navigated successfully down our street and their fate was out of my hands. I went to the hallway and dug around in my purse for my phone. I had three new emails, but none from Jeff. I felt a tinge of disappointment, surprise, then that worry again.

I racked my brain, trying to remember if he'd told me about something that might explain the absence of an answer. I hesitated for a moment before texting him because we almost never do, but I was worried the firing had gone badly, that he was taking it too much to heart.

Everything go okay? I typed, listening to the words whoosh away from me. Again, I held the phone in my hand for a minute or two, waiting for a response, but there was nothing. I put it down eventually and tried to put it out of my mind. He'd answer when he could.

But he didn't.

I spent most of the day cleaning the house with increasing obsessiveness. The air smells very clean as I lie here, trying to tell Julia enough to justify this phone call without telling her everything.

As the hours crept by, I began to carry my phone around like a talisman. My heart leapt every time it pinged with an email or text, but they were never from Jeff. A few were from Brian and Zoey, updating me on their progress, letting me know they'd gotten there, that her first round had gone well. These I responded to. The rest, I ignored.

But what I couldn't understand, and can't explain to Julia, is what made me so worried, why that worry grew as the hours passed, why it became so all-consuming. All I can come up with is that it isn't just the silence but its quality. Something about our usual connection seems missing, and that absence is tugging away at me. Part of me knows I'm being completely irrational, and the other part is terrified I'm not.

My phone pinged for the last time last night around nine. My breath caught. It was a Google Alert for Jeff Manning. My hands shook as I opened it, but it was nothing. Some other Jeff Manning was getting married. How nice for him. My panic subsided, and I smiled as I remembered setting up the alert in the first place.

It was right around the time of a big mine disaster that dominated the news. In the buzz of media attention, it came to light that one of the miners had a wife and a girlfriend. Jeff and I were emailing about it at work.

Not the best way for something like that to get out, he wrote.

Uh, no. "Something like that." Funny.

I'm glad I amuse you.

I keep thinking about the girlfriend.

What about her?

Well . . . and okay, this may be stupid or paranoid or whatever, but . . . I keep thinking about how the only reason she even knows what happened to him is because it's this big media event. If he'd disappeared or died for some ordinary reason, it's not like anyone would tell her.

I sense a deeper thought here.

Yeah, well . . . how would I know if anything ever happened to you?

Inter-office memo.

Ha!

I went back to work, but the idea stuck with me. How *would* I know if something ever happened to him? Not that anything should, but still.

Have found a solution, I wrote a few days later.

Solution for?

Miner's girlfriend problem.

You worry too much.

Like you're the first person to tell me this?

What's the solution?

Google Alert.

You think technology is the solution to everything.

Because it is.

So I'd set up a Google Alert for Jeff Manning, the theory being that my friend Google would crawl the net for me and send me a message any time his name was mentioned online.

It ended up being a joke between us. Turns out there are a lot of Jeff Mannings out there. One won a blue ribbon at a state fair for having the biggest pumpkin. One was a professional downhill skier who liked to party when he wasn't in training. There were even Jeff Manning obituaries once in a while, old men dying peacefully or after a long illness. And once, tragically, a young boy.

Whenever there was a particularly funny one, I'd let Jeff know what his namesake was up to. If one of them died, we'd hold a minute of silence, or make an anonymous donation to the charity specified in the obituary. A really big one in the case of little Jeff Manning.

But underneath, there was always that niggling worry, one I couldn't even explain to myself, especially since it was so close to the feeling I had about Zoey sometimes, particularly when she was a baby and I was sure I was going to drop her at any moment.

After getting the false Alert, a weariness passed through me, the product of tension and little food. I chewed my thumb, contemplating whether I should send one more message. In the end, I couldn't help myself from emailing: *Worried. Please answer whenever you get this.* I didn't bother waiting for a response. Instead, I brought the phone upstairs with me and left it on my nightstand.

If it buzzed in the night, I wanted to know.

Today, I woke with the sun, exhausted and certain in the knowledge that there was no message.

Lying there in bed, I flipped through the possibilities like they were index cards. One or two of them made me angry, and the rest made me so sad I'd flick them away only to have them return moments later. Others seemed irrational, but what if they weren't? I don't possess any special immunity against bad things happening to someone I care about because I can't handle it.

And all the while, I couldn't help thinking about the deadline, still weeks away. Clearly, I'm not ready for it. Maybe he figured that out? Maybe this is like agreeing to count to three, but dunking your kid on two, so they don't see it coming? Well, fuck that. If this ends up being some kind of test, I'm going to kill him.

A final check of my phone confirmed what I already knew. He hadn't answered. Again, I couldn't keep myself from emailing: *Really worried. Please, please reply.* After I sent it, I didn't know what to do with myself. All I knew was I had to talk to someone. I had to try to steal someone's rationality. But talking would mean telling, and I struggled with that for the next several hours as I wandered aimlessly around the house. Eventually, I decided I didn't have a choice. Someone had to be told, and Julia was the only possibility.

So here I am, on the floor, phone in hand, putting out as few words as possible, trying to downplay, to couch, to duck and cover. But Julia isn't stupid. And after I hem and haw, she asks the question I was trying to avoid all along.

"Tish, are you having an affair with this man?"

CHAPTER 3

Homecoming

I met Claire soon after I moved home from college.

I grew up in Springfield, an almost-a-city town set in the middle of a vast plain of flatness. They used to grow wheat here a century ago, before the land was used up and the farmers moved farther west. Old barns and grain silos still dot the landscape, empty now except for the history they hold.

My parents' house was equidistant between the only wooded area in town — called, imaginatively, the Woods — and the public golf course. I spent an equal amount of time at both, allowed by my parents to roam free with my older brother, Tim. We learned to swim in the cold pools in the river, and played Pirates, Capture the Flag, and a game of our own invention called "You Can't Get There from Here" in the Woods.

When Tim tired of me, I'd sling a bag full of my dad's cast-off clubs over my shoulder and walk to the golf course. Everyone knew me there, and many of the grown-ups would let me join them, cheering me on if I made a good shot, helping me search for my ball in the tall grasses that waved along the side of the course when I didn't.

Winter meant snow forts and snowball fights, skating on the rink my dad made in the backyard: Fueled by his dreams of having at least one son in the NHL, he'd be out there late most nights smoothing the surface by applying a fresh layer of water with a garden hose. It also meant shuffling to the golf course to look out over the snowy undulations and frozen water hazards, waiting longingly for spring.

When it was time to apply to college, Tim was already in his second year at State, but I decided to cast a wider net. I had good grades, so why not? And if the schools I applied to tended to have less winter and be in proximity to affordable golf, or have — nirvana — their own golf course, all the better.

I got into a smaller liberal arts college several degrees latitude south, and my parents were amenable to helping me out, so that's where I went.

I came home six years later.

I knew a few things about myself by then. The first and foremost was that I was never going to make the PGA Tour. Okay, I already kind of knew that, but a guy can dream, can't he? But I also knew I didn't want to be anything I'd imagined being as a boy — fireman, teacher, lawyer. What I really enjoyed was numbers, the certainty of 2 + 2. In my junior year, I'd switched from history to accounting, stuck around for a few extra years to get my CPA, and worked on how to make "I'm going to be an accountant" sound intriguing enough to get a couple girls to go home with me.

As much as I'd enjoyed my time away, I also knew I wanted to go back to Springfield.

Maybe I was homesick, but I felt like I knew that most of all.

After I got back, I spent enough time living with my parents to change my leisurely plan of looking for an apartment while I set up my accounting practice into a thing of urgency, then borrowed some money from them to buy a condo in a newer building close to what passed for downtown in Springfield.

And that's how I met Claire.

I needed a lawyer to work out the paperwork for the condo, and to set up my new business. A bit of asking around told me that James & Franzen were the best, so I called to make an appointment. The receptionist asked me if I minded working with one of the newer members of the firm.

"Sure, that'd be fine."

"Great. Claire James has an opening tomorrow at eleven thirty, would that do you?"

The name seemed familiar, but I couldn't place it. "It would."

The next day I put on a pair of pressed khakis and a sport coat — a hand-me-down from my father that had the golf course's crest embroidered above the right-hand pocket — and strolled across the town square. As I passed person after person I knew, and smiled and nodded and said, "Yup, I'm back for good, you need an accountant, you give me a call," I wondered what it was about the name Claire James that was so familiar, but I still couldn't get there.

I cast those thoughts aside as the Claire James in question came out to meet me. She was about my age, maybe a bit older, and pretty. Wearing a navy-blue skirt and jacket, she had chestnut hair that touched her shoulders, pale blue eyes that were a little close together above a straight nose, and medium-full lips covered in a light gloss. She smiled and her whole face lit up, exuding warmth and confidence.

I felt tongue-tied as I followed her down the corridor. Although I was still in the process of breaking up with my college girlfriend, Lily — she didn't want to move to Springfield, but we weren't quite prepared to give up on the idea of us having a future together — I knew immediately that I really wanted to ask Claire out.

But first, we had some business to attend to.

"Did Tim give you my name?" she asked as she sat down behind her desk, kicking off an uncomfortable-looking pair of high-heeled shoes. "You don't mind, do you?"

My brain fogged with confusion until I realized she was referring to her stockinged feet.

"No, of course not. But how do you . . ."

Her face fell as memory clicked into place. Claire *James*. Shit. This was Tim's law school girlfriend, who happened to be from Springfield too. The one I didn't meet because Tim and I never seemed to be home at the same time anymore. The one I never met before that because she went through the private school system and was Tim's age. And, most importantly, the one Tim broke up with around graduation and had been tight-lipped about ever since.

"Oh," was all I could manage.

"I'm guessing that means Tim didn't send you?"

"I'm sorry, I called the general line and they put me on to you."

"Why are you apologizing?"

"For not making the connection, I guess."

"That's all right. Have you heard from Tim lately?"

She was trying to act casual as she asked this, but the way her neck flushed gave her away. Problem was, I hadn't spoken to Tim lately. None of us had. He'd fucked off a few months after finishing law school to take a "spin around the world," and his communication since then had been infrequent and short. *In Spain* read one postcard, sent from Seville and depicting a bullfight. *Old buildings.*

"Not really."

"Me neither."

"If this is going to be awkward, I'm sure I can find someone else to handle my stuff."

"No, no," she said, and waved off my suggestion. "That's all *done* with. And it's not your problem."

But it was.

When I was twelve, my dad decided it was time to give me the Talk.

I'd been caught folding my stained Matchbox-car sheets into the washing machine early one Sunday morning. I stood there, frozen, while my dad watched me over his coffee cup with a look of deep understanding. My ears went hot, feverish. I thanked God my mom was a late sleeper.

He beckoned me into the kitchen, poured me a small cup of joe, and stumbled his way through a version of the facts of life that was so alien to what I already knew from TV and the schoolyard I was pretty sure he didn't know what he was talking about.

When he finally let me go hide in my room, Tim came to find me. Tim was fourteen. He'd grown. I had not. The weight of him as he sat down on the side of my bed reminded me of my father. But his voice still cracked.

"Nice try, loser."

I pulled the sheet down. He was smirking at me, but in a friendly way.

"Ah, fuck off."

"You gotta wait till they're out of the house."

"I was kinda figuring that out."

"Dad talk to you?"

"Yeah."

"Predictable."

"Whatever."

"Bet you can't wait to get a girl now."

His mild sarcasm made me wonder whether what my dad had said might've been accurate after all.

"No way. Girls are gross."

"Right. Till they aren't."

"Huh?"

"What do you think you were dreaming about, dummy? Unless . . ."

I picked up my pillow and threw it at him. "I'm not a homo."

"Sure."

"I'm not."

"So girls won't be gross forever, then."

I thought about the girls in my class. How my friends and I made fun of their "best-friend" necklaces. How they held hands when they walked down the hall. How they'd cry over the breakup of their friendships.

Who needed that kind of drama?

"Maybe."

"Trust me."

"What do you know about it?"

"More than you, Mr. Matchbox Car."

"I've asked Mom like a thousand times to get me new sheets."

"Well, maybe she will now that you're a man and all."

My stomach clenched in panic. "Dad's not going to tell Mom, is he?"

"I think you can count on it."

I pulled the covers back up over my head. Tim left me in my fortress of embarrassment wondering whether what he'd said about girls was right, but it soon became clear. Almost overnight, girls stopped being "girls" and became Sara, Allison, and Christie. And the scuffle that resulted a couple months later from John kissing Brendan's "girlfriend" led us to adopt the Rules.

Well, there was just the one rule, really: Once a girl was stupid enough to go out with one of us, she was off-limits.

Forever.

Because forever seemed like a real thing then, something that had to be respected.

Loyalty to my brother — and the certain knowledge that acting on my growing feelings for Claire would be a gross violation of the Rule — kept me from asking her out for months.

I held it in check while she helped me buy my condo and set up my business and became a friend. I worried that becoming her friend would mean I'd lose my chance to be something more. I spent way too much time thinking about the whole thing, to be honest, which really wasn't like me. With the exception of Lily, I'd flitted in and out of relationships without much thought, and had been attracted to girls who I instinctively knew would tire of me in short order or wouldn't be that upset if I tired of them.

So I knew I was in trouble.

I just didn't know how much.

In the midst of all this thinking, I finally broke up with Lily, driving twelve hours to do it in person. Six hours there, a two-hour prolonged and tearful — on her part — conversation, then six hours back, knowing I'd done the right thing but still feeling shitty. Would I have tried harder to work things out if Claire wasn't in the picture? But Claire wasn't really in the picture, so why was I acting as if she were? My brain wheeled round and round until I took the exit off the highway for home and my spirits began to lift.

I was twenty-four, free, and half in love with my brother's ex-girlfriend. I did a few stupid things to try to get her out of my system. Like hanging out in the local hookup bar, taking home girls I knew I was never going to ask out again, who'd become someone I avoided in the grocery store. I was having fun, but I was brooding too. Assuming Claire did want to go out with me, how was I ever going to get past the Tim factor?

Then she did it for me.

About six months after we first met, we were having lunch at a deli that had opened recently near her office.

I'd received a postcard from Tim. *Welcome to Coolangatta* it read, with the words *Learning to scuba* written on the back. I had to look up the name to figure out he was in Australia. It was in my pocket, and I was fingering it nervously, wondering if I should show it to her. I eventually decided to do it, and tried to act casual as I pulled out the slightly moist card and slid it across the counter.

"Heard from Tim," I said, taking a large bite of my sandwich.

"Oh?"

She picked up the card, staring at the azure ocean, the cloudless sky, the red sand beach. I watched her out of the corner of my eye as she turned it over and read the words on the back.

"Well, that's that, then." She pushed it back to me.

"What's that?"

"Tim wanted to go to Australia. That's why we broke up."

"You didn't want to go?"

She shook her head, looked away.

"I know how that feels." I took a sip of my Coke to wet my drying throat. "Lily, I told you about her, right? Anyway, she didn't want to move here. So . . ."

"So?"

"We broke up."

"I heard."

I wondered what else she'd heard. Not too much, hopefully.

"Small towns."

She played with her napkin. "The funny thing is, I would've gone with him if he'd really wanted me to, but the minute I expressed some reluctance he blew it up into this big thing, like he was looking for an excuse to break up."

"Idiot."

"Pardon?"

"I said, my brother's an idiot."

"Yeah, well, some things aren't meant to work out. I mean, if he really loved me, we would've figured it out, right?"

Did that mean I hadn't really loved Lily? Because I thought I had. It certainly felt like love during the good parts. But one thing was certain: Claire loved Tim enough to move around the world for him. I'd better put my dreams away if I knew what was good for me.

She put her hand on my knee. Thoughts of Tim receded.

"You won't tell Tim about any of this, will you?"

"Of course not."

"Thanks, Jeff, you're a really good friend." She leaned forward and kissed me on the cheek, then pulled back, looking confused. "I'm sorry."

"No, don't be. I . . . I've wanted that for a while now."

"You've wanted me to kiss you on the cheek?"

"Among other places," I said, hoping I was striking the right flirty tone, my heart racing against my chest.

"Well, then, maybe we should do something about that," she said slowly.

"What did you have in mind?"

She thought about it for a moment. "Do you like Asian food?"

As I stood in the shower two nights later, a riot of rationalization skipped through my brain. *He* broke up with her. *She'd* asked me out. He'd barely communicated with any of us for months. Maybe he was never coming back. Besides, if I even wanted to ask his permission, he'd made that impossible. We had no address, no phone number, no way of contacting him. He'd untethered himself from us. How could he complain if things happened? How could he be surprised if life moved on?

I toweled off and climbed into fresh clothes: a new pair of jeans, a collared shirt, and my trusty blazer. Maybe it was too dressy for the occasion, but it felt like a time to dress up.

I drove to Claire's, wishing I'd taken the time to clean out the inside of my beat-up Toyota. She was waiting on the stoop — something I took as a good sign — wearing a wool skirt and a turtleneck sweater. She had on some makeup and her hair was shiny. I was glad I'd gone with the blazer.

We went to dinner at the only Thai restaurant in town, and the conversation flowed in an easy way I hadn't felt in a while, maybe never. She teased me about my lack of knowledge of Asian cuisine, and I ate whatever she put in front of me, struggling with my chopsticks. Some of it was slimy, and some of it was too spicy for my taste. I washed it all down with too many Chinese beers, and by the end of the meal I was slightly drunk.

After dinner, we took a walk through the town square. The bare trees had lights strung through them, a leftover from Christmas. They glinted off Claire's hair, and to me, she looked perfect. It was coming on spring and the air was warm, though there was still some snow on the ground. A gentle breeze blew through the trees, and I breathed in the loamy smell of wet earth, dead grass, and old snow. I'd be golfing in a month if I was lucky.

I felt light on my feet and happy.

Happy in my soul.

Claire strolled next to me, her hands clasped behind her back, like she was keeping them to herself. I wanted possession of her hand — I wanted more than that, but the hand would do for now — so I said something silly to distract her, and it worked. Her arms fell to her sides and I seized the opportunity. She started slightly, looking down at her soft white hand encased in mine, then up at me.

By the smile on her face, I knew we'd be kissing soon.

Any moment now.

Any moment now.

CHAPTER 4

A Shot through the Heart

One of the police officers (the one I can't place) tells me he'll check on Seth. The other leads me to the couch, giving me the barest of details before asking if he can call anyone for me. I mutter something about the emergency contact list taped next to the kitchen phone. And all the time I'm feeling stunned, detached, a million miles from the tragedy that's unfolding in my house like space after the big bang.

Time passes. People start arriving. My mother. My father. My doctor. Friends, friends, friends, until the house is full, there have never been this many people in the house, I couldn't get away from them if I tried.

At one point I begin calling Seth's name and my mother, I think it's my mother, shushes me and says Seth's fine, Seth's being taken care of, what do *I* need? I give her a look that says, *Are you seriously asking me that?* She knows what I need. Everyone knows what I need, but I'm not getting that again. Not ever.

More time passes, and now I have to go to the bathroom, but I seem glued to the couch, kept there by the prison of people talking low, some fighting back tears, some crying openly. They all want to hug me, but the feel of their skin on mine, the words they say in my ear, make me feel worse. I'm convinced in this moment that if I choose to, I can leave my mind and never come back again.

A family friend and my lifelong doctor, Dr. Mayer, sits next to me and presses something into my hand. Pills. I don't want to take them, but he guides my hand to my mouth and gives me a glass of water to swallow them down with. I do it and he nods approvingly. He takes me by the elbow, maneuvering me through the throngs of people (do I really know this many people?) and up to my bedroom.

Without asking, he takes me into the bathroom and suggests I use the facilities. He leaves me alone long enough to pee, and to register, as I stand up, that whatever he gave me is acting fast, that I really am in space now.

I wobble as I come out of the bathroom. Dr. Mayer catches hold of me and walks me to my bed, removes my shoes, pants, and sweater. He folds me into the covers, and in an instant all is black but the stars.

I spend most of the weekend in bed, in proper pajamas now, courtesy of my mother. Every couple of hours someone comes to check on me, or bring me food I can't swallow, or more pills, which I reluctantly do. My bedroom's been transformed into a hospital ward, all the comings and goings, the checking on the patient. It reminds me of the days I spent in the hospital after Seth was born by emergency Caesarean. It was too loud to sleep, and food and meds were pushed on me there too. All I wanted to do then was hold Seth, and that's the same now. He's spent the last two nights sleeping next to me, in Jeff's place, his body in the same half-pike position his father sleeps (slept, slept, it's slept now, Jesus) in.

My sister, Beth, arrives Sunday night. I can hear her downstairs talking to my parents, asking how I'm doing. Unlike everyone else, she makes no effort to talk low, despite my mother's shushing. Instead, she takes the stairs two at a time and, in an instant, she's climbing into bed next to me fully clothed, curling onto her side like we used to do as kids.

"You look like shit," she says.

"God, Beth. Jeff—"

"It's awful, so awful, I'm barely functioning myself. But I think you might feel better, I truly do, if you get up and take a shower, maybe change into some real clothes. Eat something. Mom tells me you haven't had anything since Friday."

"Not hungry."

"Will you try, sweetie? For me?"

I glance at the bedside clock behind her. Two more hours until someone arrives with the magic pills that keep the world at a safe distance.

"Funeral pills," Dr. Mayer called them yesterday when I asked what they were. Then he went bright red, like he couldn't believe the words had escaped his mouth. He apologized, but I told him it was okay. I mean, it wasn't, it was never going to be okay, but there's going to be a funeral, and as much as I thought I was done with taking pills, it's clear to me now that I'm going to need them to get through it.

"I don't have anything to wear," I say to Beth.

"Of course you do, hon. You've got a closet full of clothes."

"I meant for the . . ." I pause to gulp in air, not sure I can get the word out. "Funeral."

Beth brushes my tears away. "Oh, Claire. I'm so, so sorry."

Sunday night is a fog of drugs and bad, vivid dreams. Seth's still sleeping with me, and though he hasn't said much, his sleep speaks for him. He thrashes and kicks and moans, behavior I've never seen before, not even when he was a tiny thing. I rest my hand on his chest, above his heart, and it seems to calm him. But if I drift away and my hand follows suit, it's only minutes until he's back at it again, a whirling dervish of grief who doesn't have access to the medicinal solace I've been allowed.

When I asked Dr. Mayer if something could be done for Seth too, he told me it wasn't standard procedure. Kids are resilient, he said.

Meaning what? I almost asked.

And if I need the drugs, what does that make me? Weak? Pliable?

All I know is that we're both broken and it's too soon to tell if it's beyond repair.

I open my eyes in the early light of morning. Seth's face is inches from mine. He's also awake. He looks so like Jeff in this moment, same chocolatey-brown eyes, same dark, unruly hair. I stop myself just in time from using his name.

"Were you having a bad dream, baby?"

Usually this term of endearment is met with an eye roll and a reminder to *never* call him that in public, but today all he says is "Yeah."

"Do you want to talk about it?"

"Nah."

"Maybe if you told me, it wouldn't seem so bad?"

"Don't think so."

"How do you know if you don't try?"

A tear rolls down his face. "Because when I woke up the dream was still true."

Whatever pieces of my heart that are still intact break in this instant. I can't make things better for my son. I can't take away his nightmares because life is a nightmare now.

Jeff, Jeff. How could you leave us like this?

"I'm sorry, baby."

He buries his head in my neck. We lie there like this for a while, the room brightening around us, the day marching on, even if we're frozen.

Around seven, Seth sits up abruptly. "I want to go to school."

"I don't think that's a good idea. Not yet."

"But there are so many people here, all the time."

"Won't school be full of people?"

"I'm used to that."

"Things might be different now."

"I think I'll feel . . . better there than here. Can I? Please, Mom?"

I nod. "Don't feel like you have to stay if things are hard, okay?"

"Okay. Are you going to be all right?"

"Beth's here."

He kisses me on the cheek. "Thanks, Mom."

Seth gets up. I stay in bed, wishing he hadn't wanted to go. I keep imagining what it will be like for him, wondering (because I can't keep my mind from going to dark places) whether it will be like my first day back at work after we lost the baby.

· · ·

About four years ago, we got pregnant again. We'd been trying for years. We never intended such a large gap between Seth and our second. We'd even discussed having three, but we tried and tried and nothing happened. We saw Dr. Mayer. He tested both of us and found no medical reason for my inability to conceive. These things take time, he said, sometimes. We shouldn't stress about it. In fact stressing about it would be a bad thing. Stressing about it could make it not happen.

But how do you not stress about something like that? Especially when it's your body you're constantly looking for changes in. Do my breasts feel sore today, or is it the usual premenstrual soreness I get sometimes? Do I feel bloated? Is this the way I felt when I was pregnant with Seth?

These thoughts would tumble around and around every month until I was sick of it. I didn't want to try anymore, I told Jeff. It was driving me crazy. He was disappointed but supportive. He wouldn't admit it, but I think the pressure was getting to him too. And it was so nice to have regular sex again. When we wanted, without thinking about timing and body temperature and keeping my legs in the air for minutes afterward. Just sex. Sometimes good, sometimes great, sometimes rushed in between Seth's various activities, sometimes languid and slow and tender. Just us, again.

Then we got pregnant.

I didn't believe it at first. In fact, I never really believed it. Not when my period was weeks late. Not when I finally peed on a stick and the second blue line appeared, or when the doctor confirmed it with a blood test. Jeff was elated, and I pretended I was too, but deep down, I knew there was something wrong. I didn't feel pregnant. Not like I had with Seth, not even like I had sometimes all those years when we were trying.

Jeff wanted to tell people right away, too early, but I convinced him to hold off until we passed the third month. That way, if something went wrong, no one would have to know. Nothing was going to go wrong, he said confidently, and in his certainty, I almost found belief. Then night would come, and I'd hold my hand on my still-flat belly and wait for that feeling, that flutter, that extra rush of blood that was supposed to be bringing sustenance to the cells supposedly dividing inside me. I never felt it, not once.

The three-month mark came, and Jeff was pressing me to tell someone, anyone, Seth, our parents, our friends. Wait until the ultrasound, I said, it's only a few weeks away. Then we can tell. He looked at me for a long moment and asked me in a very quiet voice whether I wanted to be pregnant.

"Of course I do. You know I do."

"Then what is it? Why won't you tell anyone?"

"I'm just worried—"

"No, Claire, I don't want to hear that again. There's nothing wrong with the baby."

"You don't know that."

"You weren't like this with Seth. Why are you so convinced ... what's going on, really?"

I gathered the breath to tell him, to confess to my nightly vigils, but in the cold light of day it sounded absurd.

"It's nothing. I don't know why I'm so ... we can start telling people, it's okay."

"Are you sure?"

"Of course. Who do you want to tell first?"

We told Seth, my parents, his, our friends, and soon it felt like the whole town knew. They were all happy, so happy, for me, for us. I accepted the congratulations, the hugs. I told myself that the night flutters would come, that everything was fine.

Then, one of my friends would say in a certain tone of voice, "You don't even look pregnant," and a shot of doubt would go to my heart and stay there, joining the others, building, building.

As the ultrasound drew nearer, I started sleeping less and less. I know now that I was in the first throes of depression, but somehow, in the daylight, I was able to put on a happy face and keep it all inside. I was pregnant at last. No, we didn't want to know the sex, we preferred the surprise, thank you, thank you, oh, right, I'm sure I'll be blowing up any day now. Any day now.

On Ultrasound Day I woke up at four. I turned my head away from

Jeff's and watched the darkness shift to light. When it was a passable hour to get up, I pulled off the covers and hid in the shower. Looking down at my still-flat belly, I counted out the hours like the beats on a metronome until I'd know what I already knew.

Our appointment was at eight. We were in the waiting room at a quarter to, me almost catatonic, Jeff's knee bouncing up and down with excitement. The nurse called us in. I put on one of those awful hospital gowns and lay on the table.

Dr. Mayer entered the examination room — "Morning, morning" — his technician had called in sick so he was doing the exam himself, and he spread the cold, thick gel across my abdomen.

I cringed reflexively as he moved the wand around. We were all staring at the screen, me, Jeff, Dr. Mayer, looking for that rapid, whooshing heartbeat, that cluster of cells taking on a proto-baby shape. After the longest minute of my life, he frowned and held the wand in place, staring at a dark spot.

"I'm sorry," he said eventually.

"Sorry?" Jeff said. "What do you —"

I took Jeff's hand in mine. "It's okay. We're going to be okay."

It always struck me, afterward, that he was supposed to be reassuring me, but I never gave him the chance. I'd had so much longer to prepare, you see. I was ready, in a way.

Or so I thought. Dr. Mayer booked me for a D & C the next day, and then, at his and Jeff's urging, I took the rest of the week off. The message (abnormal cells, no heartbeat, etc.) spread through our family, our life, our town. A week was enough time, everyone said, for me to move past it, to resume my life, to forget. I agreed with them because what else could I do? Tell them I'd had three months and three weeks to get over it? That now, when I put my hand on my stomach at night, I finally felt the flutter I'd been searching for, for so long?

Of course, I couldn't. When Monday morning came, I put on a suit and ate a banana and drove my car to my office. I made it through the front door and started walking down the hall, aware of the stares, the murmurs. I felt like an arrow moving through the building, sharp and lethal.

The people around me felt my lethalness, I'm sure they did, because they moved out of my way as fast as they could. No one reached out. No one tried to stop me.

Before I knew it, I'd walked the length of the building and was outside again, through the emergency exit, gasping for air next to a big green Dumpster.

And as I count out the minutes it will take Seth to get ready, sling on his backpack, and climb onto his bus, I can't help but wonder, *Will my son be that arrow today? Or will he attract the support he needs, rather than scare it away?*

CHAPTER 5

Safety Minute

After I get off the line with Julia, my phone remains eerily silent for the rest of the day. I can usually count on several emails from some overeager newbie working on a Sunday, and the inevitable reply-alls that follow, but I don't even get any spam. The only message I receive is a straightforward text from Brian. *She won! Heading back now.*

Instead, I ride an emotional roller coaster, cursing myself for calling Julia in the first place. Jeff is fine, he is, and there'll be some explanation, some funny, crazy story, about why he hasn't answered me. We'll laugh about it, and I'll keep this weekend to myself.

Feeling like I'm going to jump out of my skin, and knowing the golf course doesn't open for another week, I decide to take a hike up the mountain behind my house.

The mountains were the first thing I noticed about this town, twelve years ago, when Brian and I were trying to decide where to move when he was setting up his practice. The first thing I noticed, that is, once I could see past the sameness of the houses, the gently curving streets meant to slow down traffic to keep the children safe, the blond Scandinavian look most of the denizens seemed to have.

I already felt like my darker features made me stand out, like a Hungarian invader. And I wondered if I could ever feel at home in a place so different from the concrete modernity I'd grown up in.

The town is built in an ancient caldera, created when a meteor crashed into the earth long, long ago. The result is a round, flat plain, surrounded by mountains that must once have been craggy and sharp but are now smoothed and tame. Mountains that change with the seasons, the time of day, that cup the light and fill the eye in every direction above the asphalt roofs of the never-ending three-bedroom split-levels.

"What do you think?" Brian asked me as we stood on the steps of the fifth nearly identical house we'd seen that day. This one had a spider plant hanging from a hook at the edge of the porch roof. The Spider-Plant House, I thought, had a slightly different bathroom configuration from that of the Eggplant-Appliances House or the one with that strange smell in the third bedroom.

I gazed past him at the mist clinging to the mountains, thinking dreamily about how my best words always came while I was hiking somewhere, pushing my body toward something.

"I think . . . this is it," I said.

"You sure?"

I kept my eyes on the mountains, mapping out a ski route on a particularly inviting slope.

"If you are."

"I am."

"You sure you don't want to take that research position in Toronto?"

"Nope. Or the ER position in Chicago. Not interested."

We'd lived in both places for a couple of years while Brian finished his training and built up his skills to the point where he felt he could go out on his own.

I smiled at him indulgently. "All you've ever wanted to be was a real doctor. A small-town jack-of-all-trades. Like your dad."

He hated the anonymousness of the big-city hospitals, never seeing the same patient twice except for the chronic hypochondriacs and the drug-seekers.

His face lit up. "Imagine all the good I can do, really getting to know my patients, following them through their lives. But . . . I want you to want it too. I don't want you to give anything up to move here."

I let this thought trickle through my brain. Would I be giving anything up? Although I'd paid for college through a sports scholarship, golf was over for me. Natural ability and no drive, my coach always said, pun intended. And though I loved to write, poetry mostly, I wasn't going to make a living writing shaky lines about the way my heart felt either. The words were already coming less often, the tumult of teenage-hood giving way to the prosaicness of my mid-twenties. I'd had four jobs in four years. I was directionless. I needed an anchor, something, someone, to hold on to before I drifted any further out to sea.

And Brian, sweet, smart, determined Brian, was the steadiest person I'd ever encountered who wanted to put up with directionless me.

"I'm not giving up anything," I said.

And in that moment, I thought it was true.

After the hike fails to calm my heart, I do the only thing left I can think of. I slip into Brian's office and root through his medical bag. I gave it to him when he started his practice, soon after we moved here, making some joke about him being the subject of a Norman Rockwell painting. It's stamped with the words *Dr. Brian Underhill* in faded gold letters. My fingers probe through its contents until I find the bottle of Ativan he keeps in it. I hold it in my hand, wondering briefly which act is worse: the stealing of the medication or the reason I need to.

I press my palm into the safety cap and twist until it releases. I shake out four pills, hoping Brian won't notice their absence from the almost-full bottle. I hesitate for a moment, but I can't go on feeling like this, so I swallow one down with a glass of water and tuck the remaining pills in my pocket, just in case. Then I lie on the couch and wait for the pill's effects to start. After a while, I feel my heart start to slow and a sleepy calm comes over me. My eyes slide shut, my thoughts float away, and I know I'm asleep the moment before I am.

I'm still like that, my head to the side, a bit of drool running down my chin, when Brian and Zoey get home. I make a half attempt to get up, but Brian puts a practiced hand to my forehead and professes me slightly feverish. He raises me enough to slip an aspirin and some water into my mouth, then eases me back down and pulls a blanket over me, like he's done with Zoey countless times.

Only tonight, I'm the one who's helpless.

I wake early the next morning feeling groggy and disoriented till it hits me, the dread rushing back like water released from a dam.

Brian's already up. I can hear him rattling around in the kitchen, making coffee, toast. I push my hand into the pocket of the jeans I slept in. The pills are still there. I feel relieved and ashamed, but that doesn't stop me from breaking one in half and taking it in the bathroom after I brush my teeth.

Up in my bedroom, I dress haphazardly with the first things I come across. I twist the half pill into a Kleenex, shoving it into the pocket of my skirt, and hide the remaining two in my sock drawer.

When I go back downstairs, Zoey's sitting at the breakfast table, the newspaper propped in front of her while she munches on a piece of toast slathered with butter and jam. She's wearing her school uniform. Her long dark hair flows across her back in a messy tangle. I sit down next to her and apologize for not having been up to hearing about how the competition went the night before.

"'Skay," she says between bites of toast. "Feeling better?"

"A bit."

"You should eat something," Brian says, plunking down a glass of juice and a plate of toast in front of me. "It'll settle your stomach."

I bite off a small corner of the toast, and wash the cardboard taste out of my mouth with a sip of orange juice.

"Was it fun, Zo? Were you happy with how it went?"

"I screwed up a line in 'Trees.' I said, 'The way is gracious / when your leaves tumble down' instead of 'The gracious way your leaves tumble down.'"

"I kind of like the new version better."

"But that's not what we're being graded on. You have to stick to your original poem *exactly*."

"You'll nail it next time, Zo," Brian says.

"And it's not like it kept you from winning," I add.

"*Mommmm,* that's so *not the point.*"

Zoey was born forty weeks and a day after we moved to the "other Springfield," as it's called at work. She's the result of the second honeymoon feeling that consumed us the minute we went into escrow.

Zoey was a beautiful baby. With my black hair and her father's blue eyes, she looked like I always imagined Sara Crewe did when she was still A Little Princess. But mostly, she was an incredibly observant child. Able to hold her head steady from an early age, she would follow us around the room with her eyes, as if she was trying to figure out how we did whatever it was we were doing.

Turns out, she was. Zoey's first word wasn't a word, it was a sentence.

"I want milk," she said clearly at eleven months. I nearly dropped the plate I was holding, certain I was hearing things.

Then she said it again: "I. Want. Milk." Then she paused and added, "Mama."

Brian was extremely excited. He'd never admit it, but he had that fear a lot of smart people have that their children won't exhibit the same kind of intelligence they possess. So her precociousness was a relief. She spoke in full sentences before she was one. She was obviously a genius!

I met this news with wonder and trepidation. I'd been a quasi child prodigy myself (at golf), and I knew that wasn't always a good thing. It marked you out, kept you from hanging out with your friends, and came with expectations. At some point you grew up, and what you did, whatever it was, wasn't remarkable anymore — unless you lived up to your full potential, which I hadn't, not by a long shot. Another pun intended from my college golf coach. He had a bag full of them. Ha!

I read somewhere that many adults with advanced IQs are often less happy than those who test average. Like how there's this optimal money/happiness equation. Once you pass a certain amount of household income, life isn't any better.

Apparently, money can't buy happiness, or it does, but it costs less than you imagined it would.

Anyway, Brian was excited, I was happy but cautious, and Zoey was, well, Zoey. She'd observe, listen, absorb, then issue these comments on what we'd been doing. First in short, declarative sentences ("Mama opened the fridge."), then increasingly in an almost lyrical way ("These blocks are beautiful." "The sky is floating.").

Brian taught her to read and write when she was three, and she produced her first poem at age four years and seven months. It's framed and hanging in the stairway in between shots of her at various ages. Written in orange crayon, it reads, *The rain falling against my window / is scratchy / It makes the world / blurry / It's hard to sleep / when the rain is falling / against my window.*

Four-going-on-five Zoey wasn't Shakespeare, but she delivered her poem with amazing force, standing in the party dress she'd insisted on wearing before reading it to us, her shiny Mary Janed feet a body-width apart, keeping her steady.

And what do you do in this day and age when your child performs some marvelous feat? You ask her to do it again, of course, and this time you make sure you have your video camera ready. If you're me, you email that video to a few friends and family, or post it on Facebook with a proud caption. But if you're Brian, and you've been tracking every sign of prodigiousness since her first demand for milk, you spend hours editing the video, buffing it here and splicing it there. You study how videos go viral, and you make sure this one does.

And you don't tell your wife because, well, you say sheepishly when she learns what you've done by overhearing two people talking about it in the grocery store, you thought it would be a nice surprise, you weren't sure it was going to work. Isn't it amazing that it's up to ten thousand views already?

And he looks so excited, so proud, this man you love, who loves your daughter more than anything, that you squash down the anger that's been building since the produce aisle and you smile and say, of course it's a great surprise, and wow, that's amazing.

So that's what I did. And I did it again when he showed me the spoken word competitions he'd found, a couple of them really close by. They weren't beauty contests, he was quick to assure me. No tiaras. No spray tans. Only the spoken word, spoken by our daughter. He was excited, she was excited, I couldn't say no.

We went. Zoey back in her party dress, her hair French-braided, our video camera at the ready.

She lost.

I was worried she'd be devastated, but instead of putting her off the whole thing, which I think I was secretly hoping for, it made her more determined. I'd find little scraps of paper scattered around the house full of misspelled words and half-rhymes written with thick colored markers, and it wasn't long before she started winning those competitions, her room filling up with ribbons and trophies.

I'm not sure when I became less involved. Maybe it was always essentially her thing with Brian. I went to those early competitions, my stomach clenched as she spoke. I dried her tears and shared her joy. But it was Brian who planned for the next one, who knew the other competitors, who strategized her rise through the ranks.

The irony of it being Brian who was the one who encouraged her writing came up during our first interview with the local morning news show. Zoey was eight. She'd just won the National Spoken Word Competition in her age category. We were sitting on a three-seater couch, the arc lights above us casting a hot glow. The host, who looked handsome and young for his age on television, but grubby and older up close, leaned forward.

"I understand Zoey gets her talent from you, Mrs. Underhill?"

I blinked a few times, caught off guard. "I wouldn't say that."

"Aren't *you* the poet in the family?"

"No, I —"

"You were the editor of your college poetry journal, right?"

"Yes, that's true, but —" I stopped myself from saying, "She's so much better than I was." I'm not sure why, exactly. Maybe I wanted to protect the teenage/college me.

"Yes?" the interviewer prompted.

"I meant . . . I can't take credit for what Zoey's done. What she's doing. She does it all on her own, truly."

I could see the skepticism in his eyes, could tell he believed me to be the worst kind of stage mother. But until that moment, I'd never connected my poems, which I hardly ever wrote anymore, with Zoey's. She was passionate, directed, focused, while I started and abandoned career after career.

There was no contest, really.

Brian drives me to the office, worried about me in my weakened state. He drives slowly, cautiously, and I'm almost late for an early department meeting. There's another round of cuts coming, Art Davies was just the beginning, and we have to establish what our severance strategy will be.

Why we have to have a meeting about this every time we start a round of layoffs is beyond me. Our severance strategy is always the same. Offer enough money so the majority of the employees being cut will accept the offer, no questions asked. Set aside a contingency fund for the small percentage who seek legal advice and demand more. Have a firm ceiling above which you cannot rise during your negotiations with said lawyers. Make it clear that you will see them in court if necessary. Chance that someone will institute litigation, according to the consultants: 0.02 percent.

I wish I could skip the whole thing, but what choice do I have? So here I am, completely freaked out, half an Ativan in the bag, skulking into the conference room with the rest of my department.

I take a seat next to my supervisor, Lori Chan, a tiny woman with straight black hair who's been at the company about as long as I have, just in time for the Safety Minute presentation — the SMP.

If these meetings are pointless, the SMP is in a category all its own. Implemented two years ago when, as Jeff would say, the consultants started taking over, every meeting begins with one. A minute-long presentation about safety in the workplace. It's why all the cars are parked ass inward in our parking lot. Why you'll see employee after employee swing their legs out of their car and make sure both feet are planted firmly on the ground before exiting their vehicle. That, and an infinite number of other acts of conformity that are supposed to make us safer, but only make me think of the Two Minutes of Hate in *Nineteen Eighty-Four* every time I'm forced to listen to one of them.

I'm sure I'm being subliminally programmed for something; I'm just not sure what.

As Casey Durham, today's lucky contestant, rises to tell us about water fountain safety, my mind drifts to the one fun Safety Minute I ever attended.

I don't know how, but Hector Valenzuela knew he was about to get whacked. But first, he had to deliver his SMP. And boy, did he go out in style. He was supposed to be speaking about how to avoid paper cuts, but instead, he gave a very instructive, and very graphic, presentation on how to skin a moose. Apparently it depends on what you want to use the skin for, and all kinds of other things I never absorbed because I was laughing so hard thirty seconds in that the laughter took over my whole body. I was nearly crying by the time I told Jeff about it . . .

Is this what my life is going to be like after the deadline? Every little thing reminding me of him, and not being able to tell him about any of it?

Where is he, where is he, where is he?

I can feel my throat closing up and my head starts to spin even before it happens. Lori stands to thank Casey, then she gets this look on her face, this fake sad look, and says she has something else to add before we begin.

"I'm not sure how many of you knew him, but it's my unfortunate job to inform you that Jeff Manning, of the other Springfield, died tragically in a car accident on Friday . . ."

No. No!

"Tish, are you okay?"

I didn't realize I spoke out loud. Screamed. I think I might've screamed out loud.

"I . . ." I stand on wobbly legs and move as quickly as I can for the door.

The handle's slippery in my hand, but I have to get out of here. Then I'm out, and the bathroom is only two doors away. I'm in a stall and I'm leaning over the toilet, heaving, choking, until there's nothing left in my stomach, not even bile.

I knew it, I can't stop thinking. *I knew it.*

CHAPTER 6

The Sweet Spot

A couple years ago, I was invited to the company's annual retreat in Cabo San Lucas, Mexico.

I took it as a positive sign about my performance as the new head of the accounting department, but mostly I was happy it was slated to take place at a pricey golf resort, and that spouses were invited along for the ride. Claire and I hadn't had a trip without Seth in a while, and it was nice that we were being forced to take the time. That we needed it was one more reason to be happy to go.

My parents eagerly agreed to stay with Seth, and I brought my clubs up from the basement, dusting them off and taking practice swings in the living room. I hadn't played a round in four months, and I was feeling itchy. Not a golfer, Claire was looking forward to getting away from the dull gray winter we'd been having and seeing a bit of sun.

I don't usually think of myself as the sort of person who's affected by the weather, but I felt lighter the minute we deplaned. The sight of all that pristine grass, broken up by sandy-white bunkers and indigo water hazards, as we drove through the resort added to the bubble of happiness welling up inside me. I could tell that Claire was feeling happy too. She had a sort of perma-smile on her face, something I hadn't seen in a while.

The resort was plush, spread out over endless acres bounded by the choppy ocean. Our suite was in a building next to the newly built clubhouse. The first one we'd been in since our surprise, paid-for-by-the-family honeymoon, the suite had a large living room, an even bigger bedroom, and a bathroom that was grand enough to house a Jacuzzi. The colors were light and airy. Sunlight flowed in from the massive windows that gave never-ending views of the kelly-green golf course.

"Maybe I should go to the pool?" Claire said, flitting around our room, unpacking. "Or, I saw tennis courts. Do you think I could find someone to play with me?"

"I think you could find someone to do a lot of things with you."

"Flirting!"

"Can you flirt with your own wife?"

She rested her hands on my waist. "You certainly can."

We started kissing, pressing against each other. Thoughts of the golf course drifted away. I had my shirt off and was working the buttons on hers when the phone next to the bed rang shrilly.

"You better get that," Claire said.

I put my lips against her neck. "It'll take a message."

She swatted me gently as it rang again. "It might be one of the bosses calling."

She was right. John Scott, the VP in charge of my department, wanted me to go to the driving range with him, had heard I could help out a guy who might have a "slight" slice. I wondered how he knew that, but then I remembered some passing conversation we'd had months ago about how I'd worked as a golf pro for a couple summers when I was putting myself through college. Drinks had been involved in this conversation, of course, because the truth was that I'd worked *for* the golf pro while I was putting myself through college. But I couldn't tell him that, so I agreed to meet him in the lobby in fifteen.

"Sorry, honey, but duty calls," I said as I hung up the phone. "I have to go to the driving range."

"Since when has someone ever had to convince you to do that?"

"It shows the power you still have over me."

"Now you're feeding me lines! What's gotten into you?"

I wasn't sure, but it seemed like it had gotten into both of us.

I hoped it would last past golf practice.

"I feel happy."

"You know what?" Claire said. "Me too."

I met John in the lobby twenty minutes later. He was standing underneath a large blue banner that read *Welcome!* and was dressed like my grandfather used to, in a pink polo shirt, madras golf shorts, and tan socks pulled up to his knees. He was chewing on an unlit cigar, his shaven head glinting under the harsh overhead lighting.

"Jeff, my boy," he said, shaking my hand firmly, "let's do this thing."

He slapped me on the back and led me outside, where a white electric golf cart was waiting for us. I had started to strap my bag in when a young kid in a dark blue polo shirt and chino shorts mumbled, "Let me help you with that, sir," in nearly flawless English and snatched it from me, then did the same for John.

Having been in this kid's position, I wanted to tip him for his efforts, but I'd left my wallet in my room. John took it as part of the included service, and placed his rather large behind into the golf cart. It listed to the side under his girth.

I mumbled an apology to the kid and climbed in next to John, surprised he was letting me drive. Until he reached into his pants pocket and pulled out a silver flask. He unscrewed the top and took a long pull.

"Would you like a snort?" he asked, holding it out to me.

"I'm good."

I pressed the pedal and followed the signs for the driving range, wishing I hadn't answered the damn phone. Wishing the golf cart went faster than ten miles an hour.

These thoughts retreated when I caught sight of the nicest range I've ever been on. The grass looked like no one had ever hit a ball off it. The wooden pickets separating each practice area were whiter than the puffy clouds above, whiter even than the pristine balls filling the plastic baskets next to them. No chits, no ball machines, no marked-up, mangy range balls, just ones that looked like they'd been cracked out of their packets moments earlier. If making it to the majors meant real baseballs for practice, this was the Show of golf.

A different kid in the same uniform took our clubs and set them up. I mumbled another apology, and he thankfully placed me far enough away from John that his curses and frequent whiffs wouldn't distract me.

I spent a few minutes watching his swing—hunched over, not coming back far enough, head lifting at the moment of contact—searching for some polite phrases that might actually help him without getting me fired. In the end, I suggested he stand taller and position himself differently to the ball, and he hit a few shots that didn't arc into the woods. Satisfied, he waved me off, and I breathed a sigh of relief.

Left alone with my golf bag and enough balls to ensure I'd be in need of a session in the Jacuzzi later—hopefully with a slippery and happy Claire—I got into a zone while I worked my way from my pitching wedge to my five iron, ten balls each. When my muscles felt loose, I took out my driver and used it to stretch my arms above my head.

As I twisted my body from side to side, I noticed that John was sitting on the grass in his pen, his legs splayed out in front of him, flask in hand. He was watching the only other person on the range, a tallish woman wearing a white polo shirt and cropped khaki pants. A long black braid of hair poked through the back of her white baseball cap.

I rested my driver on the ground, leaned against it, and watched her. She had, very possibly, the most natural golf swing I'd ever seen. She was using an iron—her seven, I think—to deftly flick a ball from the green plastic basket and up onto her tee. She drew the club back and—*whack!*—it flew off the face in a perfect arc and landed within feet of the fluttering blue flag a hundred and fifty yards away. I realized that she was, incredibly, making a ring around the flag. In a few minutes, there was more white than green in its radius.

I'm not sure how long I watched, but I remember feeling like I could watch forever. This woman was amazing. She should be on the tour, she should . . .

56 CATHERINE MCKENZIE

"That girl has a perfect ass," John said, slurring his words and talking, I was sure, loudly enough for her to hear.

She turned in our direction, her features shaded by the peak of her cap. "Excuse me?"

"I was admiring your ass," John replied unabashedly, all politeness washed away by the contents of his flask. "Your golf swing really shows it to its best advantage."

Her iron swung in her hand like she was getting ready to use it. "And who are you?"

"I'm John Scott."

From what I could see of her expression, she clearly wanted to tell John Scott to go fuck himself, but something was holding her back. Then it occurred to me—she must work for the company too. She couldn't tell him to fuck off any more than I could.

I walked over to John's pen. "Maybe we should get back? Isn't the reception soon?"

"What? Oh, yes, I suppose you're right." He struggled to get himself into an upright position. The woman shot me a grateful look.

"Will we see you there, little lady?"

"Indubitably," she said, and went back to her half-empty basket of balls.

When I got back to the room, I found Claire sitting on the edge of the bed, wrapped in a plush taupe towel. The room was thick with steam, and her hair was wet and slicked back from her face. Pale skinned, she already had a slight sunburn across the bridge of her nose.

"Damn. If only I'd gotten here a few minutes earlier."

She looked away from the television and grinned. "One-track mind."

"Is that a bad thing?"

I walked toward her to give her a kiss, but her attention was drawn back to the screen. I followed her gaze. Anthony Bourdain was biting into what looked like a raw sea urchin, plucked from the crystal ocean behind him.

"Where is he this week?"

"Sydney."

"Australia?"

"Yes."

I watched the screen for a moment, listening to her breathing, feeling the stillness expand between us.

"It's beautiful," I said eventually. "No wonder Tim loves it there."

"Shouldn't we get to that cocktail party?" She stood, hugging the towel around her tightly.

"You're right, we should."

I walked past her to the bathroom and showered quickly, trying not to think about Claire and Australia and Tim. Eventually, I shifted my thoughts to the driving range as a distraction. And it worked, after a fashion.

I told Claire about John as we dressed.

"He's a jerk," she said. "But you shouldn't let it bother you."

"Wouldn't it bother you?"

"Of course. But a lot of the old guard are like that. You have to roll with it."

"Are you saying you get treated like that?"

"I used to. Sometimes."

"By who? And why haven't you told me that before?"

"Because I knew you'd want to beat the crap out of them, and that wouldn't have been good for my career, now would it?"

"I might've taken some pleasure from it, though. Seriously, who talked to you like that? Was it that Ed guy?"

"It was no one in particular; part of my old life. Now come on, we're going to be late."

I stifled my annoyance and finished tying my tie.

Outside, we walked along the path to the clubhouse. It was dusk, and as we walked, a set of lanterns stuck into the lawn snapped on, illuminating the path. Bugs and birds buzzed and twittered in the trees above us. The air smelled like freshly mown grass and new paint. Venus was rising, bright above the horizon.

Claire curled her fingers into mine. After a moment's hesitation, I squeezed her hand.

"Is this going to be excruciating for you?" I asked.

"Of course not. I'm sure I and the other wives will spend the night talking about our kids."

I laughed and felt lighter because of it. "I do work with a few women."

"Maybe I'll talk to them, then."

The clubhouse had a long wraparound porch. Little white lights were strung through the balustrade, and the din of cocktail conversation spilled into the night. We collected drinks from a waiter and spent the next hour winding through the crowd, having those brief exchanges you always have at these types of events. "Where are you from?" "What department do you work in?" "This is my wife." "This is mine." "Isn't this place great?" "It really is." "Do you work for the company too?"

Claire kept an eye out for the waiters passing with canapés, and by the end of the hour we had a good drink-to-bite-sized-food ratio going.

When the Milky Way was a streak above the now nearly invisible golf course, a gong sounded, calling us in to dinner. We searched the seating chart for our table and found out that we were sitting with John and his wife. I knew Claire actively disliked both of them, and I was pretty sure she'd hate John by dessert.

Hell, we might both hate him by dessert.

When we got to the table, John and Cindy were already seated, making inroads into a bottle of red wine. His face had a florid, other-side-of-sober look to it. He patted the seat next to him when he saw Claire. She sighed, and I whispered to her that she didn't have to sit there if she didn't want to. She told me she could handle it and sat down, her shoulders squared as if for a fight. I took the seat next to her, introducing myself to a middle-aged woman in a cocktail dress who was the chief operating officer's wife.

The COO was deep in conversation with a very pretty, very young woman, the newly acquired wife of our sixty-year-old CEO. She was the talk of the company, her "modeling" photos circulating around the office. Some of them had been enhanced and/or captioned. You can imagine. I hoped the guys behind it weren't on the outs with IT.

The seat next to hers was empty, for the CEO presumably. I couldn't for the life of me understand how we'd ended up sitting here.

"What are we doing at this table?" Claire murmured.

"I was wondering the same thing."

"I see big things in your future, young man," she said, squeezing my thigh under the table. "Big things."

The thought of that possibility made me nervous, and I decided to switch to water. Drinking as much as I wanted to seemed like a bad idea in the circumstances.

The first courses of salad and soup passed slowly. The COO's wife was very nice, but we had less than nothing in common, and I began to regret my no-drinking decision. When the waiter came to refresh our drinks, I decided to allow myself a glass of wine. One glass with each course ought to keep things reasonable but bearable.

The main course was set up as a buffet against the back of the room. As we rose to take our place in line, Claire told me to go ahead, she'd meet me back at the table. I suspected she was going out for a smoke, but I didn't call her on it. We had a sort of don't-ask-don't-tell policy with respect to her smoking.

I tucked into line behind a woman whose long, wavy black hair hung loosely over her bare shoulders. We waited next to each other at the turkey station, while a man in a chef's hat carved to order. The woman glanced at me when I asked for a large helping of dark meat.

"Oh, it's you," she said.

"Do we . . . ?"

"You were with that John guy, right? On the driving range?"

"Still am." I nodded toward my table. "Sorry about that."

"Forget it." She rolled her eyes. They were a dark green, the color of the dress she was wearing. It was a kind of loose, flowy thing made out of a fabric I didn't know the name of. "I assume he's not a friend of yours?"

"God, no," I said.

The chef handed her a plate of juicy white meat with a crisp brown layer of skin lying across it. She waited for me to accept my own plate, and we moved down the line.

"Which branch do you work at?" she asked.

"Springfield."

"Me too."

"You new with the company?"

"Nope."

"Then how come we don't know each other?" The office was big, but not that big.

"You must be at the other Springfield."

Johnson Company had recently acquired another company, located about five hundred miles away, in another town called Springfield. The name duplication was already causing problems. Mail had gotten lost, emails misdirected. There was a rumor that the CEO had tried to get the other Springfield, as we'd taken to calling it, to change its name.

The actual town.

Seriously.

"That's too bad," I said.

"How so?"

"It'd be nice to have another golfer in the office."

"There must be tons of guys who play where you are. Isn't it some golf mecca?"

I rolled my eyes. "Three courses and counting." I leaned in so I wouldn't be heard. "They're mostly a bunch of duffers, to be honest. But you, Christ, you really schooled that flagpole. You taught that flag a lesson."

I stopped, realizing I might be speaking through one too many glasses of wine.

"That wasn't my intention but . . . thanks."

"Did you play professionally?"

"College." She paused, considering. "Scholarship."

I spooned some stuffing onto my plate. She took a generous helping of cranberry sauce.

"And after college? Sorry, I don't normally ask this many questions."

"It's okay. I wasn't good enough to take it anywhere, so I gave it up."

"You could've fooled me."

"Lots of people can hit it at the flag on the range. It's bringing it together on the course that matters. Besides, you should see me putt. I suck at putting."

"I highly doubt that."

She shrugged as she ladled gravy over her meat. "You'll never know, right?"

"How's that?"

"You live in your Springfield, I live in mine. Never the twain shall meet."

"But we're meeting now."

"One-time thing. I have it on good authority these types of shindigs are going to be cut in the next budget."

"That's too bad."

We'd reached the end of the line. I searched for something else to say.

"What department do you work in?" I asked lamely.

"HR. You?"

"Accounting."

She raised her eyebrows, two dark slashes in an alabaster face. "The two most hated departments in the place. Anyway . . ."

"We should be getting back."

"We should."

"It was nice meeting you . . . I never got your name."

She shook her head. "Nope. Never the twain shall meet, remember?"

"All right, then. It was nice not meeting you, whoever you are."

"It was nice not meeting you too."

CHAPTER 7

Six Feet Under

Tuesday morning, and Beth is insisting that I get out of bed, out of the bedroom, out of the house.

"Out of the house?"

"Yes. The great outdoors. Have you forgotten about it?"

"Fuck off."

"Finally."

"What?"

"That's the first emotion I've seen you express since I got here. Those pills Dr. Feelgood has you on are too strong. I think some anger is what you need."

I tuck my knees under my chin. "What I need is for this all to be some sick joke."

"But that's not going to happen, so what are you going to do about it?"

"Hiding in here seems about right."

"I had another plan in mind."

Beth's plan involves shopping for a dress to wear for Jeff's service, and some secret mission she won't let me in on. And because she's my older sister, and I've been programmed all my life to follow her instructions, I get up, shower, and come downstairs to face the rest of my family in the bright daylight streaming through my kitchen.

My mother and father are sitting at the breakfast table with Jeff's parents. Our house seems to have become Grief Command Central, and I don't think there's anything I can do about it. Thankfully, the other onlookers or well-wishers or whatever I should be thinking of them as have left, back to their lives, leaving only their Tupperware behind. God knows how many casseroles there are in the freezer.

The one person missing is Seth, who's gone to school again. He wouldn't tell me how it went yesterday when he got back, simply grumbling that it had been "fine." This seemed like a good sign, a pre-Jeff-is-gone kind of behavior. But his troubled sleep continued, all thrashes and moans, and I held him like a baby, rocking him until he finally quieted.

After rising to hug me and tell me how glad they are I'm going out, my parents start bickering over the sections of the newspaper, as they have all my life. I feel a wave of embarrassment at their lack of tact in front of Jeff's parents, one of those couples who give the impression they've never had an argument. But they act oblivious, hug me, and start on the dishes, Mr. Manning washing, Mrs. Manning drying, their grief etched in their faces, their meticulous movements.

I slump into a chair next to my mother, resting my chin in my hands, and stare out the window at the sunny day. Beth plunks a bowl of cereal in front of me, Seth's special-occasion Froot Loops. I eat them, my hunger emerging after a few bites. Froot Loops are better than I remember.

"Josie called for you again," my mom says.

"Okay."

"Are you going to return her call?"

Josie's one of our closest friends, but I haven't been calling anyone back.

"Eventually."

"Jesus, Mother," Beth says. "What kind of question is that?"

"It's a normal question. Why do you have to be so harsh all the time?"

Beth mutters something under her breath about her that, thankfully, only I hear. Or maybe my father hears it too. I notice a smile creep onto his lips, which quickly disappears when my mother gives him a quizzical look.

I eat the rest of my cereal, then bypass Jeff's parents and put the bowl directly into the dishwasher. I always have to (had to, damn it, had to) remind Jeff to do the same, part of our normal married banter, the little rubs of everyday life.

"We're going shopping," Beth announces to no one in particular, then leads me out the door. My car's parked on my side of the driveway, where I park it every day, where I parked it Friday.

Before.

Jeff's side of the driveway is a blank expanse of cracked asphalt. It was on our list of things to try to fix this summer, if we had the money. His car must still be in the company parking lot. Should I ask Beth to pick it up? Do I even want it picked up, another reminder of his absence? Maybe I should give it to my parents, who've lived my whole life with one car, although they've never wanted to go to the same place.

I hand my car keys to Beth without speaking and buckle myself into the passenger side. I can feel anxiety creeping through my body, starting near my heart and radiating outward. The thought of actually being behind the wheel seems inconceivable. How can I ever be responsible for the tons of metal and plastic, the bumper, the hood, the windshield? The instruments of Jeff's demise?

I shudder and pull on the seat belt so it slaps tight against my shoulder. *It's going to be fine,* I think as Beth backs carefully out of the driveway, willing myself to believe it. *Just fine.*

The mall's nearly empty. It's early, and it's Tuesday, so I shouldn't be surprised, but somehow I am. On the way here, I imagined being swept up in a sea of people, jostled, slightly claustrophobic, normal. Instead, it simply smells clean, and like there's more air in it than usual. One more reminder of how different today is. How I shouldn't be here.

"What do you think our best bet is?" Beth asks.

"Huh?"

"For an outfit, for — Christ, you're not going to make me say it, are you?"

"I'm sorry. We should go to Stacy's, I guess."

"Don't apologize. Please. Speaking before thinking. You know how I am."

"Sure."

"So Stacy's is . . . ?"

"This way."

I angle in the right direction and Beth matches her stride to mine. She reaches down and takes my hand, and despite the numbing drugs, I'm almost in tears. I squeeze her hand and slide mine from hers. It's something I've noticed, these last few days. Aside from Seth, anyone else's touch, a kind word even, brings me close to the breaking point.

Beth doesn't say anything as we pass by the jumble of clothing, knickknack, and electronics stores. When we get to Stacy's, we weave through the racks of summer lines and frothy prom dresses. I don't see a dark outfit anywhere, only a riot of color.

But Beth's the older sister for a reason. She directs me to the fitting rooms, and before I have time to strip off my clothes, she's back with three black dresses slung over her arm. They all look similar, black sheaths devoid of any personality other than widow. If I slap on the strand of pearls I got for my sixteenth birthday and a pillbox hat, maybe someone will mistake me for Jackie O, time-warped to the future.

"I think this one will fit you best," Beth says, handing me one of the dresses.

She hangs the other two on the hook on the back of the door and pulls her sweater over her head.

"What are you doing?"

"I need a dress too, you know."

"There's a whole line of empty rooms."

"Are you getting modest on me? We used to do this all the time."

As she reaches down to undo her pants, flashes of similar occasions spring up. The first outfit I was allowed to buy without my mother (a pair of green striped pants I instantly regretted); my first formal wear (a turquoise gown with puffed sleeves); my wedding dress (a strapless A-line dress because Beth said you never regret the strapless A-line).

"Come on, slow coach, off with your clothes." She pokes me in the stomach as she says the word *clothes*.

I pull back instinctively. "What the hell?"

"You don't want to be here all day, do you?"

I definitely don't, so I finish undressing and slip the stiff fabric over my head. It itches where it meets my collarbone, but that seems fitting somehow. I don't want to feel comfortable on the day of Jeff's funeral.

"That looks like it will do," Beth says. "What about me?"

I look up at Beth. Four years older than me, her short hair is shot through with gray and there are lines on her face I've never noticed before. Her dress fits her well enough, but it looks uncomfortable too.

"You look like Hester Prynne," I say.

"About to face my accusers? That's exactly the look I was going for."

Back in the car, Beth clicks on the radio, but I quickly snap it off. The low bass notes feel like an assault. I expect Beth to take us home, but as she drives in the opposite direction, I remember that we still have to complete the "secret mission" she won't let me in on. I'm imagining all kinds of possibilities, but the place we actually end up didn't even make the list.

"No, Beth. I can't. I can't go in there," I say as we park outside a sprawling house with a conservative sign on the lawn that reads AN-DERSON'S FUNERAL HOME.

Beth pulls on the parking brake. "You have to. It's going to suck. It might suck worse than anything has ever sucked, but you have to be strong for a bit, okay?"

I gulp for air. My heart feels like it stopped beating a few moments ago, and I don't know how to get it restarted. I bring my fist to my chest and press it hard to my breastbone.

"What is it?" Beth asks. "You know you can tell me anything."

"If I go in there, then . . . all of this, all of this is real."

"I feel like a complete shit for saying this, okay, but all of this *is* real. You can't get any more real than this."

I clutch my purse in my lap, feeling the bottle of pills beneath the supple leather. The car clock says it's thirty minutes past when I'm allowed to take another pill. I've felt thirty minutes of pain I didn't need to feel, but I also feel more awake than I have in days. More present. I leave the pills in my purse.

"Okay," I say to Beth. "Let's go."

We walk up the cement walkway to the mortuary's front door. The new lawn is minty green, cut short and even, not a blade out of place. There are bunches of tulips poking out of the ground, light pink, almost white, tasteful. I take a deep breath, searching for the scent of spring, but the air is odorless. Antiseptic almost.

Inside, a young woman dressed in a conventional black dress that could be the twin of the one I just bought is sitting behind a spare mahogany desk with her hands folded in her lap. Her light hair is cut blunt to her chin. She seems to be waiting for us.

"Mrs. Manning?"

"Yes."

She rises. I expect her to offer her hand but instead she tucks them both behind her back like a museum docent. Maybe she understands about the pain her touch might cause.

"I'm Karen Anderson. Would you like to accompany me into the parlor?"

We follow her into a very formal living room plucked from the Victorian age. The Air from Bach's Suite no. 3 in D is playing on an iPod resting in a set of speakers on a side table, the one incongruous object in the room. We sit on a pink brocade couch. The fabric feels stiff and slippery. I hold on tight, in case the seas get rough.

Karen sits across from us in a wingback chair and opens a plain black notebook.

"I'm so sorry for your loss."

"Thank you."

"Did you and Mr. Manning ever discuss what kind of arrangements he'd like in this eventuality?"

I feel an overwhelming urge to ask her to speak in modern English, but there's something oddly soporific in her formal words, the way her tapered fingers hold the fountain pen that's hovering over the blank lined page.

"We talked about . . . we never talked about this part."

"Would you like to go with one of our standard packages, then?"

"What does that . . . involve?"

She opens a drawer in the table next to her and hands me a thick piece of cardboard. It's a menu, a funeral *menu,* with two headings: *Religious* and *Nonreligious.* I skip down to the nonreligious option: a little Barrett, a little Browning, space for speeches from family and friends if that is "desired." The music's all wrong, but I can fix that myself.

I hand it back to her. "The nonreligious will be fine."

"Good. Do you know what day you'd like to hold the service? We have an opening tomorrow."

"No!" I say way too loudly for this cloistered room.

Beth places her hand on my knee. I take several deep breaths. "I'm sorry," I say, "it's . . . his brother. His brother isn't here yet. He has to be here."

I'm not sure what it is that makes me think of Tim at this moment. I'm not even sure he's been told. I've abrogated that responsibility, like so many others. But, of course, he must've been. Jeff's parents must have called him. And despite everything, I know with total certainty that Tim will cross the distance and come. I just don't know when.

"His brother lives in Australia. I'm not sure when he's getting here."

"He's arriving on Thursday," Beth says.

I let that sink in. Tim is arriving on Thursday.

"Would Friday work, then?"

I want to scream *No!* again, but instead I look at Beth.

She nods and speaks for me. "Friday would be fine."

"Perfect." She scratches out a few words with her pen. "Is eleven a good time?"

Beth nods again.

Friday at eleven is three days from now. And then what? "If you'll follow me into our display room, you can choose the casket you desire."

I don't have to scream this time for Beth to grab my hand and hold it tight. Karen bows her head, waiting patiently for me to collect myself. She must be used to this. Has she become immune to grief? Does she slough it off like I do the petty slights of three- and four-year-olds?

Several minutes pass before I come back to myself. I can hear the soft tinkle of the Bach, feel my fingers mechanically playing the chords against my knee, and Beth's warm hand covering mine.

"We can do this another time," Beth says. "Or I can—"

"No, I should do this. I should be the one."

I rise unsteadily. We cross the wide hall to a set of large wooden doors with glass panels, which are covered by opaque curtains, hiding whatever lies beyond.

Karen opens one of the doors and stands aside. Beth's clutching my hand so tightly she's almost cutting off my circulation. I want to make a break for it and run, but that would mean having to come back here.

Karen flicks a switch and we walk into the showroom. I blink under the bright lights. The large, octagonal room has an assortment of caskets arranged a tasteful distance apart, each illuminated by a bright spot.

"I'll leave you two alone," Karen says. "Let me know when you've made your selection." She closes the door behind her with a discreet click.

I walk toward a casket on the left, and Beth goes right. The large room is full of options. How am I supposed to make a choice? What criteria are even appropriate?

"Can you believe the price of these things?" Beth says after a few minutes, fingering a tag that hangs from the handle of a shiny casket made of rosewood.

"Shh! She'll hear you."

"She knows they're overpriced. Why do you think she left the room?"

"To give us some privacy?"

"You think that if it makes you feel better."

I shoot her a look. She's chastened for about thirty seconds, till her eyes land on the name of the casket she's standing next to. It's an imposing metal affair that looks like it comes from the future.

"Time Capsule?" Beth says. "Are they freakin' kidding?"

"You made that up."

"Come see for yourself."

I cross the room till I'm close enough to read the card. That's really its name, and the description seems to imply that the contents will be so well protected that the occupant might be brought back from the dead, should science head in that direction.

"That's appalling."

"Especially at that price."

I look at the tag. The casket costs more than my car by a wide margin. "I can't afford that."

"Of course you can't, honey. But don't worry, we'll find something that works." She looks around the room slowly, sizing up the other possibilities. "That simple one there isn't too crazy." She points to a rosewood casket. "And it's kind of classic. Or you could always go with a pine box. It's going to molder in the ground anyway."

"Beth!"

"Sorry. No filter today. What do you think Jeff would've wanted?"

"He never said, but something tells me he'd say something flip like 'Lay me out like Darth Vader and light me on fire.'"

Beth smiles at me as if she's seeing someone she hasn't seen in a while.

"Pine box it is, then."

CHAPTER 8

BackOffice

Lori helps me out of the bathroom and since I am carless, drives me home. She keeps glancing at me, slumped against the car door, as if she wants to ask what's going on, but she doesn't. Maybe she's figured it out. Maybe she already knew. Something. But then why wouldn't she have called me when she heard? Why didn't she pull me aside before the meeting? Why did she let me listen to that stupid Safety Minute presentation if she knew the whole time?

She pulls up in front of my house, bringing the car to a careful halt. The neighbor's four-year-old is playing on the lawn, pushing a dump truck around in the dirt, making *beep, beep, beep* noises. I watch him for too many seconds.

"You going to be okay?" Lori asks.

I don't quite look at her. Eye contact doesn't seem like a good idea. "Thanks for driving me home."

"I should've told you before. I'm sorry, I wasn't thinking..." There's a question in that pause. A chance to confide. But that's the last thing I can do. I've already done too much.

"No, it's okay. I only met him twice ... it was ... a shock. He emailed me recently for some advice, and I've been sick all weekend, and ... I don't know why I reacted like that ..."

I'm babbling, producing the opposite effect of the reassurance I want to give, the downplay I'm attempting.

"I'll be fine tomorrow, I'm sure."

"If you need to talk or anything . . ."

"Thanks." I unbuckle my seat belt. It flies into its slot with a zippery sound.

I hesitate before I get out. I want to say, "Please don't talk about this at the office. Please don't make me, us, the subject of gossip," but there's no point. I can't stop what's going to happen any more than I could stop what's already happened.

"I'll see you tomorrow," I say.

I walk to my front door, smile at the boy with his truck, feeling Lori's eyes on me the whole time, her car idling like it's midnight and she's dropped me off in a bad neighborhood. I pull my keys from my purse, unlock the door, and glance over my shoulder, giving her a wave. I slip inside, close the door behind me, and slide down to the floor, my back pressing against its hard surface.

And now the tears are coming. I'm not sure they're ever going to stop.

I spend an hour on the floor, maybe more. It must be more because the shadows shift across me, flickering through the curtains that partially cover the window next to the door.

Time's a funny thing. Yesterday, each second was a thousand, each minute an eternity. But now it's slipping past me at the speed of light and I don't know how to slow it down.

When I can't stand the floor anymore, I drag myself up the stairs, climb into bed without taking anything off but my shoes, and pull the covers over my head. And in this half-suffocating environment, I eventually fall into a fitful sleep.

I wake suddenly when the front door bangs open in the way only Zoey does it. Her bookbag crashes to the floor with equal emphasis. She clomps up the stairs as if she were punishing them. My daughter is not a heavy girl, slight even, but she's always made more noise than she should.

I should rise, leave this oasis, greet her and ask her about her day. But I can't. I can't. Oh, Jesus.

"Mom?"

"I'm in here," I say, my throat scratchy and dry like I've been in the desert.

"Mom?"

"In here," I say again, louder.

Clomp, clomp, clomp. My door crashes open and in comes the light from the hallway, illuminating Zoey, her hair in its end-of-day mess. She spends most of her classes hiding behind it, countless teachers have told us, we should really get it cut. When I ask her about it, she says she likes it back there. It helps her think. And since her grades are more than they should be, we smile and nod at the teachers, year after year, and let her hair be.

"Why are you in bed? Are you still sick?"

I prop myself up, hoping I don't look like I've spent the last six hours crying.

"Yes."

She walks over and launches herself into the bed on Brian's side. It bounces up and down, making my stomach flip over.

"Easy, Zo."

"Sorry." She shuffles toward me carefully. "Is it your tummy?"

"Among other things."

"I'm sorry, Mommy."

This almost brings on the tears again. She hasn't called me "Mommy" in a dog's age.

"Thank you."

She puts her head on my shoulder and rests her hand on my stomach gently.

"You look sad."

"I am."

"How come?"

"Mommy's . . . a friend of mine died."

"Today? Do I know her?"

"On Friday. And no."

I'm not sure why I don't correct the pronoun. It'll come out eventually, but for these few moments with my daughter, a change of pronoun is the distance I need.

"How come?"

"How come what?"

"How come I don't know her?"

"You don't know everyone I do."

"Yes I do."

I shift so I can see Zoey's angular face. She has these amazing eyelashes, dark and long. She's had them since she was a baby. They were the first thing I fell in love with.

"Not this time."

She shrugs. "Will we be going to the funeral?"

A shiver runs down my spine. "No, I don't think so."

"Oh well. I kinda like funerals."

I let this one slide, not quite sure if she's being serious, especially since the only one she's been to is my father's.

"Would you like me to be quiet now?" she asks.

"If that's okay."

"Course."

So we lie there like that, my daughter and I, in the quiet, quiet house, and my heart feels a little less broken.

We're still lying there when Brian comes home a couple of hours later. Somewhere along the way, we both fell into a half-doze, Zoey's snores sometimes jerking me from sleep. I shake her awake when I hear Brian moving around downstairs, telling her to go greet him, I'll be down in a minute. She obeys me without protest for once, and I change out of my wrinkled clothes into jeans and an old sweater. Then I wash the tears off my face, careful not to look at myself in the mirror. I feel light-headed from the lack of food, too much sleep, and grief, but somehow I make it downstairs, kiss Brian hello, try to act normal.

I pull together a supper made up mostly of leftovers, some pasta, some Chinese takeout, a salad, and the dinner hour passes away much like it always does. Brian tells a funny story about one of his hypochondriac patients, identity protected, though I'm sure it's Mrs. Garland by the sounds of it. Zoey tells us about her day once we've asked sufficient questions to get her past her usual reluctance. I remember feeling the way she does, like it was my life and why did I have to be cross-examined about it, but it always feels as if it's the right thing to do, so we do it.

After dinner, Zoey and Brian go to the living room to prepare for her upcoming competition. I clean every inch of the kitchen as if my life depended on its spotlessness. When I'm done, the room smells of disinfectant and the skin on my hands is cracking along the knuckles. I'm rinsing out the kitchen sponges when Brian wanders in for a glass of water.

He's distracted and wants to get back to Zoey, so this is my chance. I take a deep breath and manage to tell him that a colleague of mine died, sorry if I've been in a bad mood.

"You've been fine. Someone I know?"

"No. Unless you met at that corporate thing? You remember that getaway we went to a while back?"

"In Mexico? Two years ago?"

"Yeah."

"What was her name?" He makes the same assumption as Zoey.

I wipe at an imaginary spot on the counter. "Jeff Manning."

"Doesn't ring any bells. He live here?"

"In the other Springfield."

"Young guy?"

"About my age. Thirty-nine. Married. A kid."

"Ugh. Was he ill?"

"Car accident."

"That's terrible."

I think I might be sick.

"It is."

"You know him well?"

"Sort of. We'd been . . . working on some projects together in the last year or so."

Brian squeezes my shoulder. "Sorry."

"Thanks."

He's expecting me to face him, but if I do I'll collapse against him, I'll be sobbing again, and if there's one thing I can't do today, it's rely on Brian for solace.

Another half an Ativan taken out of Brian's sight helps me fall asleep, but I start awake with my heart galloping at two in the morning. *Oh my God,* I'm thinking before I'm fully conscious, *the emails.*

I bolt upright and move as quietly as I can. Brian twitches and shifts position, but I'm not really worried about waking him. Doctors are programmed during their residencies to sleep deeply whenever they're prone, and he's never outgrown the habit.

I feel around in the dark for my clothes and take them into the hallway. Zoey's reading light casts a glow along the floor. I should stop and put it out, but that might wake her and I can't have that. I've behaved strangely enough today.

I tiptoe down the carpeted stairs, being careful to avoid the third from the bottom, which always creaks ominously. I throw on my clothes, slip on a pair of running shoes, and grab my car keys from the table by the door. The air outside smells wet and springy, like it does after a rain has come and gone in the night.

My heart starts racing again when I reflexively hit the automatic unlock button and my car chirps, too loudly for this quiet street. I ease open the door and close it behind me as gently as I can. More heart palpitations when I start the engine, but no lights snap on in the house as I back out of the driveway, almost hitting the garbage can that Brian dutifully put out. Maybe I should've parked my car ass-in, but I buck all company policies as often as I can when not on company property.

I drive through the 2-a.m.-dead neighborhood, being careful to stop at the lights, obey the laws while getting to the office as fast as I can. I don't bother parking in a space. I simply stop the car by the front doors and run to the entrance. I swipe my pass and jerk open the glass door. Moments later, I'm seated in front of my computer, waiting anxiously for it to boot up. When it does, I click on the Back-Office program and start running the protocol we have for dismissed employees or ones who are under investigation. I wait impatiently for it to collect all of Jeff's emails, then sort them by name. Sender: Patricia Underhill. Sent to: Patricia Underhill.

I scroll down the list, and there they are: the emails and emails and emails we've exchanged over the last year. I open one at random.

I think I need some more training, he wrote at 11:52 a.m. six months ago.

Uh-huh.

No, seriously, I can't remember if we're supposed to be compassionate and caring, or caring and compassionate. I need to do module 3 again.

I could explain it to you on the phone.

That wouldn't be any fun.

I'll see what I can do. The training center's pretty booked this week.

I have faith.

You gotta have faitha, faitha, faitha.

You have terrible taste in music.

I click it shut. I press the buttons to highlight them all, my finger hesitating over the Delete key.

I can't do it.

I reach into my desk drawer and remove a USB key. I transfer the emails to it, then erase the originals from the server and then the offline backup, a real delete this time. The USB key has a lanyard attached to it, which I loop around my neck. The metal feels warm and dangerous against my skin.

Now I have one thing left to do. Because erasing the emails from the office's system doesn't affect whatever he's kept in his personal account. Maybe there's nothing there, but I can't take the risk. I go to his email service, type in his address, and take a guess at his password. His middle name is Michael but that's not it. I try his birthday in all combinations, his address, the name of his favorite football team. Seth's birthday. Claire's. Nothing works.

Then my eyes track to the "forgot your password?" prompt. I follow the instructions to have a password hint sent to jmanning@johnson.com, and wait the anxious seconds before the email arrives. It pings into place and I open it. I almost laugh out loud. Jeff's password hint is *fuck off.*

It would be. I type *fuck off* into the password space, and still nothing.

Goddamnit. My only hope now is, if I can't figure it out, maybe no one else can either.

A faint hope indeed.

Twenty minutes later I'm home again and crawling back into bed, though sleep is an impossibility. The lanyard is still around my neck. I clutch the USB key in my hand like it might contain some part of Jeff that's still alive. His beating heart. His gentle brain.

"Did you go out?" Brian says, startling me.

"I, uh, remembered I hadn't sent a report to Mr. Keene that he needs first thing tomorrow morning."

"Couldn't you have sent it from here?"

"Something's wrong with the remote server."

"Sorry you had to go out."

"That's okay."

"You know you don't have to work there if you don't want to."

"I know."

He pulls the covers up to his shoulders. "I should get back to sleep, and so should you."

"Don't worry about me."

His hand snakes to my thigh under the covers. "I won't ever stop."

PART 2

CHAPTER 9

Meet Cute

About a year ago, Johnson Company did a total software overhaul. Our new email program took its cue from Facebook. Everyone in the system now had a user profile that included a picture and a mini-bio that popped up on the side of the page if you clicked on their contact information or emailed them.

My name is Jeff Manning. I like sunsets and kittens and . . .

It was meant to foster "inter-office collegiality" or some such bullshit. As far as I could tell, it was mainly an opportunity for voyeurism and ridicule, particularly for the people — almost always women, almost always of a certain age — who took the whole thing too seriously. They'd strike "alluring" poses with their faces tilted to the side, their hair salon-perfect, and post bios full of their likes and dislikes. If they were stupid enough to mention their cats — or, God forbid, pose with one of them — they were done for.

I don't know if it was spite, boredom, or low-level rebellion, but the minute the site went live, there was a small but persistent group — almost always men, almost always of a certain age — who started compiling lists.

Top Ten Most Likely to Have Their Corpse Eaten by Their Cats. Top Ten Trying Too Hard. Top Ten MILFs. And so on. If you can think of it, the list existed. While some of them were funny, those of us "lucky" enough to be management had the distinctly unfun task of trying to discover the perpetrators so they could be disciplined.

And that's how I re-met Tish.

When a particularly nasty list went around—Top Ten Facial Blemishes That Ought to Be Taken Care of Immediately—I actually felt motivated to find the culprit. My own assistant was on it, and the mole on her chin wasn't that bad, really. I had a pretty good idea who the perpetrator was, a junior accountant named Evan. Since he was someone I'd been wishing I had something on for a while—he was a dick of the highest order, and marginally competent to boot—I did some skulking around and got the proof I needed.

My boss, Gerry, was all for firing him, so he took it upstairs and came back with the okay to give him the axe. An "example had to be set," and guess who got to set it?

Yessir.

Gerry suggested I get some HR training before I did the deed, something about protecting us from liability if Evan went postal.

"I've found Tish from the other Springfield helpful. Plus, she's number five on—"

I held up my hand. "Don't say it. Then I'll have to report you too."

"Good luck with that."

He did one of those high school bird-flipping maneuvers that turned into rubbing the side of his nose before snickering his way out of my office.

I'm pretty sure Gerry's the origin of more than one list.

I almost called after him to ask "Tish who?" but it occurred to me that Tish was a pretty unusual name. There probably weren't two people named Tish in the HR department in the other Springfield.

So it proved. A couple clicks of the keyboard brought me to the contact page of Tish Underhill—real name Patricia—and I couldn't keep my face from breaking into a grin.

I'd thought of her occasionally since that chance meeting in the food line. Fleeting thoughts, mostly when HR got mentioned, but I'd never made any effort to find her. Because what was the point? She'd made it fairly clear that she didn't want to be found . . .

But when I pulled up her contact information, I admit I spent a long time studying it, her picture in particular. Not because she looked great in it — okay, not *only* because she looked great in it — but because of the whole attitude of the thing. Her dark hair tumbled over her shoulders, like she'd just released it from an elastic, and she wasn't wearing any makeup. She held her chin in her hand, a pose I usually would've found derisible, but in her case, it gave off the perfect mix of ease and I-don't-give-a-fuck. This is me, her picture said, love it or hate it.

I loved it, and found myself looking at it whenever I had an idle moment.

I may have had a lot of idle moments.

I also loved what she wrote in her profile. No embellishments or waxing eloquent about her pets. She was married, she had a daughter, she loved reading and golf.

It was, in fact, nearly word for word what I wrote in my own biography, which I'd left till the last minute and dashed off without any thought. Maybe that's what she'd done too. Whatever it was — our strange first conversation, the similarity of our thought process — I felt a sense of kinship with her.

If I'm being honest, it took me a few days to work up the courage to contact her. But like all things, it had to be done sometime. There was a firing to do, after all, and so I opened her contact page, glanced at her now familiar picture, discarded the mental drafts I'd composed, and wrote:

Patricia,

Not sure if you remember me, but we met a while back at that company retreat in Mexico. I was the guy who completely embarrassed himself in the food line. "You schooled that flagpole" is a line that's been haunting me for a while.

Anyway, I have an HR situation I need a consult on. Can we hop on the line when you have a chance?

Best,

Jeff Manning

I hit Send without reading it through, feeling like I'd asked her on a date.

Which was ridiculous.

Ridiculous.

Ping!

There was a reply from her in my inbox.

Jeff,

Please call me Tish. And how could I forget your knight in shining armor act on the driving range? If you hadn't dragged that guy away, there might've been a homicide. Besides, I was trying to school that thing, so no need to be haunted, if you were.

Hop on whenever you'd like.

Tish

A slight pause and then,

Tish,

Hop on now?

Jeff

Seconds later,

Hop away.

I glanced at her phone number and dialed it. My fingers felt shaky and I kept clearing my throat, like I had a cold coming on, which I didn't.

Ring, ring.

"Jeff," she said, a laugh in her voice. "What took you so long?"

CHAPTER 10

Playing in the Dirt

I wake on Thursday feeling something, some measure, like myself. I have a bit of that thumping energy I get, the will to do something, something, I always have to be doing something. I want to leave the house so badly I wish I had somewhere to go to like Seth does. School, I want to go to school, I realize as I'm eating my sugarcoated breakfast while trying to ignore the never-ending flow of my parents' bickering. And I have a school to go to. My school.

With Beth's encouragement and over my mother's halfhearted protests, I shower, dress, make an attempt to arrange my hair, and walk to Playthings. The day promises glorious and the trees are greening. Life, it all screams. Life.

Driving's still out of the question, but I leave the funeral pills behind. They make me too fuzzy, too lizard-brained, and if my mind's now full of racing thoughts, at least they aren't only about Jeff. The slow-motion slideshow of our life together that seems to wend endlessly through my brain has small commercial breaks. *We need some better food in the house. Seth should get a haircut. Is there any chance I might convince Beth to move home and, possibly, in with us?*

Playthings ends up being exactly what I need. Not the work, or the bills waiting for my attention, or the lease that needs renegotiating, but the kids. When I enter the building and breathe in the familiar smell of fruit-based children's snacks and papier-mâché materials, I decide to bypass my office and the red light I can see on my desk phone blinking *message, message, message* and head right for the primary colors.

I feel the strange looks aimed my way from some of the staff, but none of them tries to dissuade me. The tiny little children don't know any better. They have a new big person to pay attention to them; all's right in their me, me, me world.

I play blocks, I read the same story about Thomas the Tank Engine (*go, Thomas, go, Thomas, go go go*) more times than I can count. I roll around on the floor and let the boys take out their aggression by pouncing on me with squeals of delight. I plunk out a few tunes on the child-sized piano, all off-chords and tinny sounds. When snack time arrives, I scoot around the low plastic table, scooping little Ruby Adams into my lap. We share a cut-up apple, some grapes, and a handful of Goldfish.

We play a game with the fish-shaped crackers, pretending they're swimming in an imaginary sea. After snack comes nap time, and I'm as ready for it as the children are. Ruby pats the space next to her with her slightly yellowed fingers, and I tuck a plush toy under my head.

As I start to drift, the feel of the plastic mat underneath me knocks a new memory into my brain. And as much as I don't want to think about it, I fall asleep to thoughts of the last time I was on a mat in this room, and with whom.

I leave Playthings before the parents start arriving for pickup, wanting to avoid the uncomfortable conversations that are sure to ensue. Like the messages from my friends I keep on ignoring, *I'll leave it till tomorrow*, I think, then think it again the next day.

The air outside is cooler than when I arrived. April's been fooling us these last few weeks into believing it's spring, but winter isn't quite ready to give up its grip. I double over the front of my light coat, holding it tight against my body with my hands thrust in my pockets, and walk as quickly as I can.

It's fully dark by the time I get home. I can see small puffs of my breath in the glow from the street lamps. When I get to my front walk, Beth's sitting on the front porch in my winter parka, waiting, I assume, for me.

"Hey," she says, looking up from her iPad.

It's open to her work email, which is full of red-exclamation-mark-important messages.

Beth's a partner in a swanky big-city firm located a thousand miles away from here. She'd wanted to leave Springfield as long as I can remember. It was how she started most of her sentences growing up when we were out of our parents' hearing.

"When I get out of here . . ."

I never quite understood what it was that drove her. She's always been really close with our father, his favorite ever since she declared at ten that she wanted to be a lawyer like him. It was she who spent her summers working in the filing room, running documents to court, learning how to do easy research mandates. He even had "James & James" business cards made up when she got into law school.

But she was determined. And when she went first to college as far away as possible, and then to law school even farther away than that, I watched my father's heart crack at the realization that what he'd always taken as a given wasn't going to happen.

A few days after she'd called to say she'd accepted a job at a fancy West Coast firm that subsisted on sunshine and movie stars, I found him sitting in his study with the box of business cards in his hands. He looked so lost I found myself saying something I wasn't even sure was true.

"I'm going to be a lawyer, Dad. I've decided."

He looked up, startled, clearly having been unaware of my presence until I spoke. "That's nice, dear."

"No, I mean it. Really. And I want to come back, I . . . want to work with you."

"You don't have to do that."

"I want to."

He looked at me for a moment, like he was puzzling something out. "I always thought . . . are you sure?"

"I'm sure."

"Well, I guess I'll keep these then," he said, patting the box.

When I turned to leave, I heard him slide open the drawer to his desk, the one that squeaked, his discard drawer where old papers he couldn't quite bring himself to throw away went to live their lives in rarely disturbed seclusion. The box thunked onto the stack of brittle papers, and I imagined the dust motes floating up to tickle my father's nose. That he'd placed the cards in that particular drawer told me he didn't believe me, despite what he said.

And as he sneezed a mighty sneeze, I thought, *You'll see, Dad. You'll see.*

So Beth left and I stayed. She makes it home about twice a year, if we're lucky. She had a brief, disastrous marriage to a guy I never really got to know, which ended when he cheated on her, and since the divorce, I've heard little of her dating life. I wonder sometimes if she's lonely, but it isn't the sort of thing we ask in our family, or admit to.

"Has the firm collapsed since you've been gone?" I ask.

"It spins on without me."

"Then why do you look so serious?"

She shrugs. "How was Playthings? Still standing without *you*, or have the kids torn it down brick by brick?"

I take a seat next to her on the porch. The wood releases its stored-up cold.

"It was good, really good, actually, and it's still standing. But why did you change the subject?"

Her email pings. She frowns at the screen, which casts a greenish glow on her skin.

"Did I?"

"Yeah, you did. What gives?"

She types as she talks, her fingers moving in a practiced way across the screen. "Nothing. Did you want to go out for dinner? How about Joe's? I haven't been there in ages." She hits Send, folds the cover over the screen, and stands up. "Do you mind if we go now? I'm starving."

"What about Seth?"

"He's having dinner at a friend's."

"Who authorized that? Which friend?"

"I did. Carter someone. I thought it was a good sign. Hope that's okay."

"I suppose so."

"We good to go, then?"

I feel a knot of annoyance at the Seth thing, but it doesn't distract me from the fact that Beth seems awfully anxious to leave. Not that I can blame her. Our parents are probably in the house squabbling over the remote, or something else equally inane.

But still.

"Do you mind if I change first? I smell like Play-Doh."

"It's fine for Joe's."

I stand up. Even in flats, Beth's a head taller than me. "What's up with you?"

"Nothing. I'm hungry. You know how I get when I don't eat."

"Well, your stomach's going to have to cool it for a minute, because I need to pee."

She lurches so she's standing between me and the front door. "Okay, seriously now, Bethie. What the hell?"

She breathes in and out deeply, steeling herself for something. "Tim's in there."

"Oh, is that —" I stop and search her face for some explanation. "I mean, of course he's here. I knew that. We knew that. Today's Thursday, right? So what's the big deal?"

"What's the big deal? Come on, Claire."

The knot of annoyance grows. Or maybe it's a knot of something else.

"That's all past. It's in the past."

"Is it?"

"Of course. Jesus. Jeff just —"

She puts her hands on my shoulders, pulling me close. I can smell her citrusy shampoo. It feels too close for comfort.

"I know, Claire. *I know.*"

"I'm going to have to see him sometime."

"I know that too."

"So?"

"I thought . . ."

I take a step back. "You really think the worst of me, don't you?"

"No, of course not. I was just . . . I don't know what I was trying to do. I was being stupid, okay? Forgive me?"

I meet her eyes, a clearer, lighter version of my own. "Do *you* forgive *me*? I mean, really forgive. Not lip service."

Her hesitation speaks for her.

"That's what I thought."

I walk to the front door and stop with my hand on the knob. "He forgave me, you know."

"Do you mean Jeff, or Tim?"

I shoot her a look and enter the house. The heat is higher than we normally keep it, and I can hear the murmur of voices in the living room. My parents' voices mixed with a deeper one, only slightly less familiar. A voice from the echoey past.

As I take off my coat, sadness replaces it, a tight fit. It makes walking to the living room harder, even though I can't help myself from doing so.

When I reach the doorway, there they all are. My parents, sitting on the loveseat, forced closer together than they ever are in real life. Tim, in the wingback chair no one sits in, not ever. His face is tanned and wrinkled from the sun. He's wearing chinos, a white T-shirt, and a chunky steel watch on his wrist. His left hand rests casually on the chair arm. His fingers are long, thin, and bare.

I stand there silently, watching, listening to the tone of the talk rather than the substance.

My mother senses my presence first. "Why, Claire. How long have you been standing there?"

Tim reacts like an electric shock's passed through him, or the shiver of a ghost.

"Not long."

"Tim's here," she says.

"I see that."

Tim stands at the sound of his name, so quickly the chair tips backward and almost over before righting itself in the deep impressions it's left in the carpet.

We stare at each other for a moment before he walks toward me, quick and certain. He takes me in his arms, pressing my face to his chest. He smells of salt and an aftershave I don't recognize.

"I'm so terribly sorry, Claire," he says.

Then he releases me and leaves.

CHAPTER 11

Brace for Impact

Despite being only five hundred miles away from one another as the crow flies, there are no direct flights between my Springfield and Jeff's.

I consider driving to the funeral, but since I don't think I can stand that much time alone with my thoughts, I take a connecting flight through one of those hubs whose terminals splay out like spokes on a wheel. An hour there, an hour layover, an hour to the other Springfield, and I'll be there.

I'll. Be. There.

But what am I even doing here, on my way to Springfield, on my way to the funeral I told Zoey I wouldn't be attending?

The day after *the* day, after the shouting, the crying, what I hope was the worst day of my life, I managed, somehow, to pull a cloak of normalcy around me. I sat at my desk, answered my phone and emails, and processed paperwork for the next three unfortunates who were being terminated. I pretended I wasn't the object of stares, of whispers, of questions, of doubt. In my silence, I hoped, I'd reinforce the hasty explanations I gave on the ride home with Lori, and that would be that. If I was lucky, there'd be some other event, or someone else, to talk about tomorrow.

At midday, an email went out to the members of the HR department. It had been decided that someone from the company should attend the funeral. Be an envoy. Say a few nice things about how devoted Jeff was, how well liked. It wouldn't be a pleasant mission, so a volunteer *would be appreciated.*

The email felt like a bomb sitting in my inbox.

Were my coworkers expecting me to defuse it?

As the minutes ticked away and no one reply-alled their raised hand, my chest started to constrict and I worried I might start hyperventilating. I wanted to go, and I knew at the same time that it was the last thing I should be doing.

In the end, I couldn't help myself.

I'll go, I wrote and hit Send before sanity restored itself.

As my email pinged into my department's inboxes, I imagined I heard a collective sigh of relief. *Oh, thank God,* a dozen people were thinking. *I won't have to be surrounded by sad people, or search for the right words to say. Besides,* my thoughts ran on, *she should be the one to go, anyway.*

Shouldn't she?

I waited for the right moment to tell Brian. For many reasons, but in particular because of the timing.

Because timing is everything, and the timing here was way off.

"But it's Nationals," Brian said once I managed to get the words out in the kitchen after dinner. I'd poured him an extra-strong drink an hour earlier, but the whole bottle wouldn't make him forget that detail.

"I talked to Zoey—"

"What do you mean, you talked to Zoey?"

"I explained the situation and asked her whether she'd mind if I wasn't there."

"You explained the situation?"

"I told her it was a work thing. She said it was okay."

He leaned against the counter, an incredulous look on his face. "Of course she said it was okay, but you know she didn't mean it."

"She seemed sincere."

"She's *eleven*. It's not her decision. She's competing at Nationals, for Christ's sake. Her mother should be there. *You* should be there."

The stab of guilt penetrated through the Ativan shield I was still hiding behind. I have one pill left, and I'm saving it for what's coming.

"It's not like it's the first time she's been there. Or that there's any doubt she's going to win. Besides, I almost never go anymore. It's your thing together. Your thing with Zoey."

He held his thoughts for a moment. "Maybe you're right, but it shouldn't be."

"I thought you were fine with that? You never said—"

"Honestly? I was hoping you'd realize it on your own."

He pushed himself away from the counter. I reached out to him, but my reflexes were slow and all I ended up grabbing was the edge of his shirt, right below the elbow.

"Brian."

He half turned to me. "Let's drop it, all right? You've made up your mind anyway. But it's not okay, Tish. I am not okay with this."

He put his hand on the hinged door leading into the dining room and pushed it hard enough so that it slammed against the wall.

I stood there for a long time watching the door swing back and forth, thinking that it should be creaking, that its courtesy-of-Brian-oiled silence was a rebuke, evidence that his commitment to this house, this life, has always been greater than mine.

Julia agreed to drive me to the airport, but there was a thick silence between us.

She pulled up to the five-minute unloading zone. "You have everything you need?"

"I think so."

"Will you tell me one thing?"

"What's that?"

"Forget it. You won't say, anyway."

Her face was a mask.

"I can't explain, Julia. Not now. Can't you understand how this might happen, even a little?"

"Understand how it might happen to someone else? Or you?"

"Why is it any different if it's me?"

"I'm not sure. It just is."

"I'm sorry, Jules."

"Yeah, well." She glanced in the rearview mirror. Her son, Will, was asleep in his car seat, his face flushed, his head resting at an angle only a small child can sleep at. "You should probably go. Don't want to miss your flight."

"Right."

I gathered my purse from the floor, checking it automatically for the hard shape of my phone.

"Can we talk, you think, when I get back?" I asked.

"I don't know. Maybe. We'll see, okay?"

"Thanks for the lift."

She nodded and pushed the button to release the trunk.

"Have a safe flight."

I collected my carry-on, and as I walked to the entrance it began to sink in that maybe I had lost more than Jeff.

Maybe I was going to lose everything.

Aboard my second flight, I walk down the long center aisle to my seat, and look for room for my suitcase in the full overhead compartment.

"Let me help you with that," says a man touching forty.

Before I can protest, he swings the bag away from me and up into a space I thought was too small even for the little suitcase I'd brought with me. I don't intend on staying any longer than I have to.

"All set," he says.

"Thanks."

"It's nothing. Window or aisle?"

"Oh, window I guess. But you —"

"I insist. I prefer the aisle anyway." He gestures at his height, which I place at six three at least.

I slide over to the window. I tighten the seat belt against my waist and rest my head against the cold oval of plastic, noticing a row of small holes across the bottom. I've always wondered what these holes are for. To release pressure, or to keep us from decompressing as we rise to the edge of the atmosphere?

Maybe I should drill a few small holes in my brain.

The city out the window looks like any other, particularly once we've left the ground behind. We fly over a neighborhood that could be mine — the same curved streets and newly built houses in pastel hues. I watch the cars navigate the streets, and a few tiny dots on the sidewalks.

When we've pushed through the clouds, I reach into my purse and take out a battered notebook, something I threw in at the last minute, thinking I might be able to write something about Jeff to say at the funeral. To do what I was sent to do.

I flip slowly through the pages, searching for a blank one. It's an old notebook, full of half scraps of poetry, ideas, lines, an occasional finished poem. In the last fifteen years, this is the only notebook I've needed, and it's only half full.

The teenaged Tish flashes before me, hunched over one of the many such notebooks lined up like forgotten toys on the bookshelf in our study. Her hand is flying across the page, unable to move fast enough to capture the ephemeral words that appear before her at regular intervals, unbidden.

One of the pages near the front has Brian's name and number on it, written in his physician's hand.

When I was in my last year of college, my parents were hospitalized, a week apart, in the hospital where Brian was doing the first year of his residency.

Even then, it seemed over-the-top, having both my parents on the brink of dying, so *A-Heartbreaking-Work-of-Staggering-Genius* of them. But the funny thing, if there's anything funny about it, is that I wasn't that surprised. They'd done everything together my whole life, so dying at the same time seemed like one more thing they'd managed to do right.

Together, anyway. Not right by me.

He had a bad heart, my dad, the same heart that had taken his dad at forty-six. My mom had breast cancer that advanced beyond where it should because she was too busy taking care of Dad to notice the lump forming, separate the bone-weary tiredness from nursing him from something connected wholly to her. They should've been on different floors of the hospital, but my dad, Charming Billy, worked his magic until my mother was wheeled into his room and plugged in next to him.

Brian was working nights then, and I was spending a lot of nights at the hospital. Wandering the halls, haunting the cafeteria, scribbling in my notebook.

"You're the Newtons' daughter, right?" he asked me one night as I wrapped my ink-stained hands around a cup of half-burned coffee in the cafeteria. I was sitting at my usual table, a small round of Formica tucked next to the windows where I could feel like I was sitting in sunlight during the day, and in the inky sky at night.

I looked up at him. Hospital scrubs, circles under his eyes, a face that was shaven yesterday. Twenty-six, I thought. Handsome. Even in my fog of grief and words, I was present enough to see that.

"That's right. And you're . . . ?"

"Dr. Underhill." He said the words like they were unfamiliar. "Brian. Your parents are on my rotation."

"Right. I remember you."

"Can I sit for a minute?"

"Sure."

He sat across from me. I watched him, wanting to ask what I'd wanted to ask all the others: When was it coming, really, the end? But I couldn't manage it. I never could.

"Why do you guys do that?" I asked instead.

"What?"

"Insist on using your title all the time? The nurses don't introduce themselves as Nurse Jones or Nurse Ramirez."

He looked taken aback, then he grinned at me. A wide grin, full of well-taken-care-of teeth. "Because we're the masters of the universe."

"Pardon?"

"It's this thing some of the jerks in my class started calling themselves after a few weeks in first year, but it's kind of a pervasive sentiment."

"Because of the life-saving thing?"

"There's that, but it's also a way to distance yourself from the patient. If we're not on a first-name basis, then I won't be totally shattered when I don't save your life."

"You told me your first name."

"You're not the patient."

"Right. Not the *patients*."

I looked down at the words written on the paper in front of me. They were blurry and nonsensical. The ever-present smell of cleaning products was giving me a headache.

"Sorry," he said.

"About what?"

"You know . . . the patients."

"Yeah, well. That's life, I guess. Or death."

I rubbed my hand over my eyes, trying to clear the blurriness away. When I could focus, I found Dr. Brian trying to read my notes upside down.

I shut the cover of my notebook.

"Okay, now I'm really sorry."

"No big deal."

"You write poetry?"

"Sometimes." I thought about it. "When things suck, or when they're really good."

"Kind of like the doctor thing?"

"How do you mean?"

"Writing it down distances you from it, maybe?"

"Ouch."

"Oh, man, I shouldn't have said that. We don't even know each other."

I watched him again, how his face reddened, how he really did look sorry. And even though I felt terrible, I wanted to make him feel better. There was something in that, I knew. So instead of leaving, instead of giving him any more crap, I did the opposite. I told the truth.

"Then how come this is the most real conversation I've had since my parents got sick?"

"Maybe it's the circumstances?"

"I hope not," I said, and he smiled.

My dad pulled through, in the end. My mom did not. When I finally wheeled him out of the hospital, pale as the ghost of my mother, who was his constant shadow, I had a handful of poems. I read them all one night a few weeks later, trying to decide if Brian was right about them being a way to distance myself from death, illness, from everything. I thought and I thought, and when I couldn't decide, I flipped to the page I was writing in that night, saw the phone number he'd written there in case I needed someone to talk to, and decided I did.

"Were you having a bad dream?"

I start awake, feeling disoriented. The man sitting next to me has his hand on the armrest that separates our seats. It's brushing my arm.

I move away. "Pardon?"

"You sounded frightened. I hope it's all right that I woke you?"

I straighten myself in my seat, embarrassed that my old childhood habit has come back to haunt me in a public place.

"Did I say anything . . ." *Odd,* I guess I want to ask, but don't.

"No. I thought it better to wake you before you became too distressed."

Or before I said something that would be embarrassing to the both of us.

"I appreciate it."

He holds out something. My notebook, which must have slipped from my grasp.

"You'll want this," he says.

I take it from him, letting it rest in my lap. "Yes. I . . . thank you."

"You're a poet, then?"

"I used to be. Sometimes. I was trying to get some ideas down. For work."

My words seem to stick in my throat. But I don't owe this man any explanations. I don't have to say anything, really.

He smiles briefly. "Once a poet, always a poet."

"Poetry is for the young," I say, thinking of my earnest Zoey. "And maybe, also, for the old. Though I'm not sure about that one. I'll let you know when I get there."

I cut off my babble, looking down in embarrassment. I see the one word I wrote down before I slipped off to sleep: *Jeff*. It's written at the top of the page of the only poem I've written in the last couple of years. A poem no one's ever seen. I close the notebook quickly, feeling a hysterical urge to laugh. I shove my fist in my mouth to stop it, biting down on my knuckles, almost breaking the skin.

"I'm sorry, I don't know what —"

"Think nothing of it," he says, but I sense him growing wary.

I think about how I must look on the outside. My dark hair is brushed and tucked up against my neck. I'm wearing jeans, but they're crisp and new. My cream sweater has enough cashmere in it to be referred to as such. Tasteful makeup. A few lines around my eyes. Sensible shoes. A woman in the second half of her thirties who's the same size she was in high school, give or take some redistribution. An ordinary woman. Taking an ordinary trip.

But from the way he's looking at me, I can't help feeling that he's seeing past all that. That he can see the thoughts rioting around in my brain, sense the sadness dragging at my heart.

Then he shifts away, the moment's gone, and we're back to being two people on an airplane, headed in the same direction, breathing the same recycled air.

The cab from the airport takes me past Jeff's favorite golf course, one he spoke about frequently. Then we pass a restaurant he'd mentioned, and so on, and so on. It's like all these conversations we'd had are suddenly animated, clay made into moving life.

I don't know how I kidded myself into thinking I'd be anything other than a total mess the whole time I was here. The hubris of two semi-normal days at the office? Of all the stupid things to do, of all the stupid decisions I've made, this is the hardest to bear. But maybe that's fate, karma, the way it should be. Maybe I haven't suffered enough for my decisions, and so now, in this last act, the entire bill is coming due.

I barely make it out of the cab, and the woman behind the check-in counter at the hotel asks me more than once if I'm okay. I mumble that I am, of course, allergies, the first thing that comes to mind. But I'm not, and as the heavy hotel-room door shuts me into solitude with a thud, I find myself leaning against it, sliding to the floor, almost hyperventilating the tears out of me.

And though I've already spent a day like this, though I thought that would be the worst day, I was wrong. At home, I had the familiar sights, sounds, and distractions of my life to pull me from my grief, to stay the tears and the dark thoughts. For Zoey, for Brian, I could make the effort. There'd be moments where I'd forget, whole seconds, sometimes minutes. At night, I had the stolen Ativan, broken into halves to make them last, to wipe my brain clean, to erase even my dreams.

I was surviving.

But in this anonymous hotel room, I have nothing to hold on to. And outside lies Jeff's world, a world that's familiar enough to me to wound but not enough to know what streets to avoid, which people might suddenly speak of him, where it's safe to cry.

So I stay in my room, and I make myself breathe, and finally my body's so worn out by the effort I'm able to crawl under the covers of the thick white duvet and fall into a fretful sleep.

CHAPTER 12

Rites of Passage

In a sense you could say I've already been to my own funeral.

It all started when our friend Rob died.

I was in my second year of college; Tim was about to graduate. Rob was in the grade between us during elementary and high school, a mutual snow-fort builder, Woods-player, Rule-follower.

We found out he was dying when we were home on break. Tim and I were feeling restless a few days after Christmas, and we decided to make the snowy trek across town to the small house Rob had rented when he'd dropped out of college the year before when his mom died.

We showed up as the sun was setting behind his house. It was a half-cloudy day, and the sky was streaked with orange and topaz. His street was full of mature trees, their leaves gone months ago. The air smelled cold, even though the sun had been warm earlier. I looked up at the brilliant sunset as Tim pressed the bell, so I wasn't looking ahead as the door opened.

"Hey, guys," Rob said, a mixture of surprise and fear in his voice.

My head snapped down and I took a step back before I could help myself. Rob was standing in the doorway, but I barely recognized him. He was thirty pounds thinner, had black rims around his eyes, and a yellow tinge to his skin.

It was pancreatic cancer, he told us when we were seated in his gloomy living room, untouched beers in our hands. He'd taken a leave of absence from work when he got the diagnosis and, as far as I could tell, had holed up in this fourteen-by-fourteen-foot room since then. A film of dust coated everything, even him, it seemed.

The cancer was terminal. He was, for lack of a better phrase, waiting in that room to die. He didn't say the words — he didn't have to. The pills on the coffee table, the makeshift bed on the couch, the pile of DVDs of all his favorite movies stacked up like a Jenga game next to the TV all spoke for him.

What they couldn't say was why he'd kept it to himself. How he could have kept it from us all this time. He never knew his dad, and with his mom gone, we were, for all intents and purposes, his family.

I asked, once, but he acted as if he didn't hear me. He kept on washing the dishes in the sink, slowly, rhythmically, and just changed the topic.

We spent the rest of the holiday with him. We took him on a slow walk around the block, filled his fridge and freezer with prepared food, and bought him a dozen more DVDs. I taped my numbers on a piece of paper near the phone and wrote "In case of emergency" above them. Rob saw me do it, shook his head slightly, but didn't say anything. We talked sporadically, letting him set the pace, and when it was time to go back to school, we hugged good-bye, something we rarely did. His bones felt like a bird's against me, so fragile, and my brain shivered.

He died six weeks later. Tim and I both spoke at the service, telling funny stories, trying to keep it light. What else do you do when a twenty-one-year-old dies? You say he lived his life to the fullest, whether he did or not, that you were sure he had no regrets, no things left undone.

But, of course, everyone has regrets. Loose ends. Things they could do if they had more time.

Everyone does.

Afterward, we gathered in the church basement, a depressing room with ceilings so low anyone approaching six feet had to stoop.

The adrenaline began to drop, reality began to hit, and I'm sure I would have lost it completely if Tim hadn't chosen that moment to put his hand on my shoulder and suggest we get out of there.

I agreed readily, and we moved to a dingy bar down the street with a group of our childhood friends. I remember an old jukebox, a bar-food menu, the smell of half-rotted oats and cheap detergent. We ordered pitchers of beer — a local brew that's thick and strong — and we continued on, telling every story we could remember about Rob, even the ones whose endings had been consumed by alcohol molecules or time.

When the stories petered out, Tim said how much it sucked that Rob wasn't there. That he couldn't hear how much he meant to us, what a hole he left behind. "People shouldn't have to be dead for them to hear that shit," he said, his words slurring, though that didn't blunt the ring of truth.

The idea was born from this. We should have a funeral for all of us, one we could attend. It would be a celebration of our life till then that wasn't tinged with anything other than love, brother, love.

Maybe it was because we'd reached the I-love-you-man part of the evening, but we agreed to a date there and then. A date we kept, six months later.

Our families thought we were crazy, but we didn't care. We were doing this for Rob. We were doing this for us. We were doing it.

Despite people's doubts, the town hall was packed and, pretty soon, laughter clung to the rafters. Each of us spoke of the others: the good, the bad, the funny. Tim even put together a slideshow and set it to schmaltzy music. I'm sure he was doing it to be ironic, but halfway through Leonard Cohen's "Hallelujah" we were all wiping tears away.

We swore we'd do it again in five years, and every five years after that. To remember Rob, but also to remember us.

It never happened. Life became too complicated, too busy. But because of the pre-funeral, I know a few things you don't usually know.

The last person to speak about me will be Tim. There will be laughter, a few tears. He'll have a slideshow full of embarrassing shots of me as a child in a series of unfortunate outfits. He'll remind everyone of the time I almost set the house on fire, how I'd succeeded in running the school mascot's uniform up our high school's flagpole, how I still thought I might make the PGA one day, or at least the Senior Tour. Then he'll signal to someone and they'll click to the next slide, and there I'll be. My face projected through a bright stream of light, smiling, laughing, Rob and our friend Kevin on either side of me, gussied up in tuxedos for prom, awkwardly holding the corsages we'd bought for our dates.

Oh, God, we were young.

CHAPTER 13

Speechless

When Tim has finished speaking, he walks through the stream of light that's projecting Jeff's face onto the screen behind him. His shadow crosses Jeff's younger smile, a momentary reprieve.

It's such an odd place to be. Sitting in a pew at my husband's funeral. My sister on one side, my son sitting rigid against me on the other, murmuring under his breath while he repeatedly smooths a piece of foolscap across his knees. The air smells like a botanical garden, and there's a certain quality to the silence. Even what Seth's wearing marks this day as different: gray flannel pants and a blue blazer. It's his first almost-suit, something I'll never make him wear again, like the dress I bought with Beth that is, as predicted, scratchy and uncomfortable.

I've heard Tim's stories before, of course, first from Tim and then from Jeff. I knew Tim would be telling them because they told me all about that ridiculous event they insisted on having after their friend Rob died. The "pre-funeral," Jeff called it, serious and laughing, trying to make me understand. And while I did understand what gave birth to it, I couldn't support it. I laughed at the stories when they told them to me, but inside I felt nervous. Because if you attend your own funeral, if you know what everyone really thinks about you, if you are, essentially, at peace, don't you tip the odds toward death?

Maybe it was magical thinking, but I couldn't help believing that if you were prepared for the worst, you might make it come true.

The miscarriage was one confirmation of my theory; Jeff's death is the ultimate.

The person who first taught me to believe it is sitting next to Beth, and he's barely spoken to me since he's arrived.

Tim and I met during our first year of law school when we both tried out for the annual fund-raiser talent show.

My reason for being there was piano. Despite the crushing course load, I took an advanced orchestra class each semester. The music faculty made an exception for me, and that's probably why, when the law school came calling for its yearly favor (someone who could play whatever music was needed), Professor Davenport offered me up.

I'd fulfilled the same role in high school when tryouts for the school plays were as much a popularity contest as they were about talent. I could sing and memorize lines, but the parts went to Beth and her friends, and the ones who replaced them at the top of the social pyramid when they left. I could sing in the chorus, or play the piano. I chose the latter, my back mostly to the audience, but at least I had my own minute of applause at the end of the evening.

That year the law school had decided to do a musical instead of the usual compilation of sketches, a revival of *Guys and Dolls*.

My usual early-for-everything-even-when-I-try-to-arrive-late programming brought me to the auditorium a full half hour before I needed to be there. Most of the lights were off. There was a small spotlight focused on the stage, and the running lights that ran along the rows of red plush auditorium seating were on. The score, already half memorized, was tucked under my arm.

I walked down the aisle slowly, breathing in the mustiness left by a summer's un-use.

What happened next was like in one of those movies aimed at women. The geeky background girl sees her opportunity to feel what it's like (literally) to be in the spotlight, even though she isn't the geeky girl anymore. Away from the queen bees, in this mostly new place, she has come into her own. She expresses her opinions. The boys/men don't need to be drunk to approach her. Sometimes, she even approaches them.

But something about this place brings back memories. She places her music carefully on the piano and climbs the steps to the stage. She faces the empty seats, shadowy in the half-light. She takes a deep breath and sings a plaintive love song, the love song from the show she'll never audition for.

She gets lost in the music, her voice growing confident, the score she isn't playing loud and bright in her mind. She nails it.

If only there was someone to hear her.

There is. The room is not empty. The music director is standing stage left. When she stops singing, there's complete silence, followed by the sound of one person clapping. Startled, she blushes to her toes and apologizes. *No, don't,* he says. *That was beautiful. What's your name?*

She gives it, and he writes it down. *Oh, no,* she says, *I'm only here to play.* He raises an eyebrow, but before he can say anything else, the doors burst open, a gaggle of giggling young women tumbling through them.

She backs into the dark, and when you next see her she's sitting at her usual place, like Anne in *Persuasion,* ready to play for others' amusement.

Cue the hero, who's been dragged to the audition by his soccer buddies in his gray sweat shorts and a polo shirt whose collar is all stretched out. She recognizes the face sticking out of the polo shirt. He's from her hometown, though she doubts he'll remember her, if he looks at her. If he wasn't so preoccupied with acting like he doesn't want to be there. But he's been caught singing in the shower after practice one time too many, and he's been man-dared, mad-dogged-dared into it.

He waits his turn while she plays for the women with big egos and mediocre skills, for the serious guys who ignore the jocks' catcalls. If she glances at him, in between the beats, she sees his foot tapping, keeping time. She speeds up to test if he really can keep time or if it's a coincidence. He can, but the poor guy onstage can't.

A voice barks from the audience to pay attention, and the blush is back, her face angled away permanently.

His name's finally called. His friends are whistling and stamping, but he asks her to play "Sit Down, You're Rocking the Boat" anyway, and when she does he sings it well and with confidence. His friends stop their carping, respect creeping in. That respect snakes around the room and up to the music director, cast in his half shadow, as he should be.

It's no surprise when, a week later, she checks the cast list out of curiosity (she tells herself) and there his name is next to the part of Sky Masterson. And she pretends to be surprised, though she isn't really, when hers is set down for Sarah Brown, the missionary who falls in love with the gambler who eventually wants to change for his love of her.

She thinks, briefly, of turning it down, but fuck that, right? Fuck that.

They meet properly at the first rehearsal. She's about to mention their hometown connection when he does it for her. She wasn't as anonymous as she thought, after all.

In that first exchange there's already an undercurrent of flirting. And by the time they sing the song she sang to get her here, long before opening night, they're already in the love they are singing about.

The church organ is slightly off-key, something that makes me wince. Then the minister is speaking again, words that are meant to soothe, words I can't really hear. Is it simply the usual platitudes, or something he really feels? He knew Jeff, knew him all his life. He married us, and chastised us on the occasions when we ran into him for not attending church. But he says that to everyone, so I can't tell. I only know that the timbre of his voice is the same as it's been every other time I've heard him speak at a funeral. The same cadence governs his speech, the rise and fall of his voice almost hypnotic. But maybe that's the point. Maybe that's how you get through these terrible moments? Being lulled into the brief silences between old words.

Then he says a new word and I'm snatched from the somnambulant place I've been hiding.

"Seth," he says. "Did you want to speak?"

My son nods silently next to me, his hand still smoothing the piece of foolscap resting on his knees. I put my hand on his arm.

"You don't have to if you don't want to."

"No," he whispers. "I have to. For Dad."

He stands up and walks to the dais. He's just tall enough to see over the pulpit, and reaches for the microphone to adjust it to his height. He's about to grow tall like Jeff, but it's going to come too late.

"My dad was the best dad," he says, his voice cracking. "He was always . . . the best dad. I wish I could say more, for him, but I can't. So, Dad, I hope you understand that if I was any good at saying what I really felt, this is what I would say."

He looks up from his paper, and I wonder what he's looking at, if he sees anything beyond his fear. His lips tremble and my heart breaks all over again. *He's not going to be able to do it,* I think, half rising from my seat to go rescue him. But Beth holds me in place, and, after a moment, he bends his head and starts reading:

> *I don't need my heart anymore,*
> *you can have it.*
> *Cut it out,*
> *put it in a box,*
> *bury it in the hard ground,*
> *next to you.*
>
> *My eyes are useless too.*
> *They only show me a world*
> *without you.*
> *Color blind,*
> *color absent,*
> *colorless.*
>
> *And my mind screams, Not fair!*
> *Not right.*
> *Not what I was promised*

on the swing set
as you pushed me
toward the sun.

None of the stories you read me
schooled me for this.
I didn't learn this lesson
in the moon,
or on the train,
or as a thing to be curious about.

So I don't need my heart anymore,
you can have it.
Let it be buried,
in the hard ground,
next to you.

CHAPTER 14

Into the Middle Distance

I wake in my anonymous hotel room on the morning of Jeff's funeral feeling closer to control, but not close enough. I need to punish my body into some sort of submission, something that'll hold together through the funeral, the burial, the wake.

I call from the hotel room phone to check in with Brian and Zoey. They're leaving for Nationals today, a five-hour drive in the opposite direction.

"I have a bad feeling about this one," Zoey says, sounding uncharacteristically nervous.

"What do you mean, sweetheart? You'll do great."

"Dad's been pacing all morning."

"You know he gets nervous for you. We both do."

"I flubbed that line last time."

"What's up, Zo? Really?"

"Nothing, I . . . Are you okay?"

I try to keep the catch out of my voice. "I'm just sad, that's all. I'll be thinking of you."

"Dad wants to talk to you."

"All right. Good luck."

"*Mom!*"

"Sorry, sorry. Break a leg."

She thunks the phone down on the counter and yells for Brian. A few more clunks and he picks up.

"I tried calling last night . . ."

"Yeah, sorry. I realized this morning my cell phone was dead. I forgot to charge it."

"Got it. How is it there?"

"It looks a lot like home. Sans mountains."

"No, I meant . . . Anyway, Zoey is freaking out."

"Yeah, she kind of said. Look, if she doesn't want to go, don't make her, okay?"

"Don't forget your knapsack, Zo. What? No, no, she wants to go. God, can you believe it, but I think it's about a boy."

I looked out the window at the colorless sky. A boy. A boy.

"Our Zoey?"

He chuckled. "Who would've thunk it?"

"Do we know this boy?"

"That Zuckerman kid, maybe."

"Zuckerberg? The one from the western region?"

"Yeah, that one."

"Why him?"

"Not sure. He seems like the most likely candidate."

"Mmm. Well, hopefully it'll all blow over. Or maybe you can ask her on the drive?"

"I think that's your territory."

A reproach. If I were where I should be, I could ask her myself.

"Make sure she's got enough warm clothes."

"It's coming on summer here. Like someone flipped a switch over-night."

Not here. Not here.

"Drive safe, then."

"Will do. Check in later?"

"Yes."

We hang up and I flip through the town directory kept helpfully next to the telephone until I find what I need. A public golf course that isn't connected with Jeff as far as I know. I call to check if they're open, and when they say they are, I pull together a passable outfit and ask for directions from the twenty-something at the front desk.

"Cold day for golf," she says in the local twang that sometimes crept into Jeff's voice, the words slowed down, like the batteries running out on a music player.

The course is a twenty-minute walk away. The morning still holds the chill of the night I never saw. As directed, I walk along the local bike trail, still muddy from the just-gone snow. It was built on an old rail bed, and there are sections where the overhanging trees form a canopy that blocks out the weakly rising sun.

It ends at the golf course. The clubhouse and pro shop are deserted.

They're happy for the business, renting me a bag full of semi-decent clubs and giving me enough tokens for several hours' worth of hitting. I sling the bag on my shoulder, feeling the familiar weight, steadying my body against it, and trudge over the bike path to the range. The pickets haven't even been set up yet, and the ball machine groans like an old Coke machine that doesn't want to give up its treasure. But eventually the balls fall into the rusty wire basket, and the one after that.

I take out my seven iron and tee up a ball. My first swings are as rusty as the ball basket, the shaft clanging against the ground, sending shudders of protest up my arms. Soon enough the rhythm returns, but not the hum. That blank-mind state that Brick's searching for in *Cat on a Hot Tin Roof.* He used alcohol, but for me, that click from consciousness to only breathing, existing, comes from pushing myself as hard as I can physically.

I was counting on this today. I need it today, but it doesn't come. Instead, all the memories, the conversations, the words said and unsaid stream in and speed up until I'm hyperventilating again, barely able to catch my breath.

I keep on as the tears start. I swing and I swing, and I wait and I wait, but I never get there, not in the first hour, or in the second either. My back screams, my knees complain, my stomach and shoulders throw out aches and pains, but I'm not stopping for anything.

In my sorrow I've found the drive I needed all those years ago.

I want that click, I need that click, and I'm going to keep swinging until I find it, or my body gives out beneath me.

Back at the hotel, I strip my sweat-saturated clothes from my body, and I do, finally, feel a sort of calm. I feel strong enough, anyway, to climb into the shower and stand under the scalding stream until my body is as red as my face.

The rest is mechanical. Drying my hair, hiding the dark circles under my eyes with concealer, pressing the black dress I pulled from the back of my closet, purchased for some forgotten event when I was a dress size smaller. Or, at least, a dress size smaller than I was last week; now the dress fits fine.

I get to the church almost an hour early. I'm never early for anything, but I guess I shouldn't be surprised that I'm early today.

The day has become bright and sunny. I find a bench in a park nearby to sit on and stare into the middle distance. When I try to check the time on my phone, I realize I still haven't charged it.

As I clutch the useless device in my hand I briefly consider pitching it into the duck pond glimmering a few feet away, but I stifle the impulse. Throwing it away isn't going to change anything. Instead, I try to count the waves rippling gently against the pond's edge, matching the slow thud of my heart.

When I've counted what feels like enough waves to fill up three hours, I walk slowly back to the church. Cars have arrived, the parking lot's filling up, a fleet of black limos are parked in the circular drive. I reach into my purse to find the piece of paper torn from my notebook that I'd stashed there, full of words I can't read aloud, but that I will, if able, place with Jeff.

My pupils dilate in the vestibule. As I look down the long row of straight-backed pews, I know immediately that I'll be denied this too. The casket's lid is firmly shut, and in the minute it takes to register, I'm happy for it to be. I don't need that kind of personal encounter, not with him, not with anyone.

I take a seat in the back row and dig into my purse again for something I will definitely need, the last Ativan in my possession. There's a chance that in my current state it'll put me into a semi-coma, but it's the only way I'm going to survive the rest of today. I swallow the whole thing dry and am thankful when I start to feel its effects.

Sad-postured bodies in dark clothes pass me by while I stare fixedly ahead at the large, stained-glass window behind the altar depicting some biblical scene I could identify if I could focus. No one sits next to me, the stranger, the outsider, so I'm alone in my pew, a collection of worn hymnals available for my perusal if I thought a bombastic song would fix what ails me.

An organ starts, the family is ushered in. Claire looking shell-shocked and stoic. A woman who, from the looks of her, must be her sister. Seth, who, if he knew how much his father loved him, might be able to forgive him anything. Two older couples, then another face I recognize, Jeff after forty if he lived in the sun and on a larger scale. His brother.

The minister asks us to stand, to sing, to sit, to bow our heads. Jeff's friends speak, telling stories I'd heard from Jeff, as I knew they would. When he told me about it, I thought the pre-funeral was brilliant and only wished I'd had the opportunity to do one with my own childhood friends before we'd grown up and drifted apart.

When the projection of Jeff's smiling face is looming over us, I feel a sense of relief. Surely we must be almost done. A few more solemn words and I'll have succeeded in my impossible task of not causing any more harm than I already have.

But then Seth rises, pale, terrified, his head shaped like his father's, the slight diphthong in his voice one I thought I'd never hear again, and he says something totally unexpected.

"I don't need my heart anymore / you can have it . . ."

The words crash down around me, the threads that have been holding me together snap, and there's nothing I can do to save myself but head for the exit.

An hour later, I'm sitting huddled against a tree. It's half in leaf. When the wind blows, the loose buds plunk down around me like fat drops of rain.

I watched them lower Jeff's coffin into the hard ground, but I

couldn't get close enough to hear the words. I couldn't make myself
do this, even if it would've been a good idea. The act of watching was
enough to drive the Ativan from my system, and my brain feels clear
as a bell. Ringing out a warning.

Now they've all started to disperse, to walk solemnly back to their
cars, their lives. I know from the program still clutched in my hand
that there's a reception at the house, but right now the most likely
option seems like I'll be staying here overnight.

A shadow crosses above me.

"Are you all right?" a man asks.

I look up; it's Tim. It must be. His hands are stuffed in the pockets
of his suit. He looks like he hasn't slept well in days.

I ought to know.

I run a hand across my cheek to wipe the tears I cannot hide away
and edge myself to a standing position. "I'll survive."

"Were . . . were you a friend of Jeff's?"

"We worked together. I'm the company representative, I guess,
here to show the flag."

I wave my hand like I'm holding a flag, looking to surrender, hoping for clemency.

"How do you know Jeff?" I ask, playing along.

"I'm his brother. Sorry, I should've started with that."

"It's all right. I'm so sorry for your loss. So very sorry."

"Thank you. I didn't get your name?"

"Patricia, but everybody calls me Tish."

"Tim." We shake hands. In the awkward silence that follows, we
start to walk away from the gravesite.

"There's a reception at the house now, right?" I say, trying to fill
the silence, something I always do when I'm nervous.

"Yes. Are you going?"

"I should. That's why I'm here, after all."

We've reached the parking lot. The only car that remains is a
bright red Ford sedan, the kind you always get from rental compa-
nies at the airport.

"Is your car near here?" Tim asks.

"I walked."

"How about I give you a lift to the house?"

No, no, no, no, no.

"Okay."

He pulls the key from his pocket and unlocks the doors, the chipper tweet of the automatic unlocker a bright sound in the quiet world. It's as if the whole town slipped into silence out of respect.

I open the door and slide into the passenger seat as Tim starts the engine. He drives carefully, like he's not entirely sure where he's going, though he must be. We stay silent for a few streets as I watch the center of town flash by, a small-town Main Street that's survived better than most.

"Did you know Jeff well?" Tim asks as we take a left away from the town square.

What can I say to this? That sometimes I felt like I knew him better than myself, and sometimes I felt like I didn't know him at all? And now I'll never know which is right?

"Fairly well."

"From the accounting department?"

"No, I'm in HR. We met when Jeff needed some HR training. A year ago."

"Have you lived in Springfield long?"

"I don't live here. I live in the other Springfield."

"Pardon?"

I shift in my seat. I'm gripping my hands together tightly in my lap, and they've gone white. I loosen them, feeling the blisters forming from too many golf swings.

"It's this work thing. The company bought a company in another town called Springfield. So there are two, which is confusing, and mine's always called 'the other Springfield.' Anyway, that's where I live. With my husband and my daughter, Zoey. She wrote that poem Seth read."

I pause for breath, cursing myself. What the hell did I say that for?

He frowns. "I don't follow."

Of course he doesn't. I barely do, and it's my own life unfurling.

"It's this thing she does. This spoken word thing. She won Nationals last year, and one of the prizes was publishing some of her poems." I swallow, my brain whizzing. "It's about my father. The poem. That's what Zoey was writing about. He died two years ago. That's why I was so upset, I guess."

"Does Seth know your daughter?"

"No, they've never met."

"Then how did —"

"Seth get a hold of the poem? I'm not sure."

Crap, crap, crap.

"Jeff had a copy," I add.

Which is true, a hundred percent true. But which is also proof that telling the truth to get yourself out of a bad situation isn't always the best policy.

Tim puts the blinker on and takes a left. I don't know how close or far away we are to the house.

Please let us be close. Please let us be far away.

"They were given away at this office thing we were both at a couple of weeks ago," I blurt, still trying to cover up my earlier words with new ones. "We played golf together."

A small smile. "Jeff did love golf."

"He did."

Tim parks the car at the end of a quiet street. He shuts off the engine and pulls the key from the ignition. We get out in unison and I follow him up the block. Cars are parked here, there, and everywhere, and there's a steady stream of people climbing the front steps dressed in solemn clothing.

He takes the walkway and trudges to the front door, looking like he dreads going in there as much as I do. I stop at the edge between the concrete and sidewalk, staring at the house, fighting once again for self-control.

He turns back to me as he reaches the front door. "You coming?"

"I'll be right there."

CHAPTER 15

The Creaking Dark

My brother's been home twice in the last fifteen years.

Two years after Claire and I started dating, we received an unusual piece of mail. It was a postcard from Tim, again from Australia, with an address and an invitation — albeit cryptic — to write to him.

Drop me a line were the words he used, if memory serves.

It was, actually, my mother who got the postcard, and she's the one who responded. In fact, I'm pretty sure she sat down at the kitchen table and pulled out several pieces of her personal stationery minutes after the postcard came shooting through the mail slot.

Tim was open to communication and she was ready to communicate.

Boy was she ever.

Writing to Tim became a nearly daily occupation for her, narrating the small details of her life.

I don't know for certain, but I'm fairly sure she told Tim about Claire and me in that very first letter. It had taken her a while to accept us when she first found out, which was unfortunately from some local gossip before I'd had a chance to tell her myself.

"I just heard the strangest thing," she said to me on the phone, where she'd caught me at work. "I'm sure Betty must have it wrong..."

"Have what wrong, Mom?"

"Well, honey, she said that you and Claire James are dating."

She gave a nervous laugh, trying to convey a that's-so-ridiculous air, but not quite managing it.

When I fessed up and told her it was true, she went into flutter mode. "Well, I . . . If you think . . . Are you happy?"

I assured her I was and that I knew it was a bit weird but that it was a good thing. Eventually, she believed it, but she couldn't quite let it go until she found out how Tim felt about it.

When the next postcard arrived from him, three months later, the p.s. he added after saying he was working at a bank was: *Tell Jeff and Claire I said hi.*

There were two ways to take this — as a passive PFO, or a tacit acceptance that things had moved on without him. I chose the latter, at first, and though it wasn't with my mother's speed or frequency, I wrote him back, writing of surface things. My practice, the latest town gossip about the boys we grew up with. Not much about Claire, but enough to let him know we were together and we were serious. That it maybe wasn't the best situation there ever was, and that my happiness was tinged with moments of regret.

He didn't answer my letters, or my sporadic emails when he finally divulged his email address. He treated my mother's correspondence with more respect; emails were usually answered within a week. He's a busy guy, after all, my mother would say, making excuses for him, as she had during all those years of virtual silence.

Tell Jeff and Claire I said hi.

I waited a while to tell Claire about that one. When I did, casually over breakfast one morning, she went quiet, still, before asking me if I was going to write him back. I told her I wasn't sure, and thought about asking her if she was planning to. But somehow I couldn't get the words out. I'm not normally a jealous guy, but jealousy has a different texture to it when the woman you love used to be in love with your brother. I held my tongue, and if she wrote him, she never said.

I don't know if I expected him to answer me, or what the answer would be if he did. Instead, all I got was radio silence, the absence of words telling me all I needed to know. Tim was pissed, and whatever it was that had driven him halfway around the world, well, the blame for that was now shifted to me.

Eventually, I stopped writing. Maybe I wanted to send my own signal. Maybe I was tired of the lack of response. And there was life to live too. It was a good life; one I hoped was about to get better.

When Claire accepted my proposal at the Thai restaurant where we'd had our first date, we decided quickly that we didn't want a big wedding. Family, a few close friends. If we went beyond that we might have to invite the whole town. I didn't really care one way or another, so long as she showed up and said yes, but Claire didn't seem interested in the spectacle.

She was the one who sent Tim the invitation. I saw it sitting on a stack of ones to mail near the front door of her apartment. Right on top of the stack like there was nothing unusual about it. And maybe there wasn't, but it led to our first big fight, one we'd probably been putting off since the beginning, one you didn't really want to have two months before your wedding.

"What the fuck is this?" I asked, holding Tim's invitation by the corner, standing over her in a way I knew was more aggressive than it should be.

She glanced up from the kitchen table, where she was making her way through a pile of case law. "A wedding invitation."

"Come on, Claire."

She put her pen down. Two spots of color appeared on her cheeks. "Come on what? He's your brother."

"Right. *My* brother. *Your* ex-boyfriend. The guy who hasn't spoken to either of us in years."

"I thought he should be here, or at least have the option to be."

"And you didn't think to tell or ask me?"

"No. I did."

"The hell you did."

"I meant, I thought about it."

I threw the envelope on the table. It skipped like a pebble across a pond, once, twice, and landed on the floor with a soft whooshing sound.

"So you thought about it and decided not to tell me?"

"That's right."

"What am I supposed to do with that?"

She reached down to retrieve the envelope. "I don't know why you're getting this upset."

"You don't? You used to sleep with the guy!"

I knew as soon as the words left my mouth that I'd said the wrong thing. This had always been unspoken. That he'd touched and kissed her lips, her breasts, and the soft, wet folds between her legs. But it was something I was all too aware of the first few times we were together, when I was trying to figure out how to unlock the sighs and cries I craved.

Of course, I'd been with women before who'd been with someone else. There was often that feeling the first few times, before the present began to erase the past.

Someone's been here before me. Was he better? Did she cry out his name? Did he make her come easily, the first time?

I always shoved these thoughts down with the reality that I too had practiced on others. That this particular swirl of the tongue, or rub of her clitoris, might not satisfy like it had done in the past.

Adjustments were necessary.

Adjustments were made.

But I'd never had to adjust for the fact that one of the men before me was my brother. That if I disappointed her, if I continued to do so, her lack of satisfaction could always be compared with him, another man who'd been in my place, the place I hoped to make mine exclusively.

She gave me a cold stare. "You've known that from the beginning, Jeff. What does it have to do with us now?"

"You're the one bringing him into it. Sending him that invitation is bringing him into it."

"Inviting him to our wedding isn't bringing him into it, it's keeping him out of it."

"How'd you figure?"

"He's your *brother*. If he isn't at your wedding, people will talk. And your mother would be heartbroken if he didn't come. You know that."

"I don't give a shit what people say. I only care about—"

"That we were together? Is that it?"

I stuffed my hands in my pockets and looked down at the floor. "I don't know."

"Seems like that's something you should've figured out a long time ago."

"What does that mean?"

"Do you think I'm still in love with him?"

"No, I . . ."

She watched me stumble, unable to deny it.

"If you feel that way, I don't think I should be sending these out."

She picked up the invitation and walked out of the kitchen. I followed her down the hall. She placed Tim's invitation back on top of the pile and straightened the stack, making the corners neat.

"You want to call the wedding off?" I said, my throat closing in panic.

She looked me straight in the eye. "No. I don't."

"You think I do?"

"I think you need to figure out if you can live with this. With me. The person I was and the person I am now. You go figure that out and let me know."

I felt like I'd been punched in the stomach, but there was anger there too. So out the door I went to spend a miserable night at my own apartment, a place I barely spent any time in anymore, a place that no longer felt like home.

In the morning I crawled back to Claire's, begged her forgiveness, and, when she gave it, buried my jealousy of Tim deep within.

Besides, I told myself, *it's not like he's actually going to show.*

He did, of course. Not that he returned the reply card. Instead, he sent a cryptic email to my mother, which she decoded as his arrival time in Springfield two days before the ceremony.

I knew for sure by then that my take on his silence, his absence, wasn't paranoia. It was all connected. But what I didn't know was whether he was coming home to try to do something about it or to accept it.

I watched him closely in those first twenty-four hours after his arrival, looking for signs that might point the way. He looked older, tanned, and less restless. Australia agreed with him, I thought, as we sat across from each other at my parents' dinner table, as we had all our lives, eating lemon chicken, because Thursday was lemon chicken night, rain or shine.

He'd kissed Claire briefly on the cheek when we arrived and told her she looked well. Claire's face was like glass, reflecting back the expression of whomever she was speaking to. When she looked at Tim, the few times I caught her looking, she seemed calm, impassive, and slightly distracted; a woman having dinner with her in-laws a few days before her wedding.

After dinner, Tim cornered me in the living room, passing me a Scotch glass with an inch of liquid in it, neat.

"So, brother, have you been properly feted?"

"Feted?"

"I'm talking bachelor party. Has it occurred, or will you be in need of sleep and half drunk on your wedding day?"

I smiled, remembering the weekend with my college buddies, the golf, the drinks, and the drinks after that. "It's been taken care of."

"Good. Sorry I missed it."

"No worries."

It was his turn to smile. "That sounds like home."

"Home is Australia now?"

"That's right. For now. Maybe for always. We'll see." He paused to take a sip of his drink. "You should . . . come visit sometime."

"Sure, we'd like that."

If he flinched, it was only a tick of the clock. He glanced around the room. "This place looks the same as always."

"Nothing ever changes in Springfield."

"A few things do. One or two."

"Right. Sure."

We stood there sipping our drinks in silence, both of us probably wishing the women would reappear and fill the room with chatter.

"Where did Dad get off to?" Tim asked eventually.

"Lodge meeting, I think."

"Of course. Lemon chicken and lodge night. He inducted you yet?"

"Me? No, no. Never."

"Never say never, brother."

I didn't like this new way he had of calling me "brother," like he needed to remind himself of who I was. Or maybe he was reminding me.

"I guess. What about you? Any thoughts of settling down?"

He laughed. "You sound like Mom."

"No one's ever said that before. No one special?"

"Nothing on the horizon at present. All the good girls seem to be taken."

I sipped my drink. "Mmm."

Silence crept over us again and I thought about refilling my glass.

"What do you say to a private celebration?" Tim said.

"What? You and me?"

"You got anything better to do?"

"No. I'm just . . . forget it." I put my glass down. "Where'd you want to go?"

"Hurley's maybe?"

"Sure. Let me tell Claire."

He nodded thoughtfully and twenty minutes later found us ensconced at the local bar. Tim ordered two rounds of shots, which proved to be the right amount of lubrication to wash away the years. As the drinks disappeared down our throats, we talked about safe subjects: remember-whens from our childhood.

When last call sounded we were both cut, and for my part, I was feeling more warmly about Tim than I had in years. I hadn't realized how much I'd missed him, my goddamn older brother, the man I always wanted to be when I grew up.

Tim seemed to feel the same as he slapped me on the back and suggested we walk the long way round to our parents' house. I agreed, and as we stumbled home, we passed the edge of the Woods, its thick trees silhouetted against the sky.

"Man," I said, "I haven't been in there in ages."

"Do you remember all those times we played . . . what was it again?"

"You Can't Get There from Here."

"Right, right. Say, let's do it."

"What, now?"

"Sure."

"But we don't have any flashlights."

He reached into his pocket and pulled out a thick ring of keys. A silver cylinder hung from it. He flicked a switch and a bright beam of light pooled around our feet.

"This'll do, won't it?"

"Aren't you the Boy Scout."

He held up his hand in the three-fingered salute. "With merit badges and everything. You game?"

I hesitated for a moment, but why not? The night seemed to be all about memories, and these were good ones.

"Okay. Who's spotter?"

"We'll flip for it." He pulled out a quarter, getting ready to toss it. "Call it."

"Tails."

"Interesting choice."

He launched the quarter into the air and we watched it flip upward, twinkling in the street light, disappearing into the dark, then reappearing in slow motion to land in the palm of his hand. He slapped his palm against the top of his other hand.

"You sure about your choice?"

"I'm sure."

He unveiled the coin. It was heads.

"Do you think the old bell's still there?" he asked.

"Only one way to find out."

We walked into the Woods, our eyes quickly adjusting to the darkness. The half-full moon was enough to light the well-worn path. After a few minutes we came to a large, distinctive rock, our usual starting place. I sat on its cool surface.

"Give me five minutes," Tim said.

I nodded and he started off down the path. I checked my watch for the time: 2:12.

The rules of You Can't Get There from Here are simple. It has to be played at night. Spotters are placed in the woods with flashlights. The Crawlers have to try to get past them without being lit up, to reach a bell that hangs from a tree a half a mile ahead. The first person to ring the bell is the winner.

To be a good Crawler you need patience, silence, and a willingness to become one with the wet, boggy ground. To be a good Spotter you need good night vision and a sense of direction that allows you to hear past the disorienting sounds of movement in the dark. We all had our moments of glory growing up, but Tim was always the best, especially at spotting.

Two seventeen. Regretting the suit I'd considered appropriate for what I thought this night would be, I lowered myself to the moist ground about ten feet left of the path. My plan, such as it was, was to go in a semicircle around the path to arrive at the bell — assuming it was still hanging from the tree where we left it ten years ago — and hopefully avoid Tim.

Within a few minutes, I was soaked through to the skin. My nostrils were full of the smell of decomposing leaves. I moved slowly, stopping often to listen to the sound of my own breathing, willing my ears to reach out into the dark and identify the other sounds. Was that Tim, an animal, or an old tree shifting in the night?

I checked my watch, cupping my hand over its face to hide the light.

Two thirty-two. I was half hoping my slowness and the amount of alcohol we'd consumed would lull Tim into a slumber.

I should've known better. Within seconds of the numbers fading back to darkness I was enveloped in light.

"Got you, brother," Tim said, way closer than I expected. And why was the light so fucking bright?

I flopped onto my back to find Tim standing over me, shining the flashlight in my eyes. All I could see was his outline against the sky, like an actor in the floodlights. He looked enormous, a bear of a man, though I couldn't see his face well enough to tell if he'd become fully Yeti.

"Will you shut that goddamn thing off?"

"Not until you say it."

"Say what?"

"You know what."

"Jesus Christ, Tim. Who cares? You won. Enough. Help me up."

I held out my hand and the light snapped off. But instead of giving me his hand, Tim was on top of me, pinning me to the ground like he had so many times before, when he wanted to beat on me or teach me a lesson.

"Say it," he said. I could feel his hot, malty breath against my face.

"What the hell is wrong with you?"

"Say it," he repeated, and pressed my arms deeper into the mud.

I could feel the back of me becoming as wet as the front, and I was starting to get pissed off.

"Jesus, fuck, fine. You can't get there from here."

"Too bloody right you can't." He gave me a final push, then released me and stood up. "You shouldn't even be trying to."

I opened my mouth to answer him but stopped when I heard him walk away. I knew it would be fruitless to call after him, that he was content to leave me there and let me find my own way home.

So I lay there like that, watching the moon, trying to make sense of it all.

Just me and the creaking dark.

CHAPTER 16

The Plot Thickens

When we get home from the funeral, the house is already thick with people. It feels like the whole town's here, though of course that isn't possible. The whole town did send food; everyone's hands and mouths are full of something. They seem to have forgotten to send alcohol, though. A vital omission.

I wander through the house, being stopped and hugged every few seconds, like a repeat episode of *The Day Jeff Died*. I think this show should be canceled. It's always been a terrible show.

I nod and thank and agree. I'm becoming inured to hearing Jeff's name in connection with his death. At least, I hope I am.

I have an awkward discussion with Art Davies, all mumbled words and expressions of guilt.

"Maybe Jeff was distracted because he felt so bad about firing me," he says. "Maybe —"

"No. Don't put that on yourself, okay?"

Don't put that thought on me, I want to say. I don't want to think about whether Jeff's death was avoidable, who's to blame. I don't want to feel the emotions that would come with those kinds of thoughts. I'm already feeling too much, and too little.

"But —" he says.

Art's wife tugs at his elbow. "This isn't the time, Art. Come on, let's go."

He sighs and mumbles an apology and then they are gone.

The friends whose calls I haven't been returning surround me, a buzz of protectiveness. But their sorrow is more than I want to feel too, and so I don't really listen, don't really say anything, don't really feel anything.

At some point, Seth tugs at the sleeve of my scratchy dress.

"Yes, honey?"

"Was it . . . okay what I read?"

I turn to him. He looks small and embarrassed in his jacket and tie.

"Of course it was. It was perfect."

He stubs his toe at the floor. "It wasn't . . . cheating?"

"What do you mean?"

"Like at school. How you have to do your own work?"

"Darling, of course it's not like that. Think about the minister. He was reading something someone else wrote, right?"

"But that's his job."

"I don't think it's so different. I'm really proud of you . . . that you were able to get up and speak. It was . . . more than I could do."

"Don't feel bad, Mom. Dad would understand."

I pull him against me, hoping he's right but still feeling disappointed in myself. His bones feel small, not quite sturdy enough to shoulder this present life.

"I hope so."

I release him. He rubs his cheek where it connected with my dress.

"Where'd you find that poem?" I ask. "I've never heard it before."

"Dad had it."

"He did? Where?"

"In this book I found . . . please don't be mad."

"Why would I be mad?"

"'Cuz I found it in his stuff."

"What stuff?"

"His travel bag. In his office."

"Why were you looking in there?"

"It's stupid."

The house is loud and full, but we're in a pocket of quiet, Seth and I.

"Tell me."

"I feel like I'm starting to forget things, about, you know, *him,* and I thought if I held some of his things . . ."

"It's okay. I understand."

"You do?"

"I do."

"Are you forgetting?" he asks.

"I'm sure I am, but I have so much more to remember, so I haven't noticed yet, you see? We knew each other for a long time."

"My whole life."

"And then some. Are you hungry? You should eat."

"Do you think I could go upstairs instead? There are too many people down here."

"Of course."

I realize there's no one Seth's age in the house. Only a few of his friends were at the church. Did they not want to come to the funeral, or did their parents think they weren't old enough to deal with what's been thrust upon my son?

"Why don't you take off those clothes and put on something more comfortable? I'll come up soon and we can be quiet together."

He agrees and walks toward the stairs, a hitch in his step.

I stand there for a moment, uncertain of where I can stand to go next. I move eventually in the general direction of the kitchen, only to be stopped by Connie, my piano teacher.

She stands rigidly in front of me, her arms crossed. She's wearing a severe black jacket and skirt.

"Hi, Connie. Thanks for coming."

She nods curtly. "Lessons start again next week."

"What?"

"Next week."

"I don't think I'll be able to. I mean—"

"You will come to the conservatory. We will see if you can. It is time to see."

She talks like a tennis ball machine, firing words at precise intervals.

"I'll try."

"I will expect you at noon."

"I don't—"

"It is your choice. Do as you wish." She places a large, mannish hand on my shoulder. "You are strong, Claire. Come to the conservatory so you can remember."

She walks around me, headed to the front door. Tim's standing there, shrugging off his coat. I catch his gaze. He holds it for a moment, then looks away. I watch as he stares into the sea of people in the living room. He raises his hand in greeting to someone and disappears from view.

Several more people circle me, hug me, tell me how sorry they are. When I manage to escape, I go to the kitchen in search of a glass of water. I run the tap till the water is cold and start to fill a glass. I look out the window, wondering if I'll ever be able to do so without thinking of the police car pulling up to divide my life in two.

Today it all looks innocent, despite the unusual number of cars parked on the street. There's a woman who looks vaguely familiar standing at the edge of the walkway. She raises a cigarette to her lips and inhales deeply, letting out the smoke in a long, slow stream.

A cigarette. Yes, that's what I need. I let the glass I'm holding slip from my hand and hurry to the hall closet and my coat. In a moment I'm out the door.

"Please tell me you have another one of those," I say.

The woman looks at me, startled. She's been crying.

"Of course. Hold on." She clamps her half-smoked cigarette between her teeth and peers inside her purse. She pulls out a red-and-white package and hands it to me. "Here you go."

I take the crinkly package and tap out a cigarette. The act of putting it in my mouth, catching a whiff of the tobacco, makes me want a drink, but I never did manage to find one inside.

The woman holds a lighter at the end and flicks it on. I inhale quickly, twice, to make sure the cigarette is lit. The warm smoke sears my lungs. I can tell the exact moment the nicotine hits my bloodstream. Eight seconds, the time a rodeo cowboy has to stay on his bucking bronco.

"These are getting hard to find," the woman says. Her voice is vaguely familiar too.

"Cigarettes?"

"No, lighters." She flashes the green plastic cylinder at me, then puts it in her coat pocket. "Used to be, everyone always had a lighter, even if they didn't smoke. I had to go to three stores to find this one."

I take another haul, enjoying the illicit pleasure.

"We probably should be hiding behind the shrubbery. If my parents see me with this, they'll throw a fit."

A thin smile. "I know what you mean. My husband's a doctor and if he only knew . . ." She takes a last drag, throws the cigarette to the ground, and grinds it out with a black ballet flat. "God, these things really are terrible. I thought it would help, but it doesn't. Sorry, I'm babbling."

"It's all right."

"The service was beautiful, by the way. I guess I should've started with that. I'm so terribly sorry for your loss. It's a . . . terrible thing."

"Thank you . . . you look familiar to me, but . . . do we know each other?"

"Oh! I'm the company representative. Patricia Underhill, from the other Springfield? You can call me Tish."

Tish. *Tish.*

"We met once," she continues in a breathless rush. "You probably don't remember? At that company retreat in Mexico, a couple of years back? We only spoke for a few moments . . ."

Mexico. Right. The first trip Jeff and I took alone together in forever. Things were mostly normal then. Things felt good. At dinner, like today, I'd slipped outside for a cigarette and found a woman about my age sitting on the edge of a retaining wall under the bright bougainvillea trees, crying.

"Are you all right?" I'd asked.

She looked up, embarrassed, hastily wiping her tears away. She was wearing a cocktail dress in a pretty color (green?), and her long hair was loose and black against the moonlight. She obviously belonged to our party, but we hadn't been introduced.

"I'm sorry," she said.

"Why are you apologizing? I'm the one intruding on your privacy."

"This place isn't very private."

"I'm not the one who made you cry, right?"

"No, of course not."

"So, then, no apology necessary."

"Thanks." She stood up and wiped the dirt off her backside. "I'm Patricia. But people call me Tish."

"Claire. Wife or participant?"

"Oh . . . participant, I guess. My husband's inside."

"Mine too."

"What about you?"

"I'm a wife. At least, on this occasion."

She nodded. "I know *exactly* what you mean."

I pulled a cigarette from my skirt pocket. "Do you mind?"

"Of course not. I wish I could join you."

"You can if you like."

"I don't really smoke. And my husband wouldn't like it."

I held a flame to the end of my cigarette. "Why do you think I'm skulking out here?"

She smiled, and she was quite lovely, in an understated way.

We stood there in silence for a bit before Tish said, "This is going to sound strange, but . . . do you ever wish you could do your life over again?"

"Everyone wishes that sometimes."

"I mean really actually do it, start again. See if you can get it right the second time around." She shook herself. "I'm sorry. You don't need to hear the inside of my brain. I'm having a weird night."

"Stop apologizing. I've had my share of weird nights. And yes, I think about that sometimes, but I don't think it's helpful."

"No, of course."

"I mean, I don't think you have to do your life over to change it. I think it's wrong to think you can't change things in your life now be-

cause of decisions you've made in the past. Most things aren't permanent — except children, of course." I smiled, thinking of Seth, missing
him.

"I wouldn't give up my daughter for anything," she said fiercely.

"You see. Your decisions can't have been all wrong."

"You're right."

"Don't be so sure. It might be the cocktails talking."

"No, thank you, this has been helpful." She tugged at the bottom of
her dress, straightening it. "I don't have mascara all over my face or
anything, do I?"

"You're fine."

"I guess that stuff really is waterproof."

"Good to know."

"Thank you . . . Claire. I should be getting back."

"Of course."

She smiled again, wanly this time, then walked up the torch-lit
path.

"You were outside crying, right?" I say, then instantly regret it. "I'm
sorry —"

"No, that's all right. I *was* crying. And you were . . . great. I was in
a bad place and . . . I don't know if you remember what you said that
night, but it helped."

"I remember, and I'm glad, but I can't take any credit. It was probably something I'd heard on a talk show."

"I doubt it."

"So . . . did you do it?" I ask.

"Do what?"

"Change the thing you were regretting . . . Wow, that was way too
personal a question, you don't have to say."

"No, it's fine." She bites her lip. "The answer's yes. In a way, I did."
Her face becomes incredibly sad.

I look over her shoulder, trying to give her some privacy.

A police car rounds the corner onto our street, driving cautiously.
It stops in front of the driveway. A man I know is at the wheel.

"Anyway, I should be . . . go inside, I guess," Tish says, but I'm only catching every other word. My heart's beating so loudly it's drowning everything else out.

"Thank you for coming," I say, my eyes fixed on the vehicle.

"It was important to me to do it."

The driver kills the engine and it's déjà vu all over again, as Jeff would say. But it can't be more bad news, it can't be. Everyone I know, everyone I love, is in the house behind me.

The officer opens the door and gets out. My eyes track to the one thing that's different from last time. The plastic bag he's holding in his hand.

This time my body doesn't fail me when I realize what it must contain, and because I can't get away fast enough, I turn on a dime and sprint to the house.

CHAPTER 17

Decision Maker

My conversation with Claire leaves me feeling short of breath. I tell myself it's the cigarettes, but they have nothing to do with it.

Claire.

I feel like I'd recognize her anywhere.

Which is silly, and not what history relates, because when Jeff sent me a picture of her and Seth, early on, when we were trading pictures of our offices, our streets, little snippets of our lives, I didn't recognize her. Not at first.

But I couldn't shake her face from my brain. Something about it was haunting me, until it finally came to me one night when thoughts tumbled through my brain like clothes being dried.

We'd met. In fact — and, of course, because when else could it be? — we met at the same time I first met Jeff.

I remember how excited Brian was when I told him we'd been invited to the retreat.

"Mexico! Wow. You're moving up in the world," he'd said, ruffling my hair and looking proud.

I smiled back though felt a flutter of unease. Truth be told, my original instinct was to refuse the invite, but the shocked look of a coworker, a look I knew Brian would repeat, quickly put an end to that fantasy. At least there was a sweet-looking golf course in the bro-chure. It had been a while since I'd made it out for a real round.

And there was the potential of Brian's excitement. He'd been giv-ing me "helpful" nudges for a while. Were there any openings above me? Could I move from HR to another area of management? Wasn't the merger a great thing? A whole new world of opportunities?

Brian's a great doctor. He's patient and interested and will deliver your baby at two in the morning in a snowstorm. But, despite the fact that he eschewed a big-city practice, he's ambitious. For himself, for me. And while I got that about him, he never seemed to understand or believe it when I told him I wasn't like that. That I was happy to coast. To drift and somersault like a dried-out leaf in the late fall, hoping to avoid the rake, the collecting pile, the compost heap.

And by this time, there was something else too. A growing feel-ing that I had to *stop* drifting along, although I didn't know how to. That I'd been letting life act itself out on me when I should have been directing it. I'd wake up in the morning sometimes, disoriented, not sure where I was. When it would come back to me — Springfield, house, Brian — I couldn't help wondering how it had happened. How I'd ended up in this place, with this man, this life. How?

But how do you say that, really, to your husband? How do you even say that to yourself?

We went to Mexico. And when I got back from the driving range full of indignation about the crudeness of that jerk, John Scott, Bri-an's reaction had been to tell me to "calm down."

"Think about your career," he said, and, "It's not that big a deal, is it?"

When he said these things, I couldn't help but think about the man whose look said he wanted to pound that fat fucker into the ground whether it meant the end of his career or not.

And maybe it was because of him, knowing there was someone close by who I was pretty sure saw things the way I did, that made me tell Brian I didn't care about my job. It wasn't a career, and I'd already blown any chance at the careers I ever cared about because I didn't care enough.

"Don't you get it, Brian? It doesn't matter to me. Any of it."

"What are you saying? Are you only talking about work?"

"I don't know."

"You don't know?" Brian's voice moved up an octave. "What don't you know, Tish? What?"

"Don't push me. You're always pushing me."

"What are you talking about?"

"You're always trying to get me to be something I'm not."

He sat down on the edge of the bed. "Do I really do that? I don't think I do that."

He put his head in his hands, and he looked so defeated, I couldn't continue the fight. Even though I knew there were things that should be said. Even though I knew I might never work up the courage to say them again.

I sat next to him and took his hand in mine. He looked at me and I could see there were tears in his eyes.

"I'm sorry," I said. "I didn't mean . . . I was so mad at that guy."

"I'm sorry too. I should've offered to beat him up, right?"

"Maybe. Maybe that would've been good."

"I'm not really dressed for that." He was in a suit, ready for dinner.

"No."

"Or built for it either."

"True."

"Are you . . . are you unhappy? With our life? With me?"

"No, of course not. I love you."

"And you know I love you, yes?"

"Yes."

"Is this because we never had a second child?"

"No, it's not that. I didn't . . . I didn't want that."

Brian was never around, particularly when he started his practice, and I felt so overwhelmed in those first few years with Zoey, so sleep deprived and not like myself, that I couldn't imagine having another child. Brian was an only child, like me, and had never expressed the desire to have a second. But that he thought I did want more than one was a shock. Had he thought that all this time and never said, never asked?

"You and Zoey are the most important things in the world to me," Brian said. "If I thought . . ." His voice shook. "If I thought I was failing you . . ."

But the thing was, I never brought it up either. I let my silence decide for us, like I'd been doing all my life.

"No, Brian, no. I'm the one."

"The one what?"

"I don't know."

I rested my head on his shoulder. His arm circled me, holding me close.

"You don't have to work at that company if you don't want to. Or if you want to write, or go back to school, or whatever you want to do, you can do it."

"I know."

"I mean it."

"I know you do."

His eyes searched my face. "Are we good?"

"We're good."

He held me to him tightly, and his familiar scent, as familiar to me as my own, drove my anger away.

"You should—" he said.

"Take a shower? Yes."

I kissed him quickly and untangled myself. I closed the door behind me in the bathroom, turned on the taps, and slipped under the spray. And then the tears started to flow, hard and fast, dropping as fast as the water. I shoved my fist into my mouth to keep the sounds of my weeping contained. All I could think the whole time was *Why am I crying? What is wrong with me? What?*

When I regained control, I dressed quickly and we walked to the cocktail party. I was relieved to see that we were seated with a couple of people from our Springfield, people I knew well enough to skip over the usual intro chat. I stifled the rising feeling of panic with too many glasses of wine, and when I went through the food line, there he was again, being all awkward and fanlike. I didn't feel like myself and I didn't act like myself. I flirted, we flirted, but I left it at that. I didn't even tell him my name. I never expected to see him again.

Later that night I ran into John Scott again, red-faced and reeking of liquor. He made a pass at me, and I slipped out a side door and sat on a retaining wall near some bushes I thought would hide me from view. The tears came again, less intense this time, but still inexplicable to me.

And then, after a few short minutes of inconsequential talk, I found myself telling some semblance of the truth to Claire, who I didn't know, who I also thought I'd never see again. It felt good to tell someone something, and her words comforted me. They stayed with me, like her face did. They worked their way through my brain until they became one all-encompassing thought.

I could change my life if I wanted to.

I had permission.

I gave it to myself.

I watch Claire run, and when I see what's in the police officer's hand, I want to run too. But I stay put, letting him pass me by, walk up the steps, knock on the door.

Only once he's inside do I force myself to enter the house. I have a condolence card signed by the office with me. I will find the pile of them and add my card to the stack. I will do my duty and then I will leave. I will go back to my life, my family, my friends, like I'd already decided to do before any of this happened. I will try to put all of this behind me.

A woman with short graying hair wearing a black dress opens the front door. Claire's sister, if my guess at the funeral was correct.

She looks distracted and angry. Over her shoulder I can see Claire leading the police officer into the den and closing the door behind them, but not quite completely.

"Fuck," Claire's sister mutters.

"Pardon?"

She shifts her attention to me. "Apologies. Were you trying to come in?"

No, no, no.

"Yes, I . . . wanted to leave a card."

She takes a step back, leaving enough room for me to pass. We brush shoulders as I do, releasing the faint smell of gardenias. When it dissipates, the real smell of the place filters in. It's not familiar, as I feared it might be, just the smell of too many bodies packed together, too much food. Sweat and cumin. Red wine and sausage. A store full of flowers.

"Were you . . . who are you?" she asks.

"I'm Tish. I work . . . worked with Jeff. The company sent me."

"I'm Beth. Claire's sister." She closes the door and gives me a speck of her attention. "Your lot, they're all in there."

She motions to the living room to the left of the door, where I recognize a few faces. John Scott, of course, with an unhappy-looking woman at his side who must be his wife. The CEO and his very young wife. Others I've only seen in photographs. I feel light-headed at the prospect of going into that room, talking to those people, wondering if some rumor has reached them about me, if my presence there will bring it to mind, bring it to light.

"Are you all right?" Beth says.

"Yes, I . . . It's been a long day. Could I use your bathroom?"

"Of course. It's down there, on the left."

I walk slowly past the guests clogging the hall, catching snippets of conversation focused on the police officer Claire is hidden away with.

"Do you think that's . . . ?"

"What else could it be?"

"What's wrong with him, bringing it here today?"

My thoughts exactly.

I stop in front of the bathroom's closed door. I try the handle, but it's locked.

"Someone's in here!" a shrill voice admonishes me.

"Sorry!"

I lean against the wall, waiting. The door Claire and the police officer disappeared behind is across the hall, slightly ajar.

I edge across the hall. Voices float out.

" . . . investigation?"

"It was an accident . . ."

More words, then silence, then a creak of the floor, heading toward the door I'm standing too close to.

I jump back, taking up my station waiting for the person who seems to be treating the bathroom like it's her own.

The police officer leaves, followed by Claire holding the plastic bag. I scan its meager contents. A wallet. A wedding ring dulled by use. Jeff's watch. His phone.

I lift my eyes and meet Claire's for a second, but she's not seeing me, not really. In an instant, Tim's by her side, leading her away to the back of the house.

Without thinking, I slip along in their wake, like a magnet's pulling me. They stop in the solarium that leads to the backyard and I hover in the doorway, ten feet behind them. Tim tells her to wait there, turns, and walks past me. He gives me a puzzled look, like he's already forgotten where he knows me from, and doesn't slow his step.

I stare at Claire's back. Her posture's perfect — straight, with square shoulders. I feel schlumpy inside my coat, my head more naturally looking down than straight ahead at life.

Tim passes me again, a bottle in his hand, and in a moment he and Claire are outside, walking across the brown lawn, passing a small stand of crocuses, heading for an old swing set in the back corner.

As the screen door clangs shut I step into the room. The same force propels me to the doorway and keeps me standing there long enough to see them sit in the too-small swings and pass the bottle back and forth with the ease of old intimacy.

I finally force myself to look away, to fix on something else. A cell phone charger is plugged into the wall above the counter. Underneath it sits the bag of Jeff's effects.

I pick it up. Everything's intact except Jeff's cell phone. Its screen is cracked. I press the power button through the plastic, as if bringing it back to life might revive Jeff in some way. But this is foolishness. It looks broken beyond repair. And its damaged state is probably a blessing, really.

I put the bag down, and now I want very badly to talk to Zoey, to check in. But when I dig my phone out of my purse, I remember that it's dead to the world too. I plug the charger into it and wait, but it's gone so long without power that it'll need a few minutes before I can even turn it on. Which leaves me with enough time on my hands to do one more thing I shouldn't.

Like in my own house, the stairway in Jeff's displays a series of framed photographs, mostly of Seth through the ages, but also some early ones of Jeff and Claire, back in the day, purely happy, before life intruded.

The top stair squeaks loudly and I stop, nervous as a burglar worried about waking a sleeping family.

"Mom?"

I'm about to bolt when Seth pops his head out of a doorway. He's taken off his funeral suit and is wearing a hoodie over a pair of surfing shorts.

"I thought it was my mom."

"She's outside with your uncle, I think."

"Who are you?"

"I worked with your dad."

He looks at me for a moment, turning that over like a worry bead. "A lot of people worked with my dad."

I take the last step into the hallway, and now, for the first time, I can detect, faintly, the smell I associate with Jeff. This is what I was looking for. This is why I came up here. For one last breath of him.

He was here not so long ago. Not so long ago.

"Yes, they did," I say.

He edges backward, and I take this as a sign to follow him, at least to the doorway. The room he's in is set up as an office. A wall of bookshelves full of the detective fiction Jeff loved to read. A filing cabinet. A large desk made out of a piece of plywood held up by two sawhorses.

Seth is sitting at the desk in front of a large-screen laptop. He has a couple of browser windows open, including one showing his Twitter feed, updating every few seconds.

Sick trick in this video!

Does Mr. H. suck or what?

@trixli yolo!

"It's Seth, right?"

He glances at me briefly. "Yeah."

"I was wondering . . . where you found that poem? The one you read at the funeral?"

"Why?"

"Well, my daughter wrote it actually, her name is —"

"Zoey, right?"

"That's right. How do you know about her?"

"I don't. My dad did. I found her book in his stuff."

"Oh, I thought maybe . . ." I stop myself, because what am I thinking? Honestly, what am I thinking?

"It must be weird," he says.

"What's that?"

"Having something you wrote out there in the world for everyone to read."

"Is it any different from that?" I point to the computer screen, where a trail of words is scrolling it.

@connorsallright Dude, I just saw the FUNNIEST video.

"Nah, that's only, no filter, you know? Nobody's really saying anything. They're just . . . what's that word? Narrating."

Oh, Jeff. Your son is bright and perfect.

"That's an interesting way of looking at it."

"You worked with Dad?"

"Yes." I pause. "He was a great guy, your dad."

"Yeah."

He opens a new navigation screen and types something. The landing page of an email service. The one Jeff used.

"I'm doing this thing," he says, looking shy. "This kind of collage thing? You know, like the AIDS quilt?"

"What do you mean?"

"There's this mosaic site where you can load in photos and stuff like that, and it makes these awesome collages, but like mosaic tiles. But you know what sucks?"

OMG. That's hilarious. What a loser!

Check this version out! Even better with music! xtylorsm.com.

"No, what?"

"We don't have enough pictures of Dad. But I have an idea."

"What's that?"

"I'm going to email his friends, and ask them to send stuff, like pictures and whatever. But I can't get in."

I bet that's going to get, like, a zillion views . . . like Star Wars Kid.

"Into his email?"

"Yeah. I've been working on his password for *days,* but I can't get it."

My heart squeezes and I raise a hand to my chest.

"Well, maybe there was . . . stuff in there, private stuff . . . There must be another way you could get his friends' email addresses."

"Not without asking my mom."

"I'm sure she'd want to know what you were doing."

"But then it wouldn't be a surprise. You won't tell her?"

Before I can answer, or think of some other way to try to discourage this precious boy from trying to crack into Jeff's email, an IM pops up on Seth's screen.

Mike_Boarder: Sethie! Have you seen this?

Seth types quickly.

Sethsamillion: What?

Mike_Boarder: Watch this. Immediately. xtylorsm.com

Seth clicks on it and a video loads, ready to play. There's a blurry still shot of a girl in black standing at a microphone. The caption reads: *Poet Girl Takes a Nosedive!*

Oh, God . . . no, no, no.

I take the mouse from Seth's hand, move it to the play button, and click. It starts to play.

"Hey, what are you doing?"

But I don't hear anything Seth says after this point. I'm out of his room and down the stairs and into the solarium, where my phone is now charged. I pick it up and it's vibrating. The revived screen tells me I have twenty-one missed calls and eight messages, and texts from Brian, from Zoey, from Brian.

I dial the last number, Zoey's cell, and she answers before the ring even finishes.

"Mom?" she says. "Mom?"

"I'm coming, baby. Right now."

And then I do the first unselfish thing I've done in a very long time. I go home.

PART 3

CHAPTER 18

Piñata

Claire got kind of lost for a while after the miscarriage. That day, when she ended up in the stinking alley, leaning against a rusty green Dumpster, she said she knew she couldn't go back inside, that she'd never practice law again, that something essential inside of her had shifted, left, disappeared.

"But you love the law," I said, a tease in my voice because I didn't know yet that it wasn't the time for teasing.

"I did."

"Maybe you went back too soon. You should take a couple weeks off. We could go somewhere, if you like."

"That won't change anything."

"How do you know?"

"I just do," she said, with a level of certainty that drove the teasing from my voice.

"Let's really think about this, Claire. I don't want you to do anything you'll regret."

"It's not a question of regret. I can't go back there. I can't. I'm not sure I ever should've been there in the first place."

"I thought you loved working with your dad."

"It's not that, it's … what I do, it's so … hard. You have to be so hard, and I'm not that person anymore."

"You're the strongest person I know."

"No. Maybe before, but now, now I'm soft."

I took her in my arms and held her, but it didn't seem to help. And the longer I held her, the more I could feel the loss inside, as if an elemental part of her had been taken away.

But I couldn't tell her that. I could only reiterate my suggestion to take a few more weeks off. She agreed and said that, if we could, we'd try to get away.

But we didn't go anywhere, only Claire did.

Her departure was a gradual thing, like a watercolor left in the sun, every day fainter until one day the canvas was bare and you had to rely on memory to recapture the image.

The worst thing is, I didn't notice at first. I beat myself up about that. I could give excuses about how easy it is to miss things that are right in front of you, to take them for granted, and that I was doing my best, that I was grieving too.

But no excuses.

I didn't notice at first.

I beat myself up about that.

When I did notice, there didn't seem to be any fixative I could apply. I had nothing in me to keep her steady, steadfast. If I held her too close, she pushed me away. If I kept my distance, I felt her eyes accusing, uncertain. My suggestions that she try, again, to go back to work were met with stony silence or the rational, well-reasoned arguments that made me miss her all the more. Because they were so Claire, so the way I knew, deep down, she wanted to be, convincing me why she couldn't be that way anymore, and why I shouldn't ask her to be.

Those first few weeks — when we were both still pretending this was only going to last a few weeks — she kept it relatively normal in the mornings. She'd make breakfast, pack Seth's lunch, and see us out the door. But the rest of the day? The hours between nine and four? When I asked her, she spoke about them like they were as empty as the space between two goalposts.

One day, I went looking for her on my lunch hour, thinking I'd take her out to eat for something different. She wasn't home, so I drove around the neighborhood and eventually located her in a park a few blocks from our house.

She was sitting far enough away from the jungle gym to catch the drift of the children's laughter. She was smoking a cigarette — something I thought she'd given up years ago — and I couldn't help feeling like I didn't recognize her. Like how you look at your own face in the mirror sometimes and it feels as if there's a stranger looking back at you.

I sat in my idling car, only fifty feet away from her, but she never noticed me. After a while, I just drove away and went back to work. I didn't tell her I'd seen her. I pretended I didn't know about the smoking, the lost hours. I stopped expressing how helpless I felt, how I didn't understand what had started this and that I wished I could fix it.

We spoke about it less and less, but as the weeks became months my worry was growing like a physical thing. It was this barrier between us, thin at first, but thickening by the day. Eventually, even when I tried, I didn't have the strength to push through it.

And then Tim came home.

It was about six months into Claire's dark period. She'd started taking antidepressants a couple months back, and they finally seemed to be working. There were a few smiles, fewer tears, even a laugh or two. As spring turned the corner into summer, I felt her turning that corner with me. Her recovery was fragile, like a bluebell pushing through last year's grass, hoping there won't be another frost.

The ostensible occasion of Tim's visit was our parents' fortieth wedding anniversary. At least, that's what he told me when I found him on my doorstep, travel satchel in hand.

When I got over the shock of seeing him unannounced and ten years older, I invited him in. Claire was out running errands — another good sign.

I brought Tim into the living room and went in search of some beers. When I came back, I found him standing in front of the mantelpiece, his eyes wandering over the usual collection of family photos. Our wedding photo was tucked in there among school shots of

Seth and a great day on the beach. We looked young and happy, but if you got in close enough, you could see a slight smudge of dark under my left eye, where I'd rammed into a tree after Tim left me in the Woods. A mar on the day, and a reminder too.

"When did you get in?" I asked.

"Just now."

I handed him a beer. "You didn't go to Mom and Dad's?"

"Nope."

"But you're staying there, right?"

He shrugged and raised the bottle. When he finished his long pull, half of it was gone. He let it swing loosely between his fingers.

"Is Claire around?"

"She should be back soon."

He sat on the edge of the couch and downed the rest of his beer. I watched him sitting there, tanned, and relaxed in his jeans and pullover, a fully grown man. He seemed both intensely familiar and strange, like hearing your own voice on an answering machine.

I sat across from him. "So you're really back for the anniversary?"

"Sure enough."

"Why?"

"Pardon?"

"You've been home twice in the last ten years. Why now?"

He took a beat. "Forty years together is a serious thing. It should be celebrated. Proper respect should be paid."

"If you're implying—"

"I'm not casting stones. I know you've been stressing about the party."

I wanted to protest, but he was right. I had been stressing about the party. Mostly because it was something to stress about that wasn't Claire but also because basically the whole town was coming, and I was shit at organizing things.

"How did you even find out about it?" I asked.

"The usual way."

"So forthcoming, as always."

"Mom told me. How do you think I found out?"

"Right."

He looked around the room. "Nice house."

"Thanks."

"And Seth . . . well done there."

"Yeah," I said. "You should meet him. You know, since he's your nephew and all."

"Now who's casting stones?"

"What the fuck, Tim? Honestly, what the fuck?"

He looked at me for a long moment, a look I might've understood twenty years ago but which was impregnable then.

"Maybe I'm here to make amends . . ."

The front door slammed open.

"Jeff?" Claire called in a voice that rang out like it hadn't since before.

"We're in here," I answered, but my throat felt dry, and I knew it wasn't loud enough.

"Jeff?" she called again, walking through the house. "You're never going to believe this! I've got the perfect idea. The perfect thing."

I heard her voice trail off at the same time as I felt her presence behind me. Tim shifted his dark gaze from me to her, and something about him softened.

"Tim."

I was ready with a sarcastic "Tim's here, honey, isn't it awesome?" which was always how we spoke of this possibility, the few times it had come up. But something in her expression stopped me.

"Hello, Claire."

"When did you get here?" she asked.

"A few minutes ago. Jeff and I have been . . . catching up."

"Great, great. You'll stay here, of course?"

"I'd be happy to."

We fought that night. In low voices, through clenched teeth. A half year of disappointments and things unsaid came pouring out, filling up our bedroom until it felt like a window had to be opened or there wouldn't be room for one of us anymore.

It was Seth who ended the fight. His soft rap at the door was like a fork hitting a glass at a wedding.

"Yes?" Claire said, her voice shaky.

"Had a nightmare," Seth replied, his own voice wavering.

I stood up quickly and was at the door in an instant. Nine-going-on-ten Seth stood there in his footy pajamas that Claire wasn't ready to give up, his round face streaked with tears.

I picked him up. "You're getting so big."

"Not that big. Not as big as you."

"You will be soon, little man."

"Can I kill the bad guys, then?"

"Were you playing that video game at Cory's?" Claire asked from the tangle of sheets where she'd retreated as my words got angrier and angrier.

Seth nodded. "I lost."

I kissed the top of his head and walked him over to Claire. He slipped from my arms and into hers with a lack of hesitancy that struck me. When was the last time I'd taken Claire in my arms without thinking about it, or sought comfort in hers?

I sat down on my side of the bed as Claire settled Seth in between us. He lay on his back, the covers pulled up to his chin.

"Will you stand guard?" he asked.

"Of course we will, honey."

Claire met my eyes over his head and we each propped ourselves up on an elbow, forming a wall of family around Seth.

"That's good. That'll teach 'em."

"Shh, now. Close your eyes."

He obeyed her in a way that was becoming rare and was almost instantly asleep. We stayed like that for a while, listening to him breathe.

"What were you saying when you came home?" I said eventually, speaking low.

"About what?"

"When you came into the house, you seemed all excited about something."

Her face cleared. "I figured out what I want to do."

"What's that?"

She told me. That she was thinking of opening a daycare, that she thought it might be what she needed right now. It seemed to me like the opposite of what she needed — to be surrounded by other people's babies — so I stayed silent while she talked more than she had in months. I knew her well enough to know that the more I protested, the more she'd dig in her heels. I thought if I gave noncommittal "hmms" at appropriate moments, the thought would pass, sink back into her brain, and be gobbled up.

But apparently not.

Apparently, I didn't know her as well as I thought I did.

But I didn't think about that then, because Claire was smiling at me, and our son was warming the space between us, protected by the fort that was our family.

I never did get a clear answer from Tim as to why he chose that particular moment to come back. In truth, I spent a lot of time avoiding him over the next couple weeks. It was the company's year-end and I'd just been promoted, and that provided enough of an excuse to spend longer hours than usual at work.

Tim, to his credit, spent a lot of time with Seth, trying to get to know him. He took him to the local single-A ball team's spring training sessions, and helped him become proficient at riding the new bike we'd bought him. These were things I should've been doing but were good for Tim to be doing too. Seth had always been curious about Tim, and I was happy that he was there to fill in.

Claire was also busy. She was serious about the daycare thing, and seeing her sense of purpose, her determination, made me rethink my earlier opposition. Some of the color had come back into her face, and the circles around her eyes were fading. I even heard her singing in the shower once, a few bars that she cut off suddenly, as if she'd surprised herself.

When I wasn't at work, I was planning my parents' party. I'd originally intended it to be a small affair, but now that Tim had made a big show of coming all this way, I had to take it up a notch. Rent the town hall, have it catered, though the thought of the hole it was going to make in my credit card kept me up at night, listening to Claire's regular breathing.

It was one of those nights when she had what I can only describe as a wet dream. Her breathing got shallow and her hips rose and then her whole body tightened and released. It had been so long since we'd had sex, watching her made me hard, but all thoughts of waking her and bringing some reality to whatever fantasy she'd been experiencing disappeared when I saw the peaceful smile crawl onto her face and take up residence. Instead, I went to the bathroom and took care of myself, feeling like a furtive teenager as I came into a washcloth, then rinsed it out.

The town hall was located in an old grain silo that had been converted years ago, but still smelled of wheat and chaff if you breathed deeply enough. My parents made appreciative noises about the long buffet tables groaning with food, the small votives flickering on the tables for eight covered in light blue fabric, and the DJ who knew not to play anything past ABBA's heyday.

After dinner, Tim rose from his seat by my mother and tapped his glass. A hush fell over the room.

"Some sort of toast at these kinds of things is inevitable. And so, on the long flight here, and off and on for the last couple of days, I thought to myself, what should one say at a moment like this? How does one pay proper homage to the commitment you see before you? Forty years. That's a beautiful thing." His eyes scanned the room and found a place to rest. "A beautiful thing. And what more can you say than that, really? I can't think of anything. So raise a glass, mates. Stand up even. To Mom and Dad. To forty years."

We all stood and drank and mumbled what he told us to, and I felt both diminished and like I wanted to punch him in the face. That was my speech to give, damn it, even though I hated giving speeches.

"One more thing," Tim continued. "I also want to say thank you to my brother, Jeff, who's the reason you're all drinking and eating so well this evening." He held his glass held out to me like a peace offering. "I haven't been around, and you've been doing more than your share. Thank you." He raised his glass again as the room chorused, "To Jeff!"

Goddamn Tim. Right when you want to hate him forever, he goes and does something unexpected. Something that had me feeling way more emotional than I thought possible.

Claire took my hand and leaned into me.

"You did a good thing. A really good thing."

"Thanks."

She took my face in her hands and kissed me. "I mean it. I love you."

"I love you too." I kissed her back until there were a few whistles and catcalls telling us to "get a room." We broke apart. Claire gave me her crooked smile and excused herself to go to the bathroom.

"Good show tonight," Tim said to me a few minutes later, catching up to me at the bar.

"Right," I said, taking a sip of my drink. "You too."

"Sorry, did I steal your thunder?"

"No. Forget it."

"Damn."

I looked at him. His tie was askew and for some reason he looked younger than me. Or younger than I felt.

"What's that supposed to mean?"

"Stealing your thunder was kind of the whole point."

"Is that right?"

He laughed. "Jeff, Jeff, when did you get so serious? I came over to apologize. I thought I was doing you a favor. I remember how much you hate public speaking, but when I saw your face I realized . . . anyway, sorry."

I sipped my drink, trying to figure out if he was being genuine. It made me feel empty that I couldn't tell anymore.

"Do you really mean that?" I asked lamely.

He cocked an eyebrow. "And everyone always said you were the smart one."

"No one ever said that about me. You're the one they said that about."

"Then why do you have all this?" He waved his hand around. "How'd you get so fucking lucky?"

I rested my hands on the bar. "I ask myself that all the time."

"Uh-huh."

"I do."

"See you around, brother."

He started to leave and I grabbed his arm. "Don't do that."

He shrugged me off. "I can do what I want. Whatever I have, I have that."

"Why'd you come home, Tim? Just tell me."

"You know Claire's not doing well, right? You at least know that?"

My heart started to pump. "Don't tell me about my wife."

"But you asked me to," he said, and then he walked away.

CHAPTER 19

Swing Low

It's only when he's sitting across from me in the den, holding the plastic bag full of Jeff's effects, that I realize the police officer is Marc Duggard, a guy who was a few years ahead of me at Springfield Prep. The fact that I never realized who he was the day Jeff died underscores how out of it I was. At least now, it only takes me five minutes to recognize someone I was in school with for a decade. A baby step of progress.

"Sorry to have to do this, Claire," he says. "But we have to dot all the i's and cross all the t's. You understand."

"Yes," I say mechanically.

"I'll need you to sign this form," he says, handing me a release form in triplicate.

I sign the copies, and then he sits there, staring at me, as though I might hold the answers he's presumably here to give me.

"We've concluded our investigation," he says eventually.

"There was an investigation?"

"Standard procedure with vehicular homicide."

"Yes, of course. I remember."

More echoes of my past life. They'd have to make sure the driver wasn't drunk, or high, or reckless. But careless was okay. Careless was just a part of life.

"We've concluded it was an accident," he says. "With the sun in her eyes, and Jeff walking into the street suddenly like that, well, it could've happened to anybody."

I've always hated that expression. It didn't happen to anybody. It happened to Jeff.

"What's her name?" I ask.

"Pardon?"

"The driver. Do I know her?"

"She's from out of town. Passing through. Terrible luck. Terrible luck for everyone. Maybe I shouldn't tell you . . ."

"What?"

"She's still here. In the hospital, actually."

"Was she hurt?"

"No . . . a mental hold. It's common in these types of cases . . . well, you can imagine, I guess."

"I guess."

He slaps his hands on his thighs. "I should be going."

"Okay."

I shift in my seat and the plastic bag slips around in my lap, tinkling. Is it Jeff's keys? Loose change? Am I ever going to be able to open it?

Marc stands and pauses. He seems to be expecting me to thank him, for Jeff's effects, for the information about the woman who killed him, such as it is. Instead, I give him back the thousand-mile stare he's been giving me.

He holds it for a moment. "I'm real sorry about all this, Claire."

"Yes."

"I can see myself out."

I nod but rise anyway. Out in the hall, there's a line waiting for the bathroom. Tish is at the head of it. She looks like she wants to say something to me but before I can ask her what it is, Tim's at my side, leading me to the back of the house.

We come to an abrupt stop in the solarium that overlooks the backyard.

"Wait here," he says, as if I had anywhere else to go, then takes the plastic bag from my hands and places it on the counter.

He leaves the room and I'm alone. Seth's yellow rain jacket is hanging by its hood over Jeff's larger red one. Their baseball gloves are resting on the bench, a mud-caked baseball half slipping out of Seth's newer glove. When was the last time they played catch? Was it this year, during a thaw? Or have the gloves been sitting there all winter, waiting, waiting, waiting?

"Come with me," Tim says from behind me. He reaches over my shoulder and pushes open the creaky screen door. The sound of a million summers.

We go outside. It's late afternoon, the sun is low, and the air is heavy with the smell of impending rain. He directs me toward the rusting swing set tucked into the corner of the lot. Jeff spent hours assembling it, cursing, sweating, even slicing his hand open, resulting in a long wait in the emergency room. But when it was finished (slightly off-kilter, the swings always listing to the left) and he revealed it to six-year-old Seth, all the stress and toil were worth the expression of pure joy on his face. Jeff hoisted him into the seat, and Seth swung and swung, too high for my liking. Later, he and his friends scampered up the slide, dangled from the crossbeam. For a while I always knew where to find him, but then he grew, and the swing didn't, and Seth moved on to other things.

I used to find Jeff out here sometimes a few years ago, and again lately, stuffed into a swing, his arms wrapped around the metal chains, staring off into space.

Tim sits in a swing and motions for me to sit in the other. The stiff rubber gives under my adult weight, cutting into the backs of my thighs, reminding me of the scratchy dress I'm still wearing. The itch of grief.

Tim's swing creaks back and forth, screaming for oil. Last year's leaves are gathered under our feet, rotting into earth. A chore we never got to.

"You want some?" Tim asks as the grainy smell of alcohol hits me. He's holding out a fifth of something dark, wiping his mouth with the back of his other hand.

"I've been looking for that."

"How could you be? I brought it with me."

"No, I mean something *like* that. All the alcohol seems to be missing."

"I noticed."

"My mother," I say, and he nods in agreement.

He passes the container to me and I take a swig. Jim Beam, I realize as soon as it hits my throat. An old flavor, full of memories.

"That's awful."

"It was the only thing I could find at my parents' house."

"You think they keep it to dissuade guests from drinking?"

"Maybe."

"Sometimes I think it wouldn't take much to turn this town into the one in *Footloose*." I take another burning swallow. "Anyway. Thanks."

"Wasn't that town called Bomont?"

"It's not about the name, doofus."

"Put a girl in a swing and suddenly she's using terms like 'doofus.'"

"If the swing fits."

I twist the creaking, rusting chains, like I used to do as a child. I twirl and twirl and twirl — and release! I'm twirling in the opposite direction. The world blurs, my brain goes dizzy and feels loose in my skull.

"What did he want?" Tim asks when I come to rest.

"Who? Marc Duggard?"

"The one and only."

"To give me Jeff's effects, and to tell me that they've closed their investigation. Accident. Unavoidable. 'One of those things.' Did you know the woman who did it is in the hospital?"

"Was she injured?"

"They're worried she's going to kill herself."

"Maybe they shouldn't try to stop her."

"Tim!"

"What? You don't think she should pay for what she did?"

"What's it going to change?"

"That's a weird thing for you to say. Whatever happened to 'light 'em up'?"

"Did I ever say that?"

His feet push at the ground. He sways slowly. "Many times."

"That was a long time ago. Another lifetime."

"We only have one lifetime."

"Right."

"Do you know who she is?"

"He wouldn't tell me. Someone from out of town."

I look down at my own feet. I raise my toes up and try to dig them into the mud, but the ground won't give.

"Are you going to forgive her?" he says.

"I can't think about that right now. I'm still trying to forgive myself."

"What does that mean?"

I look at him. His face is flushed from the alcohol and the cold breeze.

"Do I have to say it?"

He holds my gaze for a minute, then takes another drink.

"It's not the same thing, Claire. It never was."

"How can you be so sure?"

He doesn't answer. Instead, he gives a big push backward, leaving the ground, arcing through the air, then jumps from the swing, landing gracefully on the ground, sticking the landing like a gymnast.

He stands in front of me, blocking the wind. And now, for the first time, the day feels warmer than it is.

When I get back inside, I decide it's time to finally get out of these clothes. And the thought of climbing into bed, pulling the covers over my head, over this day, is there too.

And Seth. I want Seth.

I pull Beth aside and let her know where I'm going, ask her if she can handle the people who don't seem to want to leave. She agrees to see that the guests get out of here eventually, sooner rather than later.

Upstairs, I go first to our room, my room, and change into an old pair of flannel pajamas Jeff always used to make fun of me for wearing.

"But they're so comfortable," I'd say.

"You look five," he'd reply, then nuzzle his face into my belly. "And you smell like the cottage. Like mothballs."

The pajamas did date from our cottage days, a rickety old house thirty minutes away that wasn't winterized and seemed to be slowly sinking into the ground. Everything in that house smelled like beach towels that had never quite dried, and the occasional mothball we found in the back of a closet, left over from its grander days when my grandmother kept fur coats there for special occasions.

We played dress-up in those coats, Beth and I, wrinkling our noses against the mothball tang, ladying around in our mother's high heels while our parents bickered downstairs. These pajamas smell like memories, mostly good ones. Ones from before life became something too complicated to be fixed by a juice Popsicle pulled fresh from the freezer.

Seth is in his room, lying on his car bed that was super cool when he was seven, and has now become almost kitsch. Something a hipster might choose if he was discovering irony. Only Seth is twelve and his father's just died and I doubt he's thinking much about irony these days. Either way, he needs a new bed.

His back is propped against the headboard, a pillow at a weird angle, and he's reading a book. A slim volume I don't recognize.

"What you got there, buddy?" I ask as I sit down next to him, my feet in the same direction as his.

"Dad's book."

I lean my head against his shoulder. "What's that?"

"That book of Dad's. You know, the one I got the poem from."

"Oh, right. Where'd you find that again?"

"In his bag."

"His golf bag?"

"Nah, his travel one. He never unpacked from that trip he took a couple of weeks before . . . Anyway, just like Dad, right?"

I smile. Jeff's the worst unpacker in the world.

"What's the book about?"

"She seems to have a thing for trees. And snow. She likes snow."

I take the book from him. It's called *Just This Side of Childhood* and contains about fifty poems. On the back is a black-and-white picture of a girl about Seth's age — the National Spoken Word Champion of the previous year. She has long dark hair and a pale face, and something about her straight-on stare seems familiar. Only with more confidence, if that makes any sense.

Zoey Underhill.

What was Jeff doing with this book?

Seth takes it from me and goes back to the page he was reading.

"You enjoying that?"

"Dunno. Makes me feel a bit better."

"Because it was Dad's?"

"Maybe."

"You want me to leave you alone?"

"No, you can stay."

"Okay, then, I'll stay."

I pull up the covers from the bottom of the bed and tuck them around us. I close my eyes and listen to Seth slowly turning the pages, muttering a word or two out loud.

The wind is rattling against the panes, and maybe it's my imagination, but I think I can hear the creak of the unoiled swing.

CHAPTER 20

Hold the Phone

Will you play a game with me? Jeff wrote to me about a month after we'd come back into contact.

Since those first few email exchanges, that first phone call, I'd felt a fizzy excitement, carbonated, letting loose little bubbles of happiness. A crush, a work crush, I'd tell myself when I opened his profile to figure out the exact color of his eyes, or when he'd race through my thoughts at odd moments. He was *fun,* and I needed that. And I was different with him, I felt different with him, and I needed that too. Friends, we were friends, and if our interactions had secretly become the best part of my workday, that was play, pretend, nothing to worry about.

What kind of game? I wrote back.

Word association.

Like in Psych 101?

Nah. Well, maybe. There's this thing I read about on the Internet and I thought . . . I'm curious what you'll say.

You were reading a women's magazine, weren't you?

I smiled as the email floated away from me, imagining his indignant snort.

If you're not going to play nice . . . he wrote.

I'll be a good girl, I promise. How does it work?

I send you a word, you write back the first thing that comes to mind, and so on.

Is there some kind of scoring mechanism?

Sure, that comes at the end.

I put my phone on do not disturb.

All right. Hit me.

Distill.

Moonshine.

Really?

I shook my head as I typed.

Aren't you just supposed to ask me the next word?

Right. Okay. Sunshine.

Day.

Off.

Crazy.

Your current score is crazy.

I thought you could only check the score at the end?

Yeah, yeah.

I glanced at his picture. It felt like he was smirking at me.

This was your idea, remember? I typed.

Motherfucker.

Excuse me?

Sorry, he wrote. *That's really the next word.*

Where did you find this thing?

The Internet, I told you. Answer please.

My answer is: Really.

Totally.

Seriously.

Yeah.

Wait, I wrote. *Are we still playing?*

We are. Yeah is the next word. Promise.

Okay. That's my next word, for clarity.

A long pause while I drummed my nails on the desk.

Hello? You still there? I wrote.

I'm still here.

Is there no next word? Or does the computer say that I'm an axe murderer?

No . . . there's a next word.

Well, what is it then?

You sure you want to know?

Of course.

Another pause. Then: *Sex.*

Sex? Really?

Really.

Huh.

What?

I never would've thought you could get from distill to sex in so few words.

His answer felt instantaneous.

I might've gotten there sooner.

My heart was suddenly racing.

What's that supposed to mean?

Just . . . God. Forget it.

What were you going to write?

The pause was so long I was about to type another prompt.

Probably better left unwritten. Unsaid.

Oh, right. Yes. Probably.

Unsaid, but not unthought?

It was my turn to pause.

Not unthought, I wrote eventually, my fingers sweaty on the keys.

When the cab from the airport drops me at home, the windows are fogged from the unrelenting rain that feels like it's been falling for days. The storm drain outside our front walk is clogged with last year's leaves, and a puddle that looks like it has ambitions to be a lake is blocking the way.

The cabdriver helps me navigate the walkway, along with my hastily packed suitcase, but without an umbrella I'm soaked through to the skin before I get to the front door.

Brian must hear me fumbling with the keys in the lock because he has the door open and is pulling me into the house before I can do it myself.

"Where's Zoey?" I ask.

He looks like he hasn't changed clothes since yesterday, or shaved. And though he hides lack of sleep well from many years of experience, I'm guessing he hasn't had much of that either.

"She's upstairs in her room. Sleeping, the last time I checked."

I move toward the stairs, the water running off me forming puddles on the hardwood floor.

"Let her be. She needs to sleep."

My hand rests on the banister. The adrenaline that's been propelling me since Zoey's tearful voice came through my revived phone dissipates. I feel like I could sleep for a week.

"Is she okay?"

"I'm not sure. Why the hell weren't you answering your phone?"

"I'm sorry. I told you. I forgot to charge it. You can't imagine how bad I feel."

"You have to be reachable, Tish, if you're not going to be … If you're not going to be *there,* you have to be reachable."

"It won't ever happen again. Forgive me, okay? Please?"

He looks at me for a minute. Water drips from me like a leaky tap.

"Why don't we get you out of those clothes," he says eventually. "Go to the kitchen. I'll get you some things."

I nod. When I get to the kitchen, there's a full bottle of liquor sitting on the table, an empty glass next to it. These must be for Brian, but we have other glasses.

I pour an inch of vodka and toss it back. My empty stomach protests, but the rest of me welcomes it.

"Will you pour me one of those?" Brian's holding a towel, an old pair of sweats, and a T-shirt I used to sleep in in college that I thought I threw out years ago.

"One finger or two?"

"Surprise me."

I pour him two fingers, hand him the glass, then strip down, letting my clothes slap to the floor.

"Aren't you worried the neighbors might see?"

I dry myself with the towel quickly, then slip the T-shirt over my head as I take in the shadows in our spotless backyard. The daffodils are up, though the rain seems to be trying to drown them.

"I doubt the little perv across the way is going to get too excited about seeing me naked."

"You underestimate the teenaged boy's mind. Besides, if it gets me excited, why not him?"

I smile as I climb into the sweatpants and take a seat across from him. His glass is empty. He looks like he wants another.

"I'm guessing not today. So what happened?"

"Zoey passed out onstage."

"I know, but why? Is she okay or was it nerves?"

"Zoey doesn't get nervous."

He picks up the bottle and pours himself another couple of inches, but doesn't drink it down.

I reach across the table and rest my hand on Brian's arm. The hair on it is smooth, familiar.

"What's going on? Is something wrong with Zoey? You're kind of . . . you're scaring the shit out of me, to be honest."

"I'm sorry. I'm scared too."

"What is it? Please tell me."

He shakes his head, looking lost. "One minute she was fine, excited, you know how she gets right before she goes on. Keyed up, distant. Then that kid, that Ethan kid, he screwed up, not in a big way, but enough of a stumble that I was thinking she's got this sewn up, and then before she could even say her name she was on the ground, out like a light."

"Did she eat breakfast? You know sometimes she forgets to eat if you don't remind her."

"That's not it. Tish . . . she was out for *five* minutes."

"*What?* That video on the Internet was only a couple of —"

"Wait, what?"

"Jeff's kid, Seth . . . he was watching it on his computer and —"

"A video? What are you talking about?"

The wind picks up outside, pushing the branches of a tree that's always been too close to the house against the glass. It screeches and moans in a way that would signify monsters coming if this were a horror movie. Which it might be.

"You don't know about the video?"

"Are you saying that Zoey's mishap is on the web?"

"I guess they were taping the event?"

He thinks about it. "I forgot. They were."

"I think they were streaming it out live, and when Zoey fainted . . ."

"Jesus. Thank God Zoey doesn't know."

"What's wrong with her, Brian? What's wrong with our daughter?"

He finally picks up the glass and downs it in one gulp.

"I don't know."

I spend the night in Zoey's room, curled up in the old squashy chair from our first apartment that ended up in here somehow, missed by my mother-in-law's decorator, who tore through the house in a burst of color wheels and fabric swatches right after we moved in. I doze fitfully, my brain stuck on the possibilities I finally pried out of Brian, but that won't be confirmed, or unconfirmed, please God, until we see the specialist on Monday.

Another weekend to face without knowing what's going on in my life. Another Monday where my worst fears might come true.

Brian passed out in the living room around eleven. When his beeper buzzes an hour later, I let it go unanswered. Somebody else can take care of whoever's calling him tonight. I tuck a pillow under his head and put the spare duvet over him. Judging by the depth of his snores, he'll be out for a solid eight hours.

When the sun's thinking about rising, I realize Zoey's gone still, assuming the position of someone who's only pretending to sleep. I walk across the room on half-asleep, tingling legs. I climb into Zoey's bed and wrap myself around her back.

"I'm sleeping."

"I know, honey."

"I don't want to talk about it."

"You don't have to." I breathe in her smell, loving how she still uses Johnson's baby shampoo on her thick tangle of hair. I can pretend, sometimes, that my baby is still a baby because she smells that way.

"Dad's freaked."

"Cut him some slack. He worries about you. We both do."

She pulls the covers up over our shoulders.

"There's nothing wrong with me."

"Well, I really hope so, but we're going to do some tests to make extra sure, okay?"

She goes silent and I realize after a moment that she's crying. Her hot tears splash against my arm.

"Why are you crying, sweetie?"

"Because I ruined everything."

"What? Of course you didn't."

"I fainted in front of . . . in front of everyone. I lost. Ethan won."

"It's only a competition. There's always next year."

"*Mmooomm.*"

"I know, I know. That's so *not the point.*"

The tears are still falling but, despite herself, I can feel her smile.

I eventually persuade Zoey to get up and into the shower. I go downstairs to make her the greasiest, most tempting breakfast I can make in a house where a health-conscious doctor lives. Bacon is out of the question, but I'm pretty sure there are eggs, and some full-fat cheese hidden in the meat drawer.

Brian's up, sitting at the kitchen counter with his laptop open. A quick glance confirms he's watching the video. Zoey standing, Zoey going gray, Zoey on the ground.

"Can you believe they've put it to music? What the hell is wrong with people? Can you tell me that?"

"Put it away, Brian. Zoey'll be down in a minute."

"We're going to have to tell her about this."

"I want to get some food into her first. Maybe let her have a few minutes where she doesn't have to think about it?"

He glances up from the screen as he closes the laptop. "Do you think that's possible?"

I look at him. At the concern in his eyes. At the pure certainty I feel that he'd do anything, anything, to keep her happy. To keep her safe.

I did a good thing here. In my whole life, this is the best thing I have done. Brian. Zoey. My family.

"I hope so, Brian, I really do."

He nods and stands. "I went to the store. I got bacon."

"Bacon?" Zoey says behind me, her voice carrying almost the right amount of enthusiasm.

Her hair's loose and wet from her shower. She looks thin, thinner than she should be. Maybe that's the explanation? Maybe we've been missing what she's been silent about because silence isn't her thing? But she's always been thin. I was all knees and arms until I was thirteen, and then I was knees and arms with hips. Zoey's the same.

"Doctor's orders," Brian says. "It's a little-known fact that bacon's a natural cure. In fact, Native Americans introduced the first settlers to it, only they called it salt pork."

"*Daad,* you are so full of . . ."

"Shit," I say, laughing. "Your dad is full of shit."

Zoey's mouth makes an O. "You are so going to get in trouble! Did you hear what she said, Dad?"

"I heard it all right. She challenged my knowledge of history. And natural remedies."

He tries to keep his face serious, but he barely gets the words out before he breaks into a full belly laugh. Then I'm laughing and Zoey's laughing and the room, the house, is filled with laughter.

The phone rings.

I'm closest to it, so I pick it up. "Underhill residence."

"Hey, um, Mrs. Underhill?"

"Yes?"

"This is Ethan. Ethan Zuckerberg?" His voice rises at the end, like he's questioning who he is.

"Oh. Hi, Ethan. And . . . congratulations."

Zoey's laugh cuts out like she's been unplugged. Her whole body is tense with focus.

"Um, thanks, I guess? Can I . . . talk to Zoey?"

"Let me see if she's free."

I cover the mouthpiece with my hand. "It's Ethan. Do you want to talk to him?"

"You don't have to," Brian says.

"No, it's fine. I'll take it in the other room, okay?"

"Of course."

I hand her the portable phone and meet Brian's gaze over her head. He raises his eyebrows, and I can see the fear of a thousand generations of fathers in his eyes. Boys. Boys! Our daughter is talking to a *boy*.

I smile at him. "Why don't we cook that bacon?"

"That's probably a good idea."

He walks to the fridge. I've got one ear on the mumble of Zoey's voice in the other room.

"No . . . it's all right . . . *what? What!*"

And now the fridge and breakfast and bacon are forgotten, and Brian and I are through the door to the dining room, but not before Zoey hits the ground.

CHAPTER 21

Falling

Two weeks after the "sex conversation" — as I'd taken to trying not to call it in my head — Tish was standing across a conference table from me, her hands resting on a lectern.

"So, we'll be starting off with module 1 today: *How to identify staff that ought to be considered for termination*," she half-read her notes with a bored tone of voice. She was wearing the woman's work uniform: a dark blue skirt, a white Oxford shirt, and discreet earrings. Her hair was parted in the middle and loose around her face.

One of the guys from marketing put up his hand. "Mrs. Underhill?"

Her jaw clenched. This was already his fourth question of the day, and we were only five minutes into the meeting.

"Yes, Mr. Dunn?"

"You skipped the Safety Minute."

Her eyes fluttered closed. "So I did."

"Would you like me to do it?"

"Sure, go right ahead."

He stood up. The left side of his shirt had come untucked, and there was a pen stain blooming from his breast pocket.

Thirty. Still eager.

I gave him six months before he'd be on the receiving end of module 3: *Firing*.

That, or he'd be the next CEO.

"Right, so, okay, I thought I'd talk about opening doors in closed conference rooms . . ."

I tuned him out, letting my gaze wander around the high-tech room until it came to rest on Tish. She shifted her body, and I swear we locked eyes for a moment. I gave her a slight eye roll. The corner of her mouth lifted in what seemed like an answering smile. For a moment, I felt like I could read her thoughts, that they were echoing my own — *What the fuck am I doing here?*

Then she turned her head away.

The lights flickered.

An error line flowed through her image, and the illusion was gone.

Around when the company made our email into Facebook, they also installed a high-tech conference room with the latest in two-way video technology. Part of the consultants' motivation — what, you thought this *didn't* have something to do with them? — was to provide a more cost-efficient way of firing people without making it too impersonal. We've all seen *Up in the Air;* Skype-firing has its drawbacks. But, apparently, a roomful of technology that makes it seem like someone who's actually five hundred miles away is sitting across the table from you is enough to trick the brain. Kind of like how Luke falls in love with Princess Leia after seeing her in R2-D2's fluttery blue light projection.

At least, until he realizes she's his sister.

Of course, the system had other applications too. More effective cross-company meetings, a flashy recruiting tool, and a good way to train incoming managers in the art of not being a wimp and firing your own people.

Which is how I found myself watching Tish's image, trying not to focus on the increasing amount of time we now spent in communication with each other, how much of a fixture she'd become in my life so quickly.

Because something that felt this good couldn't be wrong, could it?

And anything that might skip across my brain like a flat rock thrown sideways, well, we'd agreed not to say those things, to push them down.

So, no harm, no foul.

When I got the meeting invite, I felt a frisson of ... something else I pushed down. But I certainly dressed more carefully than usual that day. I wore my favorite shirt. I got a haircut I told myself I needed anyway. I gave myself an attentive shave. And when Claire said something about me looking good at breakfast, I pushed the stab of guilt down too.

The funny thing was, neither of us spoke about it in advance. I mean Tish and I. We'd been debating about best movies off and on for a couple days, and when I got to the office there was an email from her containing the case for *High Fidelity*.

John Cusack while he was still hot. A seamless transition from book to movie. The Beta Band. "Is that Peter fucking Frampton?" John Cusack while he was still hot. Need I go on?

Is the John Cusack point supposed to be determinative for me?

Not sure. Are you a guy who can appreciate male hotness from an aesthetic point of view?

I'm about three on the Kinsey scale.

Interesting that you'd go there.

?

Just that you'd take that as a sexual orientation question.

It wasn't?

Men.

That's not an explanation.

Sure. Right. Now why don't you love this movie? Lack of light sabers?

I laughed out loud and glanced at the Han Solo figurine on my desk, which was a present from Seth for my last birthday.

I don't know what you're talking about.

It's amazing how convincing you are.

Anyway, I have this meeting ...

Right. Me too.

I sat staring at the screen, waiting for some acknowledgment that my meeting was with her, wondering why neither of us had brought it up.

Whether our silence was speaking for us.

Then my computer chimed, reminding me that I had a meeting with Underhill, Patricia, in five minutes.

I stood, looking around my desk for something to bring with me for luck.

My eyes came to rest on the Han Solo figurine. I reached out and tucked it into my pocket.

I think I'm falling, I thought.

I know, little Han Solo replied.

When Dunn the Corporate Drone finished his safety stupidity, Tish resumed her lecture. As I bent my head over my notes, I tried to rid myself of the disappointment that our meeting wasn't just the two of us. But although we weren't alone, I felt acutely aware of her presence. Like how you do sometimes in a crowd of people. How you can tell exactly where they are at any given moment, even though you haven't looked in a while. Like some thread connected us.

Two hours later, the meeting was over and I looked up from my doodle/notes to meet Tish's eyes again. I smiled and started to wave at her, stopping in the middle as it struck me that it might come off as weird to my colleagues. She nodded her head and clicked a button, and then she was gone.

We all stood and made our separate ways out of the room. Marketing Guy was talking to someone I didn't know about the list Tish should be on, if she wasn't already. I smiled, but I felt restless, like there was somewhere else I was supposed to be, something else I was supposed to be doing.

I got back to my desk, and there was the usual host of emails waiting for me, but also one from Tish. The Re was:

Strange?

I clicked it open.

Well, that was strange, she had written.
Strange good?
A moment, two, then *ping*!
Strange good.
We used the conference room a lot.

CHAPTER 22

It's Not What It Looks Like

I wake up next to Seth with an almighty crick in my body. When I look over at him, I suppress a laugh. He's fallen asleep with the book he was reading across the bridge of his nose, his book light still on. I guess it's a measure of how tired we both were that we slept despite the cramped quarters and illumination.

I lift the book from Seth's face as gently as I can and leave his room, letting him sleep in, sleep yesterday off, if that's possible.

Beth's already up and downstairs, sitting at the kitchen table, working away on her laptop. Amazingly, there doesn't seem to be anyone else here, only their detritus, which I'm sure my mother will be here to start cleaning up as soon as she gets my father out the door.

"There's coffee," Beth says, not looking up.

I put the book down on the table and help myself to a large cup, keeping it black, though I generally don't drink it that way. Yesterday feels like it's clinging to my brain, and Beth's black tar might scrub it away.

"You don't have to stay," I say to Beth, "if you should be getting back."

"Ha!"

"What?"

She grins at me. "You don't really mean that. At least . . . I hope you don't."

"I don't, but I'd understand if you have to. If you're needed elsewhere."

"I can't think of anywhere else where I'm needed more than here."

"Are you trying to make me cry?"

"Little bit."

I reach for a Kleenex. "That's not really a challenge these days, you know."

"How about making you laugh?"

"That might be harder."

"I'll work on that." She picks up the book from the table. "What's this?"

"What? Oh, it's the book Seth got that poem he read from. Jeff had it."

Beth starts flipping through it and I read the title again. *Just This Side of Childhood* by Zoey Underhill. Why did Jeff have this book? Underhill, Underhill . . .

"Who's Tish?" Beth asks.

"She's . . . she worked with Jeff. She was here yesterday."

"Why would she give him this? Were they good friends?"

"I don't . . . I don't think so. She gave it to him?"

Beth holds the inside cover of the book open to me. Written on it, under a date from three weeks ago, are the words *To Jeff, I'm a proud mama! Tish.*

"This must be her daughter's book."

"Okay."

"What?"

"Nothing. Forget it."

"Beth."

"Don't you think it's . . . weird that she'd give it to him?"

"They worked together. Maybe she gave them to a bunch of people?"

She stays silent.

"You don't think —"

She shakes her head. "No. I really don't. I'm sure it's fine."

"But that might explain a few things. Like how distracted he's been. And I found her *crying* outside —"

"No," she says firmly. "Don't go there."

"Why? Rick did it. Why not Jeff?"

"Yeah, my asshole ex-husband cheated on me, but it was only a one-time thing. It's not like he was leaving me for her or anything. He only told me because he wanted forgiveness."

"As if."

"I know, right? Only . . ."

"What?"

"When he'd moved out and I'd calmed down, I missed him. And I got to thinking that I wished I didn't know about it. If he could've kept it to himself, then we'd probably still be together."

"Why are you telling me this?"

"Because sometimes it's better to leave well enough alone."

"You really think that?"

"Yeah, I do." She rises, taking her dishes to the sink. "I guess I should get started on this mess."

"You don't have to. I'm sure Mom . . ."

"I asked Mom and Dad to cool their heels for the day. For the weekend actually."

"And they agreed?"

"Yup. I think there's some big golf tournament on or something."

"The Masters."

"The whatsit?"

"The Masters? One of the four majors . . ."

She smiles. "Jeff knowledge?"

"Yeah. I bet he's pissed as hell that he's missing it."

"You mean, up in heaven."

"Ha, ha."

She hugs me quickly. "I'm only poking fun. Besides, if there really is a heaven, I'm sure they have cable."

Amazingly enough, my parents keep their word (or the golf is so riveting they're sufficiently distracted; either scenario is just as likely), and it's only the three of us for the weekend. Even Tim seems to have fallen off the face of the earth, but since that's hardly new, I don't remark on it.

Monday rolls around as Mondays always do, and it's back to work for real now. Not that I couldn't take more time off if I needed to, but Playthings made me feel more like myself the other day. It always has.

I get there in time for morning drop-off, marveling, as always, at the long line of SUVs waiting to disgorge the tiniest of cargoes. Our parents had a Ford LTD growing up, and the backseat was just big enough for Beth and me to have to lean slightly to land a really good blow on the other during the cross-country family vacations my parents insisted on taking. If ever there were two people (or four, for that matter) who didn't need to be cooped up in a four-door sedan, we were those people. But my parents have never been the most self-aware of couples.

Outside my office, Mandy Holden's got LT firmly by the hand, the sweater of her pale blue twin-set knotted over her shoulders.

"Oh, Claire, hello. Great to see you." She says this like the last time she saw me wasn't at my husband's wake.

"You too, Mandy. What can I do for you?"

She holds her finger to her lips, then points down at LT, who, as far as I can tell, is plotting how to get the Fruit Roll-Up out of Sara Kindle's little paw and couldn't care less about whatever it is his mother wants to keep quiet.

But I nod and motion for her to enter my office, our pantomime confirming that she'll come see me when she's done depositing LT in the toddler room and giving whatever today's instructions are to the way-too-patient staff.

The message light on my phone is still blinking away like it was last week. I can't believe it still has the energy. I dial into my voicemail and skip through the messages. All sympathy, all the time. It occurs to me after I erase the tenth one that I should be keeping a list for the thank-you cards my mother's going to start bugging me about writing any day now, but I can't be bothered. Instead, I hit the buttons to erase them all; if someone wants to say something other than how sorry they are, they'll call back.

Mandy enters my office as I hang up the phone.

"So, um, sorry, again, for your loss."

"Thank you. What's up?"

"We haven't found a way to tell him yet, but it's important that the staff know, and you'll probably have to implement some new food guidelines—"

"What are you talking about?"

"LT's gluten sensitivity, of course."

"LT has celiac disease?"

"Of course not! It's only a sensitivity. I told you on Friday."

She sounds genuinely annoyed that I don't remember this. As if something she told me after I put my husband in the ground should be top of mind, or in my mind at all.

"Right. Of course."

"So you'll make the changes?"

"No."

"We're talking about LT's health here, Claire."

"We went over this when you found out LT was allergic to pollen. We can't implement a whole set of rules because of one child's sensitivity. Not unless it's life-threatening."

"But—"

"LT's not the only child who isn't eating gluten. I'll let the caregivers know and we'll make sure he only eats what you provide him with, but that's as far as we can go."

She holds her enormous purse to her chest. "But on Friday you said—"

"You're not seriously trying to hold her to something she said on Friday, are you?" Tim says from the doorway.

Mandy looks startled, then smiles brightly at Tim. "Well, I . . . No, I guess I understand. But, Claire, I want to continue to dialogue about this."

"Why don't we see how it goes this week and we'll take it from there, all right?"

"Sounds reasonable to me," Tim says.

"Oh, well, yes . . ." Mandy stands and I can see the blush creeping up her cheeks. Tim is throwing her off her game, but not completely. "And who are you?"

"I'm Jeff's brother, Tim."

"I'm so sorry."

"It's all right."

"Pleased to meet you."

She holds out her tanned hand, diamonds flashing. Tim takes it briefly, and I swear she's batting her eyelashes at him. Maybe those rumors of LT's father sleeping on the couch are true.

"You have a minute, Claire?" Tim asks.

"I'm sure she does. I'll be running along. Ta."

Tim watches her leave, shaking his head. When she's maybe out of earshot he says, "'Ta'? Does she think she's a queen?"

"In the furthest reaches of her mind? Probably."

"What did she ask you to do when she found out her kid was allergic to pollen?"

"Cancel all field trips. Have the windows sealed. Have special HEPA filters installed in the ventilation system."

"Why not just put him in a bubble?"

"I thought about suggesting that, but I think it would've been too much trouble for her. I mean, if someone came to the house, and LT wasn't in the bubble, or there wasn't even a bubble, people might talk."

"She's a piece of work."

"She is. How come you're here?"

He frowns. "I hadn't seen you for a couple of days, and I thought . . . I wanted to see how this place turned out in the end."

I wave my hand around. "Here it is, in all its glory. What do you think?"

He does a full 360, taking in the primary colors, the handprints on the wall from every class I've had since I started the place, the massive jar of pennies the kids are collecting to buy books to send to kids in Africa, then back to me.

"I like it very much," he says. "Very much indeed."

• • •

When I thought of the idea of Playthings, I clung to it like a piece of driftwood that crosses the path of someone lost at sea, just about to give up. And then, because more pieces floated by, I started constructing the pieces into a raft that would take me back to myself, home.

It didn't really surprise me that Jeff was skeptical about it. I was skeptical myself. Was I really ready to give up something I'd worked toward for years? Do something that was going to disappoint so many people, my father in particular? Losing the baby had nothing to do with my job. Why was my brain connecting the two and making it impossible to disentangle them?

But six months of haunting playgrounds and feigning normalcy hadn't given me any answers. My brain was playing tricks on me, sucking me inward, away from my life, my family, myself. I might've clung on to anything that floated by. If I'd been hanging out in a coffee shop instead of a playground, I might be the proud owner of a Starbucks knock-off right now.

All I knew is that I could see land for the first time in months, and if the wind didn't change, I'd be ashore soon.

So I threw myself into the project. What it would've been prudent to take six months to do, I did in one. I scouted locations, researched licensing requirements, started seeking out disgruntled staff at other daycares to steal them away when the time was right. I even fomented dissent among parents I knew about their current daycares. Did they have a sign-in system? No? Really? Oh well, I'm sure it's fine . . .

There was a sense of unreality about the whole thing. I might've been on the raft, paddling in the right direction, but I didn't expect it to last. Like a fat person who'd gotten thin, I couldn't see the real me in the mirror yet. And also, Jeff wasn't on the raft with me. I wanted him to be, he wanted to be, but I didn't know how to make any room, and he didn't know how to climb on board.

The reappearance of Tim made it more complicated. Things were so tense between him and Jeff and me. As far as I knew, they hadn't talked since the wedding. And it had never really been normal between Tim and me since we broke up and he left.

Our breakup had been sudden. Or maybe that's not right. Maybe the truth is that the seeds of it had been there the whole time, but we were concentrating on the bright blooming things and not the choking weeds that were getting bigger by the day. But I'd promised my father I was going home, and Tim wanted nothing to do with it. So when he proposed Australia or Phuket or anywhere but Springfield, we'd finally said the things out loud that we thought we'd said before, but never had.

"I always told you I was going home," I said.

"And I always told you I wasn't."

"But I thought—"

"I thought it too, but I guess neither of us is going to compromise, are we?"

There were other words. Angry ones. A few desperate weeks where we argued, and were silent, and had frantic sex where I'd cry afterward, trying to muffle my tears with my pillow while Tim pretended to sleep. Neither of us would bend. Each of us expected the other to.

In the end, that's really all it came down to. And if we regretted it after, neither of us was willing to be the first to say so. Maybe it was for the best. No, it was. It was.

Tim seemed to be making an effort this time. He spent a lot of time with his parents. He took an interest in Seth, filling in when Jeff and I were absent. He made overtures to Jeff. They shared a beer, went on a night out with the boys, played a round of golf. And he kept his distance from me. He acted like a polite, distant brother-in-law who barely knew me. Which was, on many levels, the truth.

Then I found the perfect place. This place where I am now, where the children are laughing in the other room, where despite the Mandys of the world I was able to paddle my raft to shore, get back home and almost forget what it was like to be at sea.

After all the papers were signed and I got the keys from the realtor, I left a quick note for Jeff on the kitchen table telling him where I was and made a beeline for this building. It had been a gymnasium before and the previous tenants had left lots of useful equipment behind. An enclosed space full of balls for the kids to jump around in, bright colors on the walls, those mats we used in high school for sit-up drills, which would be perfect for the kids' naps.

I walked into what I already knew would be the toddler room, pulled a couple of the mats to the middle of the floor, and sat lotus-style, letting the room tell me what it wanted to be, letting it become my home away from home. It was pelting rain outside, the drops making a soothing hum as they plinked against the metal roof.

"Are you meditating?"

"Jeff, you came!" I opened my eyes. "Tim. Sorry—"

"I sound like him?"

"You do."

He motioned to the floor. His hair was wet from the rain and he carried a sodden jacket over his arm. "There room enough for two on there?"

"I guess."

He draped his jacket over a tiny plastic chair and sat next to me. He tried to emulate my position but stopped halfway, grimacing.

"Not as flexible as I once was."

"No way you could ever do that."

"You don't know, maybe I could."

I shook my head. "How'd you know I was here?"

"Saw your note for Jeff. Thought I'd take a spin by. See what all the fuss was about."

"What do you think?"

He looked around him. Not a cursory look, but really taking the place in.

"You going to have two kids' rooms?"

"Yes, exactly . . . how did you know that?"

"Makes sense."

"Right."

"The place is awesome, Claire. I'm really proud of you."

I don't know what it was, his tone, the word *proud,* but in an instant I was crying. Crying like I hadn't in a long time.

"Claire? Are you all right? Claire?"

I couldn't speak, could only shake my head. Tim's arm went around me and he held me to his chest. He smelled like he always smelled, like a boy at bath time after he'd been playing in the rain. His other arm went around me and I gave in to his embrace, burying my face in his chest, soaking his shirt.

I don't know how long we stayed like that, but at some point the tears dried up, as they always do, as they have to.

Tim kept holding me, though, stroking my hair, making small comforting noises like I did when Seth needed them after a skinned knee, a toy taken away, a bad childhood day. And then, I don't know why, or how, or why, but then I was looking up at him and he was looking down at me, and his lips brushed mine, once, quickly, and then again, for longer. And though my brain was screaming that I should pull away, that I had to stop this now, immediately, I didn't.

The clang of the front door did it for me. We sprang apart and I bolted to my feet, knowing, somehow, that it was Jeff, that he had seen, oh God, that he had seen.

I rushed to the front door. It was still rattling on its hinges, but when I got it open and made it outside, all I found was the driving rain and the certainty that I was too late.

CHAPTER 23

Let's Pretend You're at the Beginning of Your Career

Zoey comes around before the ambulance gets to our house, but two fainting spells in two days is enough to worry the most sanguine of mothers, which I am not, and send Brian into a worst-case-scenario level of hypochondria that I haven't seen in him since I was pregnant.

We spend the weekend ferrying Zoey back and forth to the hospital, where she's put through a battery of tests. She has a headache that won't go away, and her vision's a bit blurry she says, but each test tells us nothing, only scratches one more archaic possibility off the list, like on an episode of *House*. And maybe it's the influence of television, but I keep expecting Zoey to get worse, for more symptoms to appear. Instead, all she does is submit to each blood sample, body scan, and pupil-dilating exam with an uncharacteristic silence, and no answers emerge.

On Sunday, while Zoey's with an eye doctor to check if her problems are optical, Brian and I see the neurologist. He's come in on his day off, and though he claims to be happy to do so, the fact that he's dressed like a teenaged boy sends a different message.

We thank him for taking the time, and I sit quietly while he flips through Zoey's charts and tests results, and Brian reels off possibilities like answers in a multiple-choice exam. Dr. Coast shakes his head at each of them, and eventually Brian runs out of suggestions. The clock on his wall ticks loudly, a reminder of each second passing by.

Dr. Coast finally puts down Zoey's file. "I understand that this must've been a trying few days for you, but I think that everything that can be done has been done."

"What do you mean?" I ask.

"I don't think there's anything wrong with Zoey."

I hear the words, but they don't bring relief, not yet.

"But how can that be? She fainted twice in twenty-four hours. And her headache? The blurry vision? That's not normal, is it?"

He leans back in his chair. The hood of his brown sweatshirt reminds me of a monk's cowl.

"I understand your confusion, and if I were at the beginning of my career I'd be running a whole battery of tests to be a hundred percent sure. But I think Zoey's had enough tests, don't you?"

"Yes, of course," Brian says, concern edging out his usual professional medical tone, "but we need to be absolutely positive. Surely you understand."

"I do. Unfortunately, we often have to live with uncertainty in these kinds of situations. We know so little about the brain, really, despite our efforts. But if I had to give you my best guess, I'd say it was stress related."

"She's eleven," I say. "There's nothing stressful going on with her. She . . . she's a good kid. Things with her are good."

"The beginning of adolescence can be a very stressful time. Surely you remember?"

Brian makes a frustrated noise. "She's not like other kids. She takes things in stride. And with her IQ . . ."

"Yes, I've seen that in her file, but that might just mean she's better at hiding things. And those competitions she does must be stressful."

Brian's jaw clenches and I reach for his hand. He squeezes it and glances at me as if to ask, *Are we on the same page?*

We are.

"She likes those competitions," I say. "We don't push her to do them. And she's been doing them for years without incident."

"Perhaps she's changed the way she feels about them?"

"She would have told us."

"Maybe she didn't realize it herself."

"So that's it? We take her home and . . . what?"

"Monitor the situation. Make sure she eats well and exercises and makes time for things that are relaxing. Talk to her. If she's experiencing anxiety, I can recommend someone, but I don't think that'll be necessary. My bet is that this won't happen again."

"This is crap," Brian says. "We know her. I was with her right before this happened. And I'm telling you that if she'd been 'stressed,' we would've known. No." He leans forward, resting his hands on the front of the doctor's desk. "No. I'm afraid we're going to have to insist that you pretend like it *is* the beginning of your career."

A couple of hours later, we're standing in the sterile viewing room for the MRI machine, watching Zoey being loaded in.

The technician sits to the right of us in a white lab coat, her eyes on the screen. Thin slices of Zoey's brain appear like they're coming out of a deli cutter. The whole room feels like the future, and it is husha-husha silent except for the clicks and whirs of the machine.

Zoey looks pale and skinny and small in her washed-out blue hospital gown, the soles of her bare feet the only thing less than pristine. I can feel the tension seeping out of Brian next to me. I place my hand at the base of his neck and begin rubbing gently. Something that's always calmed him in the past. The muscles in his neck start to unclench.

"You don't blame me, do you," he asks, "for the competitions?"

"Of course not. And I agree, Zoey loves them. She always has."

"She really seemed okay. Everything was like it always is. If those damn TV cameras weren't there, no one would've had to know about it."

"Were they there last year?"

"It's something they were trying this year because of how popular those spelling bees have become."

I nod. I've watched them myself sometimes. Some of the same

kids from the spoken word circuit are involved in them too. But Zoey's never shown any interest.

"I want to kill the little bastards who put that video up," Brian says. "When this is resolved, I'm going to figure out who did it."

"I don't think that will solve anything."

"Might make me feel better, though. Might make Zoey feel better."

"I'm guessing Zoey would prefer to pretend this never happened. And then there'll be a poem about it. *Diving for the floor / for all the world to see / words failing me*."

"Yes. That sounds like her. And like you."

"No, she's better. She's braver."

"You always discount your talents. I don't know why you do that."

"Years of practice?"

He shakes his head. "Apropos of nothing, and sorry I didn't ask before, but how was your thing?"

"My thing?"

"The funeral."

I suck in my breath. "You know, in all of this, I'd forgotten about it."

And this is true. I've barely thought about Jeff from the moment I got Zoey's tearful phone call. Maybe an aftershock is coming, but for now my mind seems to be fixating on the right things. The right now.

"It was . . . sad," I say. "Do you blame me? For not being there? At Nationals? Maybe if I had been . . ."

"You're here now. That's what counts. And like you said, this wasn't our fault. There's no one to blame. Dr. Coast is probably right. Not about the stress, but about it being nothing. He *has* to be right."

"He does. He really does."

Brian takes my hand, and we twine our fingers together as another slice of our daughter's brain thunks into place on the screen beside us.

CHAPTER 24

One Minute in a Thousand

I never wanted to quit my accounting practice. I loved everything about it, really: the little old ladies with their shoeboxes of receipts; the local cash businesses that wanted you to help them circumvent the tax man just enough so that they could still feel honest; the puffed-up businessmen who were expecting you to be impressed with the size of their bank accounts, and were quietly infuriated when you refused to give in to their satisfaction.

The problem was, I couldn't make a living at it. Not really.

It held together, after a fashion, when Claire was working and we were happy living in my condo. But things got tight once Seth was born, even though Claire went back to work sooner than she wanted to. We were cramped in the condo, the three of us, Seth's colorful toys staking out more and more territory, but neither of us wanted to take up the offers of financial support from our parents.

We bumped along, staying barely on the right side of debt — I'm an accountant after all — but we wanted more kids. We needed a house. I wanted Claire to be able to take as much time off as she wanted when our next baby was born, or to stay home even, if that was her choice. And further down the road there was summer camp, and school trips, and college tuition to think of.

So I knew what I had to do. It had been selfish to resist the inevitable for so long. And if I could be happy everywhere else, I thought it wouldn't matter much if my nine-to-five wasn't everything I wanted it to be.

There was only one place that could solve my problem. Johnson Company — maker of widgets and whatchamacallits — was the biggest employer in town, and the only business that had an accounting department. It occupied a low, sprawling campus that was trying to pretend it was located outside of San Francisco, and before the consultants got a hold of it, it wasn't that bad a place, really. When the Art Davieses and the Don-What's-His-Names were running the show, I bet it was even fun on a regular basis.

You know, office fun.

I knew before I started that it wasn't for me, but it was a path to other things. We could buy a house. Less working on the weekends trying to balance the books would mean more time for the family, for me, for golf. And kids should have a house, right, with a sandbox and a swing set in the backyard? With friends on the same street whose houses they could run in and out of like Tim and I did as children?

The last remnants of the idyllic parts of my childhood were still to be found in the shaded streets in the neighborhood we'd now be able to afford to live in if I took the job, and I wanted to give that to my family.

I wanted it very much.

So I wrapped up my practice and we went into escrow. I started working for Art and found my rhythm. Then Claire got pregnant, even though we'd stopped trying, and it seemed to confirm my decision, a pat on the head from the universe telling me I'd done the right thing.

And right up until the moment our doctor was moving a wand around Claire's stomach in primordial goo searching for something that wasn't there, I really thought I had it.

I thought I had it all.

After I ran away from Claire's daycare, and Claire, and Tim, and the Kiss, I still couldn't quite believe that what I'd seen had taken place. I spent a couple hours walking around in the rain, letting it seep through my clothes till they clung to me like skin. When I stepped into the Woods, looking for a place to hide, the rain's clatter and the rustling leaves blocked out everything else but the wish that I hadn't run, that I'd stood and fought.

Fought for Claire.

Fought for the life I held in my hand for a minute.

But I'd relaxed my grip. I'd taken my eyes off the ball—just for a second—and my club was whistling through the air with no purpose. A whiff, they call it in golf, after the windy sound your club makes when you swing and miss.

That windy sound was in my head, my heart, my lungs.

That windy sound felt like the soundtrack to taking a swing and missing my life.

I had to go home sometime, I knew, even if it was only to pick up things to change into before I slunk off to some hotel room, or wherever it was husbands whose wives were cheating on them with their brothers spent the night. There had to be some place that fit the bill, right? There was probably even a greeting card for it, but greeting cards don't tell you how to feel; they assume it. Happy on your birthday. Sad someone died.

Black and white.

White and black.

But how are you supposed to feel, really, when all your worst fears, things you'd never even imagined could happen, actually do happen, actually do come true?

Hearts don't come with an owner's manual.

Someone should do something about that.

It must've been a couple hours before I got back to our house. I don't know what I expected to find there, but what I found was Tim sitting on the front steps with his suitcase by his side. He was smoking a cigarette, and I was fighting the urge to ask him if he'd gotten that from Claire too when he said, "About time you got here."

"Excuse me?"

He stood up. "You're taking me to the airport. My flight leaves in an hour."

I wanted to tell him to go fuck himself, that he could get his own self to the airport. But then it occurred to me that driving him to the airport would be an excuse to not have to face Claire yet, to not have *that* conversation, whatever it was going to be.

I nodded and slopped in the puddles that were my shoes toward my car.

Inside, I could feel the wet dripping off me like I'd stepped out of a shower. Claire would've been pissed if she knew I was in the car in my present condition, and that gave me a small measure of petty satisfaction.

Tim shoved his suitcase into the backseat and climbed in next to me. I started the engine, started the wipers, and listened to them slap against the glass as I pulled out of the driveway.

"Jeff —"

"No. I'll drive you to the airport, but that's it. I don't want to hear it. And if you don't like it, you can get there on your own."

He paused. "All right. If that's what you want."

I turned on the radio, putting it up full blast, like I hadn't done in years, and certainly not with someone else in the car. It was some stupid '80s station, playing a Rush song I hated — there's never any need for Rush, really — and I could tell by the way Tim was clenching his hands that he wanted it off.

Denying him this, even if I was cutting off my own nose to spite my face, was another notch of satisfaction in a day where every notch counted.

If I could've made the radio play "Itsy Bitsy Teeny Weeny Yellow Polka Dot Bikini" through sheer willpower, it would've made my day.

I took the airport exit. "What airline are you flying?"

"I'm not sure."

"Are you going to check your ticket or should I drop you wherever?"

"It's not that big an airport. I'll figure it out when I get inside."

"You don't even have a ticket, do you?"

"Of course I do."

"Right. Whatever. Asshole," I muttered under my breath, but not, you know, that quietly.

He cleared his throat in a way that let me know he'd heard me despite the computerized crap screaming from the car's cheap speakers.

"Pull over," Tim said.

"The terminal's right ahead."

"I mean it, pull over here."

I slowed the car and pulled onto the shoulder. The front wheel bumped against a large rock.

"Suit yourself."

Tim got out of the car, and I sat there, waiting for him to get his suitcase out of the back, thinking that it was par for the course that he was going to get the last word.

My door swung open.

"Get out," he said.

I looked up at him. He loomed large as always but also, in a way, he looked small, like Seth when he was trying to act like a grown-up.

"Just go, all right?"

"No. Get out. Let's do this right for once."

I got out of the car. It was still raining, but it was more of a foggy mist. A perfect setting for a duel, or whatever Tim had in mind.

"Are you saying you want to fight?"

"Not exactly. I want to tell you something first, and then I want you to hit me."

"You want me to hit you?"

"That's right."

"What the fuck, Tim?"

"Just . . ." *Trust me,* he was going to say. "Will you do it, already?"

"All right. Fine."

I raised my fists, trying to remember the last time I hit someone in the face. Trying to remember if I'd ever hit someone in the face.

"Hold up," Tim said. "Listen to me first."

"I don't need you to say something to make me hit you."

"That's why I need to say this first."

"What are you talking about?"

"I'm going to give you some advice, Jeff, and then you're going to hit me and I'm going to fly out of here."

"Get on with it, then."

"One minute doesn't erase a thousand."

"Of all the . . . what the . . . maybe it does."

"No, not unless you let it."

"How would you know, anyway?"

"I know, okay? Let's leave it at that."

"No, I need you to tell me."

He sighed. "I let one moment, one idea, ruin my thousand moments, all right? And I've regretted it ever since."

"And what? That's supposed to make me forget about today?"

"It should."

"What do you know about it?"

"I don't know anything. That's my whole point. She was sad, Jeff. She was vulnerable and I took advantage. And I'm a complete asshole for doing that, but that's all it was. It didn't mean anything. Not to her. And I'm sorry, okay, I'm sorry I had anything to do with it."

"You're sorry."

"Yes. I've been feeling like a jerk for a long time. Ever since I found out about you and Claire. Before that even. And when you feel like that . . . well, let's just say it's not much of a stretch to start acting like one. I fucked up. I've been fucking up forever. And I'm sorry. You're my brother, and I'm sorry. Now hit me, and go home to your wife."

I stood there staring at him, a foot away, as wet as I was now. My brother. Someone who knew things about me I'd forgotten. Someone who I betrayed, and who betrayed me in return.

Hitting him wasn't going to solve anything.

But I did it anyway.

When I got home from the airport with grazes across my knuckles and a dull ache in the joints of my hand, I felt like Grady Tripp at the end of *Wonder Boys*. Too many things had happened in too short a time span. Did people's lives really change this quickly? Years of sameness, and then a few hours, a few moments, and everything's different? But, yes, of course they can. It happens all the time.

My clothes had dried on me in the way that only happens after you've been soaked to the bone, and they felt stiff and uncomfortable. I wanted to strip them off, climb into a steaming shower, and then sleep, but I knew that might be a long way off.

When I walked through the front door, Claire was sitting on the couch in the living room under the reading lamp with her feet curled under her, staring off into space. Her eyes were red and puffy, and the wastepaper basket nearest to her was full of balled-up Kleenex.

"Where's Seth?" I asked.

"Upstairs. Asleep, last time I looked."

I checked my watch. It was seven, early for him to be in bed.

"Does he . . . is he okay?"

"He has a slight fever. He actually asked to go to bed."

She stood clumsily, then fell back to the couch, clutching her foot.

"Foot cramp," she said through clenched teeth.

"Ouch. Sorry."

"No, I deserve it."

"Claire —"

Her fingers worked at the knot in her foot, which I knew from long experience could be excruciating. "No, I do."

I wanted to go to her, put my arms around her, and wait out the cramp like we'd done so many times before, but the image of her in Tim's arms held me back.

"Will you sit for a minute?" she asked. "You're making me nervous, standing there like that."

"How am I standing?"

"Like you're wondering if you should pack your things."

I let that hang there as a deep weariness settled over me. I closed my eyes for a beat, two, then Claire was there, at my shoulder, leading me to the couch.

"You shouldn't walk on that. You'll make it worse."

She grimaced and I could see her fighting the instinct to fall to the floor and cradle her foot in her lap until the cramp passed. Sometimes it was fast, but a few times I'd found her in the hall, or the bathroom — wherever she was when the cramp hit — where she'd been stranded for half an hour or more.

She pressed on and we were on the couch, both worn out and gripped by pain.

"Can I talk? Will you listen?" she asked.

I looked her in the face for the first time. Her eyes were the color they only were when she'd been crying. They always turned this amazing shade when she was particularly upset.

"We don't have to do this now. We can wait till you feel better."

"I'm not going to feel better until I put this right. If I can."

"What did you want to say?"

She blew out a long breath. It reached my face, a sweet smell I always associated with kissing her. And in thinking this I knew — I was going to forgive her.

Probably.

Assuming that's what she wanted.

"I've screwed everything up, haven't I?" she said.

"Do you really want me to say?"

"I guess I meant it more rhetorically, but I wanted to tell you I was sorry. I mean, of course, you know I'm sorry, so desperately sorry. I won't insult you with the details, unless you want to know —"

"No!"

She started. "No, of course you don't. And there's nothing to tell. You saw everything there was to see."

"Did I, Claire? Did I really?"

Did I see what's in your heart? I wanted to ask, but didn't.

"You did. And Tim's gone."

"I drove him to the airport."

"You did?"

"You didn't know?"

"He packed his stuff and left. Said he wouldn't be back. Did he . . . you drove him to the airport?"

"I did."

"Why?"

"I wanted to hear what he had to say for himself. And punch him in the face, though that was his suggestion."

"You what? You're not making sense."

"No. Nothing is."

She fell silent, her hand massaging her foot idly. I could tell by the way the muscles in her neck loosened that the worst of the cramp had passed.

"Is that it?" I asked.

"No. I've been sitting here, trying to think of a way . . . trying to make you believe me. I know it's always been hard for you that Tim and I were together. I know you've wondered about him, about us."

I didn't deny it. How could I?

"I'm not saying that I don't understand how you feel. I've always known, really, and it's something I should've worked harder to correct."

"Because I was totally in left field?"

"Not totally, but not in the way you mean."

"So you haven't been harboring some secret wish that he'd come back? Declare his undying love for you? Beg you to take him back?"

She smiled uncertainly. "Of course I have, or a small part of me has, anyway. Just like I bet what's her name—Lily—is wishing that same thing about you sometimes, no matter how happy she is right now."

"But the difference is, I haven't shown up in her life."

"Right, but you have to let me have that, Jeff. That's the part of girl-Claire that was hurt by the first person . . . it's not real, is what I'm trying to say. It's revenge. And revenge isn't sweet. And it isn't the point."

"What is your point?"

"Do you remember why I told you I came back here? Why I wouldn't move away with Tim?"

"Because of your dad? That promise you made him?"

"Right. I know it sounds stupid, and part of me was probably just testing Tim, but it was important to me to do what I said I was going to do. But if I'm being perfectly honest, if Tim had shown up in those first few months, I probably would have left. My dad would've been hurt, but Beth had already broken his heart. He would've gotten over it. Anyway, all this to say that he might be the reason I came home, but he's not the reason I stayed."

"What's the reason, then?"

"Do you really not know?"

"I only know what you tell me."

"I hope that's not true, but I will say it. I'll say it if you promise to believe that I'm telling you the truth."

I looked into the gloom beyond the puddle of light from the reading lamp. Little balls of it reflected off the photographs on the wall leading up the stairs to where our son was sleeping, oblivious to the chaos in his own house.

"All right. I promise."

She placed her hand on my arm. "I came back for my dad, but I stayed for you, Jeff. I stayed for you."

And because I'd promised, I believed her.

And in the end, I stayed too.

CHAPTER 25

Amateur Detective

After Tim leaves the daycare, I receive a curt email from Connie that I know will be followed by a Chinese water torture of communication until I comply. So I let the staff know I'll be gone for a couple of hours and walk from Playthings to the conservatory.

On my way, I wonder, as always, what it is about this woman that removes my free will. She's had my number since the first time I met her, both figuratively and literally, and I've never known how to keep her from using either.

"Because you like it," Jeff would say. "She pushes you. And it feels crappy at first, like the first round of golf after winter, but by the back nine, you're loving it."

He was right, of course. Somewhere along the way, I'd lost the ability to push myself, to get outside myself, inside myself. Music was the way I'd always done that in the past, and Connie pushed me hard enough to realize that it still worked after all these years. It was still something I needed in my life to feel whole, happy, connected. It was a fundamental part of me and always had been.

And as I walk down the quiet side streets, empty and abandoned by the parents at work, the children at school, I realize that this too has been missing since all this happened. There hasn't been any music. None coming from the radio I won't turn on, the iPod I will not play, and the piano I have not touched. As a result, it's too quiet up there in my head, and this has let the noise in.

So after I do a few scales and runs to warm up my fingers, and Connie puts a new piece in front of me, something modern and dissonant, I dive into the score. I play it clumsily and loudly, these off-kilter notes, until they work their way inside my brain and the volume's loud enough that there isn't room for anything other than the music.

When I get home from the day, there's glue in my hair and a tiredness that's familiar, workable. Beth's left a note that she's gone to the gym, but Seth is there, and I make dinner for him for the first time since that Friday. Less than two weeks ago on the calendar, but we've been through a time machine since then. And like in the Stephen King novel I was reading shortly before all this happened, the time that's elapsed since I stepped through the wormhole bears no relationship to real time. Two weeks, two minutes, two years. Any of these is a possibility.

I throw together a mismatch of foods left by our friends and neighbors, who I still have not thanked, my mother's voice reminds me. There's chicken curry, chickpea salad, and rosemary potatoes. As Seth picks at his food (the Tupperware crew really didn't have a twelve-year-old boy in mind in their act of kindness), he tells me that two women he didn't even know dropped off the latest batch when he wasn't-watching-TV after school.

"Thought you'd slip that in there, did you?"

"But I wasn't."

"Of course not. You're a good kid, Seth."

He scowls.

"Did I say something wrong? Being a good kid not cool or something?"

"No one says 'cool' anymore, Mom. Jeez."

"What do they say, then?"

"I don't know? We don't talk about it."

"So you're saying that kids today all get along, and there are no cliques, no geeks, no loners. It's a real utopia over there?"

"No . . . I . . . what does utopia mean?"

"It's like an ideal place, the perfect place."

"I don't think that's right."

"That's what it means."

"No, I mean that's not what school's like."

I ruffle his hair. "Of course it isn't. It never has been. But it's not worse than usual, right? Are people —"

"Everyone's being *fine,* Mom. Like I told you. Nicer than usual, even."

As if to confirm this, the phone rings. Seth skips over the floor to answer it. I can hear the high tones of a teenage girl's voice coming out of the receiver.

"Hold on a sec." He lets the phone dangle. "Gonna take this upstairs. Can you hang up?"

"Sure."

He bounds from the room and I pick up the phone, slammed by the déjà vu of a thousand similar instances from when I was Seth's age. Back before Twitter and Facebook and IMs and texts, all I had was the phone, pressed against my ear for so long after dinner every night that it took on my body temperature. If I had a fever, the receiver might've melted.

"I got it!" Seth bellows from upstairs.

I raise the phone to put it back in its cradle slowly. A few words tumble out, a giggle, a how are you? Seth's voice a little deeper saying he's all right, you know? Considering.

"Are you eavesdropping?"

I jump and put the receiver down louder than I meant to. I'm busted now, and Seth'll probably have something to say about it, as he should.

"A mother's prerogative."

Beth smiles through her red face. Her hair's slicked back, like she's just had a shower, and she's wearing a loose pair of sweats. She leans on the counter and stretches her legs behind her.

"That did me some good. You should join me at the gym sometime."

"And run like a rat in a cage? I don't think so."

"There are lots of other things you could do. Besides, they say that . . ."

She bends over quickly, touching her toes, like that was her plan all along.

"That exercise is good for depression?" I ask, more aggressively than I should. But the thought of it, the thought of falling back into that dark place with no joy and no light, and no light even at the end of the tunnel, makes me feel like fighting. I have to fight that, no matter what, with everything I've got, and then some.

"I, well . . ."

"I'm not depressed, okay? I'm sad. I know the difference."

She straightens up. "I only meant, if you were looking for something to do . . . ah, hell. Forget I said anything, all right?"

"Okay."

She moves to the fridge and asks me about work. As she assembles some of the same food we just ate, I tell her about how crazy Mandy was being, and about Tim stopping by.

"What did he want?"

"To see the place. He didn't stay long."

"I see."

"What?" I ask, though I know what. I've never been able to keep anything from Beth, and she knows all about that rainy day. She barely spoke to me for months after I told her; having been on the receiving end of deception, she had trouble forgiving me. I'm still not sure she has.

She brings her plate to the table and sits, and picks up the newspaper, though that doesn't mean she's done talking. That's my sister, always doing three things at once. "I'm surprised he's still here."

"I think he feels like he should be here for his folks. And this has been hard for him too."

"Losing a brother he'd barely spoken to in twenty years?"

"That's not fair, or accurate. They'd . . . they'd been in touch again these last few years."

Beth gives me a skeptical look, but it's true. Though I hadn't spoken to Tim since that day until he came home last week, he had something to do with Jeff forgiving me, with him agreeing to see if we could try to get past it all.

And though I don't know the details (because part of our tacit agreement for trying to put it behind us was that the only relationship Tim had with our family was on Jeff's terms), I know they've been communicating off and on over the last couple of years. That Tim had reached out, and Jeff had responded. Gifts arrived sporadically for Seth. Always age appropriate and something Seth had been hankering for. And Jeff's casual references to Tim in conversation, every once in a while, were an acknowledgment that his forgiveness was real, and remained.

"Holy shit!" Beth says.

"What?"

"Have you seen this?" She hands me the paper, her finger stabbing at a small article whose headline reads: DRIVER IN ACCIDENT THAT KILLED LOCAL HOSPITALIZED.

"Oh. Yes. Um, what's his name, Marc Duggard, told me that when he came to give me . . . Jeff's effects."

My eyes track to where the bag's still sitting on the kitchen counter, half hidden by unanswered mail. A growing pile of things I cannot face yet.

"And you didn't mention it to me because . . . ?"

"I haven't thought about it that much."

"Seriously?"

"What's the point?"

"If it were me? I'd be insisting they press charges."

"I've never been you."

"What's that supposed to mean?"

"Nothing. As Seth would say, jeez."

She smiles, but she doesn't let it go. "Okay, but still. Aren't you bothered by this?"

"Of course I am. I . . . can you imagine? What it must be like for her? I mean, she killed someone. I'd be on suicide watch too."

"I don't give a shit about her, and you shouldn't either."

"It was an accident, Beth. It could've happened to anyone."

"But it didn't happen to anyone. It happened to you."

"It happened to Jeff, actually."

She stands. "That's my cue to leave."

"Why?"

"I have some work to do, but mostly because I don't feel like fighting right now."

"I'm not trying to fight."

"That's why I'm leaving." She gives me a quick hug, and then I'm left alone in the kitchen. I try to keep busy with little tasks but find myself pulled to the pile of mail and the bag sitting behind it. I lift it in my hand. Jeff's wedding band clicks against his cell phone, his watch, the only things he had on him. Where are his keys? I wonder. Did he lose them? Is that why he was walking home?

I reach for what I think will cause me the least amount of harm, his cell phone. The ring and the watch are things I gave him, things that are connected with me, with us. His cell phone is all him. Our house has been so silent since he left, and silly as it might sound, this broken cell phone is part of the reason. There are no longer any dings or buzzes or swooshes of texts being sent and received. He spent so much time on his phone that sometimes I felt like he was lost in there. And the mystic part of me wonders if he still is, if that's where he's really gone.

I sit at the table, holding the smashed device in my hand. I plug it into the charger and press the power button, not expecting anything to happen, but after a few moments it starts to whir. The screen flashes and then goes dark, flashes again. It feels warm, as if it's been placed in a microwave, and it's emitting some kind of current that makes my teeth hurt. Then it vibrates and the screen comes briefly to life. A message pops up. It's a notification of a text message from Patricia Underhill. I tap the notice with my finger, but the text doesn't open.

I lean forward, confused, trying to make out what I'm seeing, when the phone vibrates again and a black line begins crawling across the screen, eating up the pixels in its way like Pac-Man. It eats and eats until the phone goes dark and cool.

It all happens so quickly that when I'm staring at the black screen, moments later, I can't help but wonder if I've imagined the whole thing.

CHAPTER 26

Imagine Them Naked

He caught me at the right moment.

That's what I always remember thinking of Jeff in the days after we started speaking, emailing, spending time together in the ways that we could. When I was trying to figure out what I was doing. What it was about him, about me, that was pulling us together and holding us in place. Why I let him in.

He caught me at the right moment. That much was clear.

But what I still wasn't sure of a year later was what made the moment right in the first place?

The MRI shows what Dr. Coast expected it to, a normal, functioning brain with no mistakes in it. When we get the results on Monday, I can tell that Brian's both relieved and unsatisfied, but I'm only relieved. When he says she's going to be fine, my heart feels like a too-full balloon that's been popped. All my anxiety rushes from me in a few, brief seconds, and I collapse in on myself, a shrunken parody of what I once was. But then I take a deep breath, and I look through the glass of Dr. Coast's office at my bored daughter slumped in a plastic waiting-room chair, who is going to be okay, she is, and my heart starts to expand again, taking a shape that can withstand being batted about.

There isn't always an explanation for everything, I say to a still-unconvinced Brian, parroting back what he's told me plenty of times about his own patients. He nods and agrees, but he'll be spending nights up late surfing the Internet, researching her symptoms. When I'd punched them into WebMD myself, it gave too many possibilities to count, but the first one was something called "vasovagal syncope," a fancy way of saying that it's the body's way of reacting to emotional or physical stress. Dr. Coast's explanation, which I hoped he'd gotten from somewhere other than WebMD.

When we tell her we're all done, Zoey seems happy to be done with the tests and anxious to put it behind her. When we get home, she wants to go back to school today, even though the day's already half over.

"Let's wait till tomorrow, all right?"

"But I have to, Mom."

"I'm sure the teachers will let you make up whatever work you've missed."

She chews on the end of her hair.

"What is it, Zo? What can't wait till tomorrow?"

"The longer I stay away, the bigger deal it's going to be when I get back. Like, ooh, Zoey was all hiding because of that video. Check out the Freak Fainting Girl."

Goddamn that little shit who posted the video. He should count himself lucky that Brian's been too distracted to carry through on his promise to track him down and teach him a lesson.

"But won't it bring *more* attention if you show up in the middle of the day? Why not start fresh tomorrow in homeroom, like it's any other day?"

"It doesn't work like that. There's no reset button. Unless some kid decides to shoot up the school, or something . . ."

"Zoey!"

"I'm just saying."

"Okay, but it's already lunchtime. You need to shower and eat, and by the time you do all that the day really will be almost over. Let's relax this afternoon, take it easy. One more day isn't going to make a difference."

"Don't you have to go to work?" she asks hopefully.

"One more day isn't going to make a difference there either."

And if I have my own reasons for avoiding the office, that's my problem, not hers.

She shrugs, giving in, and clomps up the stairs. I call after her that I'll make us some lunch, maybe with that bacon we were supposed to eat the other day, but she doesn't answer.

Brian emerges from his study, telling me he's had a call from one of his patients, he's needed, do I mind if he goes? He looks guilty for asking, but I reassure him. Everything's all right here. I'd like a bit of time alone with Zoey, anyway.

He gets his medical bag and kisses me good-bye, and I go to the kitchen to assemble lunch things. I stop in front of the fridge. My flight itinerary's tacked to it, held fast by a Cabo San Lucas magnet, right where I left it.

Springfield to Springfield and back again.

Oh, Jeff.

I hear a *thump* from upstairs, and then another and another.

"Zoey? Zo?"

Now there's a crash, and more thumps. Something being pulled over, something being thrown. I take the stairs two at a time and find Zoey in her room on the floor surrounded by a tipped-over bookshelf, binders and notebooks, all full of her writing. Zoey's room has always been a reflection of her pinwheel mind, but never like this.

"Zoey?"

She looks up at me like she doesn't know how she came to be in the middle of this hurricane. Her face is wet with tears.

"Are you all right? What is it? Why did you ... ?" My eyes dart around the room and come to rest on her flickering laptop. A video's playing, the video of Zoey stepping up to the mike, going pale, falling to the floor, and then up again as it happens all over again. And now I understand. Although Ethan told her about the video, we've kept her from watching it, which was easy to do these last couple of days. I should've known she'd make a beeline for it the moment she was alone.

I maneuver around her things till I get to the laptop and shut the lid. "You shouldn't watch that."

"Ha! Too late."

I sit down on the edge of her bed, still unmade from the day she left for the competition.

"It'll blow over, Zo—"

"I want to throw this stuff away."

"No, Zoey. No."

"Yes. I don't need it anymore. I'm not going—"

"Honey, please. You don't have to do the competitions anymore if you don't want to, but trust me. You don't want to throw this stuff away. It's a part of you. And you'll regret it if it's gone."

She pulls her knees up to her chest. She looks so thin.

"Have you not been eating, Zo? Is that what this all is?"

"No, it's not, I promise."

"Because it's normal, you know. Lots of young girls—"

"*Mmooomm,* I'm not some stupid ana girl, okay? That's so dumb."

"Then what?"

She looks down at the floor. One of her earliest notebooks is open in front of her, from when she was maybe six or seven. Her green period, we called it, because so many of her poems were about grass and trees and *the soil they suck up through their roots.*

"You're going to think it's stupid."

"I could never think that."

She hesitates, a few tears still falling, wetting the slightly yellowed pages.

"It was the people."

"The people in the audience?"

"In the cameras. All those faces I couldn't see . . ." She shudders.

"Will you tell me?"

"If you mess up where you can see the people, you can make it all right again, because of that connection? Like, when I'm up there, in the lights, onstage, I can feel the people in the room. Especially when I'm speaking. There's this, I dunno, *link,* between me and them, and I can make them feel things. What I want them to feel. Like magic."

"Is that why you love it?"

She nods.

"What was different this time?"

"I don't know, but I could tell, when I saw the cameras on either side of the stage with their red lights blinking, that something was wrong. And I was right. In the earlier round, the semis, it was awful."

"But Dad said you did well. You scored the highest score."

"Maybe, but it didn't feel good. It felt like . . . you know how when you go into a room that you've lived in and everything's packed away and it's all echoey?"

I thought about it. "Like at Grandpa's house, you mean?"

When my father died a few years ago, we'd all gone to the house I grew up in to pack everything away. As we were leaving, Zoey's hand slipped from mine and she ran from room to room, shouting her name at herself as it bounced off the empty walls. When we got in the car to drive home, she was quiet. Sad. Grandpa was really gone, she said when we pressed her. The house had told her.

"Yeah, like that. Only, it felt like that in my heart. I couldn't get it out of my mind. And when it was my turn in the finals, I looked into the camera and it was so black in there, I couldn't see anything but me. A tiny little me. And that's the last thing I remember."

"So it was a kind of stage fright?"

"I guess."

"But, if that's what caused it, then what happened when you were on the phone with Ethan?"

She flushes. "Don't be mad, okay?"

"I won't."

"I kind of . . . freaked out when he told me the video was online, and I tripped on the sideboard and hit my head. I was so embarrassed, but when I was lying there on the floor and you and Dad thought I'd fainted again, I thought . . . I thought that if I *had* fainted again, when the cameras weren't there, then I could say it was some medical thing, like low blood sugar or something, and Ethan and everyone wouldn't have to know the truth. No one would know it was because I was scared."

This truth pulls me from the bed to the floor, the precious note-books be damned. I take her into my arms, holding her close, holding her up.

"Thank you for telling me, sweetheart. That couldn't have been easy."

"You won't tell Dad?"

"Oh, honey, he's been so worried. He'll be relieved. Not mad."

"You're not mad?"

"Of course not."

"How come? I caused so much trouble."

"Come with me and I'll show you."

An hour later, Zoey and I are standing between the peeling white pickets of our local driving range. A hundred chipped and dirty range balls sit in a wire basket waiting for us to hit them. The course is mostly deserted (it opened only a few days ago) and the grass is barely green. Giant oak trees line the range. A few birds twitter and screech from their still-bare branches. *Where is everyone?* maybe they're asking. *Did I get to the party too early?*

Zoey's holding one of my old clubs in her hand clumsily, like she doesn't quite know what to do with it. I offered to teach her a few times before, but she never showed any interest, and even today I had to insist.

I set a ball on a tee, narrating my actions for Zoey. Hold the club like this, swing back slowly, arc down through the ball like you're scooping something off the ground, follow through, follow through, turn your hips, let your wrists snap so the club is over your shoulder.

The club feels heavy and raw in my hands. They haven't healed properly from the other day, but I make good contact anyway, and the ball arcs away and up and lands within feet of the flag a hundred and fifty yards away.

I breathe in the scent of new grass and warming air and feel a piece of satisfaction, deep inside. I try not to think about the last time I was on a golf course. Or the time before that, either.

"That's awesome, Mom. You're good," Zoey says when I've re-peated the exercise a few times with the same result.

"Thanks. Now you try it."

She looks skeptical but turns gamely to her own ball, perched on its tee. She brings the club back too quickly and stabs at the ball. She's not looking where she should, and I know what will happen a second before it does. *Thunk.* Her club stutters into the ground behind the ball and stops. The ball teeters, then falls over in defeat.

"I missed."

"That's okay. Happens all the time. Let's try again."

I spend the next twenty minutes breaking her stroke down. The backswing. The follow through. Showing her how to keep her eyes on the ball. On the thirtieth try she makes pretty good contact, though her shot slices badly and lands in the tall, dead grass left over from last year.

"Nice one, Zo."

"It didn't even go near the flag," she says, feigning disappointment, though I can tell she's pleased to have made contact at all.

"No, you're doing really well. It usually takes much longer than that to make good contact."

"How long did it take you?"

I hesitate but decide to tell her the truth. "I don't remember, really, but your grandpa said I got it on my first try."

"Wow."

"He thought so."

"You were like . . . a child prodigy, right? Dad told me."

"He did?"

"Sure. He said that's where I get it from. What I do. Not just the writing, but the timing of it."

"When'd he tell you that?"

"Dunno. More than once. He doesn't understand why you gave it up, though."

"Mmm. You want to know a secret?"

"Okay."

I flick a ball into place. "I've never really told anyone this, but I quit because I was scared."

"You were?"

"Yup."

"What were you scared of?"

I swing at the ball. It hits the sweet spot on the face and curves away, landing next to the first ball I hit. Like it always does. Like it was nothing.

"Same thing you were."

"People watching you?"

I nod. "Invisible people. You've seen golf on TV, right?"

"Were you on TV?"

"A couple of times. In college." Another ball teed. Another shot at the flag. "I was there on a scholarship, a sports scholarship, and I was . . . good."

"Like, how good?"

"Good enough to get to Nationals. Good enough for people to be talking about doing it for a living."

"Cool."

"Sure, for a while. Then my first big tournament was televised. And I totally blew up. Not cool."

"You were probably nervous."

"That's what I told myself. And the next tournament I played in was a normal one, no TV, only a few spectators, and everything was fine, and I won. But then I had to go to Nationals."

"TV again?"

"Yup."

"Did you pass out?"

I lift my head and smile at her. "No, honey, but I played awfully. I couldn't hit anything." I point to the divots surrounding her tee. "It hurt when you hit the ground before, right?"

"Kind of."

"My arms were aching by the end of the day. I almost quit."

"But it was only twice. Maybe you could've gotten over it."

"That's what I thought, but it was the same thing every time. In practice, even in small tournaments, I was fine. I won. Everyone would talk about how I was the next big thing. But when it came time to perform for real, when anybody was looking, I tanked."

"What do you think it was?"

"My coach thought it was a lack of ambition, that I didn't have that killer instinct. But listening to you today, I think it was more what you said. When no one was watching, I could play for me. I connected to the ball and the course and the breeze and the birds. I hardly noticed who I was playing with. It *was* like magic. But when I knew people were watching, I couldn't feel that anymore. I felt empty."

"In your heart?"

"In my heart. So I gave it up."

"Is that what you think I should do?"

"No, Zoey, that's not why I told you that."

"Why, then?"

"Because I wanted you to know that I made a mistake. What my coach thought was also true. I didn't care enough to work through the problem. It had always been easy for me, and the minute it became hard, the minute I really had to work at it, I gave up and walked away."

I cross into her practice zone and click my club against hers, tapping out a sound like a hollow gong.

"You're better than that. You're better than me. You can quit if you want. If you hate it. If it isn't fun anymore. I'll back you with Dad. But you can't quit just because it's hard. Things are hard for most people. Life is hard."

Zoey watches me silently for a moment and then she starts to laugh.

"What is it?"

"Man, Mom, did you sign us up for some reality show without telling me?"

I almost ask her what she means before I get it. And then I'm laughing too.

"Okay, okay. I wasn't trying to be all melodramatic. But that doesn't mean I didn't mean what I said, okay?"

"Okay."

"And you'll think about it?"

"Yeah, yeah."

"I hear imagining the audience naked helps."

"Mom!"

"Try it."

She shrugs and squares herself to the waiting ball. Her arms swing back and for a moment I see a video of myself at eleven.

And I know the shot will be perfect, even before it is.

PART 4

CHAPTER 27

Romance and Sex Life of the Date

A couple months before the consultants issued the report that recommended that 1.2 people be eliminated from my department, they actually had a good idea. Morale was a bit low, they reported to the brass after conducting their usual round of impromptu interviews with a subset of employees. Business was going well, and yet there were always more cuts, more asked of them. All their perks had been taken away and replaced by Safety Minutes and uncertainty. Something needed to be done.

I'm sure the employees who were interviewed meant — in a coded way — to send the message that what needed to be done was to axe the consultants and their recommendations. Message not received. But they did have a simple suggestion that would wipe all the cares away.

This was reported to the board with a serious face, my boss, Gerry, told me. Could I believe it? When *they* were the ones responsible for the morale problem in the first place?

It was bullshit, he said, and I agreed, but still, I was curious what the solution was.

"Some fucking lottery thing."

"Like Powerball?"

Did the consultants really think spirits were going to be lifted by tricking us into a voluntary tax on the off chance of a jackpot that couldn't be worth it?

"Nah. Some weekend at a golf resort team-building thing. Like in the old days. Only, everyone will be eligible to go, and the participants will be chosen by lottery so there's no grousing about why him and not me?"

"What'd you want to bet that John Scott and his cronies all end up winning?"

"Too true, my friend. Too fuckin' true."

But the consultants, for once, knew what they were about. The lottery was announced, and a tremor of excitement rippled through the office. The prize was a weekend in Palm Springs in early March, perfectly timed for those of us who felt that winter had dragged on too long, i.e., all of us.

Fifty people were going. That made the odds good, right? That made the odds . . .

"One in twenty," Art said in the break room where it was all anyone could talk about. "A five percent chance."

"That's not so bad," one of the assistants replied.

"So they say, so they say," Art agreed, and took his coffee cup away, looking reflective.

I followed him back to his desk.

"Is everything all right?" I asked, wondering if he had an inkling of what might be coming when the consultants handed in their final report. Or maybe I was being paranoid. I wasn't sure about what was going to happen, then. Not totally sure.

He was fine, he assured me, and he hoped I'd have fun at the getaway.

"What do you mean? I haven't won anything."

"But you're the kind that does win, aren't you?"

"We all have the exact same chance of winning, like you said. Right?"

He smiled and went back to his spreadsheet.

But when my name was pulled from the spinning bingo ball cage they'd decided to use for the occasion, he looked back over his shoulder at me with an expression that said, *I told you so.*

Of course, I wanted to go. *Palm Springs,* I typed into my search engine, already knowing what I'd find. Golf courses as far as the eye could see, all kept green by the aquifer lying under the desert that was supposed to be inexhaustible. Five-star resorts, with courses designed by Nicklaus and Faldo. Hell, you might even run into Nicklaus or Faldo on one of those courses.

It could happen.

You never know.

But that's not what happened. What happened was that when I took a seat in the empty-but-for-me van they'd rented to drive us to the resort from L.A., a familiar voice spoke above me.

"This seat taken?"

I looked up, my heart in my throat. "Tish! What are you doing here? How come you didn't tell me you were coming?"

Her name wasn't on the list of winners. We didn't discuss it, but I'd checked, hopeful. I'm-not-going-to-think-about-why-I'm-even-checking hopeful.

"I didn't know."

"I'm confused."

She plopped down next to me and I caught a whiff of the apple of her shampoo. She was wearing a light green sweater and casual jeans. Her hair was pulled back in a ponytail, and she looked great. To me, she looked perfect.

"Lori Chan, the supervisor whose office is next to mine, was supposed to go, but she came down with a nasty case of the stomach flu. She got to pick her replacement."

"And she picked you?"

"As you see."

"But why didn't you say anything?"

A slight hesitation. "I thought I'd surprise you."

"Well, I'm surprised."

"Good surprise?"

"The best."

She smiled and looked like she was about to say something else when another employee climbed into the van. She looked away and said something anodyne about the weather, and once the van was full, we settled surprisingly quickly into companionable travel mode on the two-hour drive from the big city to the big desert. Along the way, we passed those windmills from *Rain Man,* and as we got closer, Joshua trees began to spring up. And that's pretty much all there was — Joshua trees, scrubby-looking brush, and rocky sand unending in all directions.

A desert, to state the obvious.

"Do you know that, every couple of years, it rains an inch or so, and the desert comes out in all these amazing flowers?" Tish said.

"How'd you know that?"

She pulled a California travel guide from her bag. "I was reading about it on the plane. Here, look." She flipped to a glossy page full of purple flowers spread among the Joshua trees. "Pretty amazing, huh?"

"It is."

"Won't happen this year, though. It's been dry as a bone. Oh, look, that Joshua tree's all burned!"

I laughed and gave her hand a squeeze, then dropped it. I looked around, wondering if anyone had seen. Two of our travel companions were reading, and the other two had fallen asleep.

Tish started speaking quickly. "A lot of them are burned. I wonder if there was a fire recently. It didn't say so in the book."

"Tish," I said quietly.

She lowered her voice. "Sorry, am I talking too much? I do that when I'm nervous."

"Are you nervous?"

"Aren't you?"

I had butterflies in my stomach, for sure, but I couldn't tell if they were more nervous butterflies or excited. I was trying not to think about it too much.

"There's nothing to be nervous about," I said.

"No?"

"No."

When we got there, the resort wasn't quite what the firm had promised. While there were three greener-than-can-be golf courses, the decor was ten years past its prime, and the whole place had a sad, yesterday's news feeling about it. We had the afternoon free until the welcome dinner. You could golf, swim, or take a tour of the area.

"Can you tear yourself away from the golf course?" Tish asked me after we'd checked in, been assigned rooms on the same floor, and were handed our welcome packages.

"You mean, this afternoon?"

She looked disappointed. "You don't have to, of course, but I thought it might be fun to go on one of the tours. And we're all playing tomorrow, right?"

I gave myself a mental kick in the ass. I'd been saying how much I wanted to explore someplace, anyplace, with her, for months, and here I was, seduced away from my promises by some green grass.

"I think it'd be awesome."

"Wow. Overcompensating. I can go on my own. Don't worry."

"No, I want to go. I do."

"Well, all right then."

The tour was leaving in twenty minutes, and we agreed to meet back in the lobby. Although we were staying on the same floor, we took separate elevators to our rooms. I didn't plan to, but she let me step on the elevator first and didn't join me. Instead, she gave me a wave as the doors closed, mouthing, "See you soon."

Alone in the elevator, I leaned back against the cool expanse of glass. My heart was beating abnormally fast, and it occurred to me that maybe I was nervous after all.

I squelched the nerves, and whatever might've been behind them, by calling home. My cell didn't seem to be working — I got this weird clicking noise after I dialed, even though I had good reception — so I used the phone in the room. I was thankful the office was going to have to pay the outrageous long-distance charges printed on the small card next to the phone.

"How's the place?" Claire asked. "As nice as last time?"

"Nothing could be as nice as last time."

"Awww. I'm surprised you're not on the golf course already."

"Well," I said, a cough catching in my throat. "I'm going to go exploring, actually. There's a tour of Joshua Tree National Park on offer."

"Oh! You have to promise to play the album while you're driving through."

I laughed. "I'd even wear my tour T-shirt, if you hadn't thrown it out."

"It was full of holes and two sizes too small."

"Bono would've understood."

"You're crazy. Have fun."

"Will do. I'm in Room 806, by the way, if you want to reach me. My phone's behaving oddly."

"Eight-oh-six, got it."

I changed into a pair of trekking sandals, cargo shorts, and a long-sleeved T-shirt. It was warm out, but not too warm. I could see why people retired here.

Tish was waiting for me in the lobby, and she'd changed too. Into practically the same clothes.

We looked at each other and laughed.

"Maybe we should've consulted on our wardrobes?" Tish said.

"That's way too girly."

"Says Mr. I'm-about-a-three-on-the-Kinsey-scale."

"Shut it."

Despite our driver waiting till twenty minutes past when he was supposed to leave, no one else showed up for the tour.

"You folks still wanna go?" he asked.

Tish looked at me and raised her shoulders to her ears.

"I'm game," I said.

"You sure you wouldn't prefer to be on the golf course?"

"I'm sure." I tapped the driver on the shoulder. "We're up for it if you are."

He started the car and put it into gear. "First stop: Joshua Tree National Park."

He drove around the long loop through the park, letting us out into the bright sun to take pictures of the endless expanse of Joshua trees. The park felt like being inside U2's album: American and desolate, and although no music was playing, there were moments when I felt like I was in a music video.

When we were tired of seeing Joshua trees — after you've seen a hundred, you've seen too many — the driver announced our second stop: the Shields Date Gardens in Indio, a couple towns over from Palm Springs.

Tish looked puzzled and thumbed through her guidebook. She read quietly for a minute, chuckling to herself.

"This is going to be something," she said. "It was opened in 1924. And they've been showing this film there ever since then that 'can't be missed,' apparently."

"Oh?"

"Yeah, the guy who made it felt that dates were the 'least understood of all fruits' and wanted to educate the public."

"You're making that up."

"No, sir."

"Takes all kinds."

Indio was a short drive away, the less posh cousin of Palm Springs. It seemed to consist of one of those long strips of highway with a million tiny malls and gas stations. The housing was mostly trailer parks. Not the kind that get swept up by tornadoes — there was grass and trees and flowers — but a long way from the white adobe mansions we'd left behind.

Next to the highway, Tish told me, reading from her guidebook again, was the wash, a huge ditch system that existed to catch the once-every-couple-of-years rains, to keep the town from flooding.

Looking around me at all the dryness, tasting it in my mouth, it was hard to imagine that ever happening.

When we got there, the Shields Date Gardens was the one old thing in a sea of new. It was protected by a grove of palm trees, and proudly announced itself as being the Date Capital of the World.

I guess everything needs a capital.

And yes, there was also the film — *The Romance and Sex Life of the Date* — which was, the sign said, "Free for Life."

It would be.

We walked around the large, run-down store, Tish delighting in the ridiculousness of it all.

"Check this type out," she said, pointing to a sign above a large barrel of dates. "'Sweet and Creamy Super Jumbo Royal Medjools.' You can't make this stuff up!"

"That's a hell of a moniker. Do you think they call it Super Jumbo for short, or Royal Medjool?"

"I'd prefer to be called Royal Medjool, myself. Much more mysterious."

"Agreed. Shall we watch the movie?"

"Hold on, we have to get a shake first."

"A what?"

"A date shake. The guidebook says they're highly recommended."

"What's in them? Wait, I don't want to know."

She went to the snack counter in the corner and ordered a large shake that looked about as unappetizing as you might imagine it would look, and we crossed over into the old, worn theater. The movie played every ten minutes or so, and the next showing was about to start.

The room was ghostly quiet except for the sound of the ancient projector wheezing to life. After a few moments, a scratchy black-and-white film that looked like it was being held together with duct tape started. The soundtrack sounded as if it were being played on a phonograph that was underwater, all echoes and skips.

Tish tapped me on the arm. "Date shake?"

I looked at it dubiously. It was really the last thing I wanted to be trying. But Tish looked so . . . so cute, really, even though women don't like to be called that, but she was, her ponytail bouncing slightly, a we-just-cut-class-successfully grin on her face, that I said:

"Don't mind if I do."

CHAPTER 28

Suspicious Minds

I spend the night going around in circles.

The text.

The book.

Tish's presence at the funeral, her odd behavior outside my house.

What does it all mean?

What does it goddamn mean?

My careening brain brings me to the computer in our study at 2 a.m. When I open it, the web browser loads Facebook, and so this is where I start. I go to Jeff's page, one he set up years ago and rarely consults. His picture is de rigueur for guys almost forty with families. A picture of him with Seth from a few years ago, a picture I took one summer at the beach. They're both wearing bathing trunks that end at their knees, sand, sunburned noses, and identical grins.

That was a good day. A day worth savoring.

I scroll down and get a different kind of emotional stomach punch. His page is full of sympathetic messages from friends, distant cousins, and townsfolk reaching out: *I'm so terribly sorry. We miss you. We're thinking of you.*

Like Jeff's going to be checking his Facebook page from the great beyond.

My heart skips a beat when I see a message on his wall from Lily, his college girlfriend. She's *<3broken.* (It takes a second till I figure out this is some kind of online abbreviation for "heartbroken." Blech!) I check. They're Facebook friends, another thing I don't remember him mentioning. Stupid Facebook. Some people are meant to disappear from your life, to remain a memory, a faded possibility. A curiosity. I ought to know. But when curiosity is so easily fulfilled, how do you avoid fulfilling it? A button is pressed and you're friends again.

I log in as him (Jeff's password for everything has always been *Abacus* — I gave him one for his first birthday after we started dating) and go to his direct messages. If I know Jeff, *if,* any message he's ever written will be there.

And so it is.

I almost breathe a sigh of relief, but there's nothing relieving about this situation. Hunched over a desk at two thirty in the morning, going through my dead husband's Facebook messages for evidence of . . . what? *What?*

The messages are sporadic, more of them at the beginning, when everyone was getting on Facebook and reconnecting with people long gone and long forgotten. A message from Lily is there, from five years ago. Harmless, harmless.

I'm married, he wrote in response to her *Hey there, stranger.*

So am I. I have two kids.

I have one. I still live in Springfield.

Still? Why am I not surprised? Anyway, I hope you're happy. I hope you're well.

I am happy, Jeff wrote. *I really am.*

Five exchanges over three days, and then nothing. The rest are all from his college buddies, and other names I vaguely recognize. Messages from a few bands or other things he's a "fan" of.

Of Patricia Underhill, I find nothing.

Jeff has 153 friends, and Tish is one of them. I scroll back through his meager timeline history and find the entry, a little over a year ago: *Jeff and Patricia Underhill are now friends.*

A year ago. So not after the company event in Mexico where we met, two and a half years back. What happened a year ago? What made them suddenly become (Facebook) friends?

I click through to her page. She's also several years younger in her photo. She's wearing a yellow rain slicker, and her daughter's sitting in her lap, a miniature six-year-old version of her. They're grinning at the camera like bandits, and I can almost imagine the muddy puddles they just finished thumping around in.

Tish works at Johnson Company, likes hiking and golf, and is married to someone named Brian, whose Facebook page is even more spartan than Jeff's. He's a doctor. He has twenty-four friends. He lives with his wife and daughter in Springfield, the other Springfield. His favorite quote is "First, heal thyself."

Jeff's not friends with Tish's daughter or her husband, of course he isn't, but her daughter's page is an open book like that of everyone her age. She has 515 friends and is fond of posting bits of poetry (hers, I imagine) between uploaded photos of almost weekly road trips to some kind of competition. I play the voyeur for a few more minutes, but there isn't anything for me to learn here.

But ... golf. I click back to Tish's page, searching for more information, but it doesn't provide any. She likes golf. So what?

My next stop is the Johnson website. Jeff's username (*jmanning*) and password (*Abacus*) get me into the employee-only section. I click around, not sure, really, what I'm looking for.

"Staff" brings me to an index where I search for Tish's name, and there she is again, dressed less casually this time but still comfortable in front of the camera. She has her chin in her hand, and her smile is half smirk, half amusement. Her biography is simple, no different from the Facebook one.

I skip over "Resources," "Announcements," and "Reports" and check "Activities." The first one listed is Jeff's funeral, and I suck in my breath. Jeff's funeral is an activity? Honestly, as Jeff would say, what's wrong with these people?

I'm grateful there are no links to pictures of the event. It seems their callousness stops somewhere, at least.

Underneath Jeff's funeral notice is the title "Lottery." It's the firm thing Jeff went to in Palm Springs a few weeks before he died.

I search my memory for mentions of Tish. Maybe her name came up once or twice in conversation, but if so, it was a while ago, a medium-term memory. Jeff certainly never said anything about her being in Palm Springs. Of that I am sure.

At least, I think I am.

And why would he mention her, anyway? my voice of reason asks. He told me a couple of funny stories about one particularly bad seminar. He said he couldn't believe that John Scott was actually there, as Jeff predicted he'd be. He talked about the few other people I knew who were there too. Of the fifty people there, most were unmentioned.

But then again, most of them didn't give him a book.

Or send him a text.

Or travel to his funeral.

There are fifty-four photos linked to the lottery, and my hand's shaking as I start the slideshow: the resort, the welcome banner, the first night dinner, lecture, lecture. Neither Jeff nor Tish are anywhere to be seen in these pictures. Was Jeff even there? Yes, of course he was. I called him there. I called him in his room because his cell was on the fritz. I left a message on his room's voicemail and he called me back. Stuck at a deadly dinner, he'd said, sounding sober and tired. Rest well, I'd said.

He was there, and lots of people were missing from these photos. So calm yourself, Claire.

First, calm yourself.

Click, click, click, the slideshow keeps sliding. A sunny day, breakfast, a golf course, and then the final shot, everyone crowded in, come on, come on, get closer, closer, and say *Johnson!*

Jeff's standing in the second row, and Tish is next to him. The *proud mama* herself.

There's only one thing left to do now, but still, I hesitate. If I go to his email, if I see what I expect to see, find what I expect to find, am I going to feel better? Right now I have suspicions and doubts, but it's the middle of the night, and all these things might have an innocent explanation. In the cold light of day, all these things might fade and disappear.

But no. I've come this far. If I don't look now, I'll torture myself until I do.

I go to his email page and enter his username and password. The page won't load. My username and password are incorrect. I try again. I must have mistyped it. *Username and password are incorrect.* Incorrect. Not *Abacus,* not anymore. And not his birthday, or mine, or Seth's, or our address or his favorite word (*motherfucker* — he could be childish sometimes), or any of the other combinations of letters and numbers I can think of.

Why would a man change the password to his email? my brain mocks me.

Why?

I feel sick and tired, so tired now, but I have to press on, if I can. I have to know if there's anything more.

I scurry downstairs, knocking into corners in the gloomy light, in my tiredness, and panic, and search through the unpaid stack of bills until I find what I'm looking for: Jeff's cell phone bill. I take it back upstairs, waiting till I'm there to open it.

A long list of calls and texts, almost exclusively to me, with three exceptions: three texts to a number I don't recognize on the weekend he was away. When his phone wasn't supposed to be working. I check the area code on the web. It's for the other Springfield.

I stumble in a daze to the corner of the room and slide to the floor. Jeff's travel bag is where he left it, still packed, where it might still be sitting even if he were alive today.

This is where Seth found the book.

I take the items out one by one: dirty socks and underwear; grass-stained golf pants; his rumpled dress clothes, in need of a dry cleaning; two golf gloves. There's nothing else. No lipstick on any of his clothes, no strange receipts in any of his pockets, no condoms.

I raise his golf shirt to my nose and all I smell is him, faded, and grass. It doesn't smell of perfume. There are no stray black hairs, or stray hairs of any kind. I hold the shirt to my face for a while, closing my eyes, trying to decide if Jeff's scent is a help or a hindrance at this point.

I put his shirt down and run my hand around the bottom of the case, thorough in my investigation, even though I doubt I could remember my own email password right now, and my hand comes up against something hard and sharp. Something I missed.

I pull it out. It's a black folded corkscrew, like the kind you buy in convenience stores or find in hotel rooms. The name of the hotel where Jeff stayed is stamped on the back.

I unfold it, one side a corkscrew, the other a knife. A small piece of cork foil clings to the corkscrew part. Burgundy colored, still smelling faintly of the bottle it protected.

The text.

The book.

The trip.

The changed password.

The corkscrew.

They are all I have to go on.

They are not enough.

Beth finds me in the study sometime at dawn. I'm leaning against the wall, the corkscrew in one hand, Jeff's clothes strewn around me, a couple of hours of tears half dried on my face and T-shirt.

"Claire! What the hell?"

"I found this," I say, holding out the corkscrew. "And he changed his email password."

A few quick strides and Beth is by my side, prying the device from my hand, moving Jeff's clothes away. "Come on, honey. Stand up."

"And there was a text. Texts. She texted him. I think he texted her. She came to the funeral. Why, Beth? Why?"

Beth doesn't answer me, she just leads me out of the study to our bedroom, mine and Jeff's.

"Do you still have those pills the doctor prescribed? What did he call them?"

"Funeral pills," I say, and the tears start again. "For a girl who mourns for someone who doesn't deserve it."

"Where are they?"

I slump on the bed and pull a pillow over my eyes. "Bathroom."

I listen to her leave the room, run some water in a glass, and crack the cap off a plastic bottle.

"Take these."

"No, Beth. I have to tell you. You have to see."

"No, not now. Take these. Sleep. I'll get Seth to school. We'll talk about this when you wake up."

"I won't be able to sleep."

"Yes, you will."

She pulls the pillow from my eyes and props me up. She's holding two pills in her hand, not one.

"That's too many."

"No, it isn't."

She holds them below my mouth and I open it like a child whose mother is playing airplane with her food. She hands me the glass and I swallow, once, twice. The pills stick in my throat at first but then they go down.

"Get into bed."

"Beth."

"I mean it, Claire. Get into bed right now."

"Are you angry with me?"

"Of course not, but you need to listen to me."

She has her sternest expression on, the one she must use to pulverize opponents in court. The pills are already making me woozy, or maybe it's being up all night, so I give in. I lie back and Beth pulls the covers up over me, tucking me in.

"You'd be a good mother, Bethie."

"Thank you. Now go to sleep. Don't think. Sleep."

Don't think. Don't think. Don't think.

But how can I not?

The text.

The cell phone bill.

The book.

The trip.

The corkscrew.

I count these things.

I count them until I sleep.

CHAPTER 29

Guess Who's Coming to Dinner?

Tuesday morning, and it's time for Zoey and me both to go back to real life. School for her, work for me.

Brian's still out on his call by the time we finish breakfast, so I decide to drive Zoey to school, rather than let her brave the bus. She puts up a bit of protest, but it's feeble. I can tell she wanted to ask, but keeping her brave face on won out.

Zoey goes to a small private school for advanced children that's housed in a building that still looks like the old rambling mansion it used to be. More modern wings have been added on, here and there, as needed.

I was dubious about the school at first. It seemed like an awful lot of after-tax dollars to spend on basic education, and I'd gone through the public system and came out all rightish, but it was important to Brian. The school dismissed my ambivalence pretty quickly, though. Small class sizes, genuinely nice people, and enough kids there on merit scholarships so that I didn't feel like Zoey was being reverse ghettoized.

But today, Zoey's first day back after the Incident, as she's started calling it, my judgment is back out. If memory serves, eleven is the cruelest age, and if that proves correct, I'm ready to mount a campaign with Brian for her to switch schools next year.

Bigger class sizes mean more places to hide.

I pull up to the curb behind a line of luxury cars. Our modest se-dan has always been out of place here. Zoey leaves the car silently. I watch her walk toward the front doors, thin and pale, her back held straight against the weight of her backpack. Her hair's in a ponytail for once, and I feel a surge of pride and awe that today, of all days, she's willing to come out from behind her curtain.

If only I can be so brave.

When I arrive at Johnson, half an hour later than usual, the park-ing lot of backed-in cars is almost full. I circle once, twice, until I find a spot. And because it's that kind of day, I pull in nose first. I'm almost certain to have a warning citation waiting for me on my windshield at the end of the day. Somehow, in all the cuts, the guy whose job it is to look for safety code violations *in the parking lot* still has his job, but fuck it. I have bigger problems.

Like sitting at my desk. Like realizing that too much of what has held me here this last year has been its pleasant association with my email inbox, my phone, the high-tech conference room down the hall. In a few short, jittery minutes, I'm thinking about requesting a transfer to a new office for an excuse I'm still working on when Lori pops in.

"You're back."

"I am. Sorry I couldn't make it yesterday."

"Of course. Is Zoey all right?"

She's seen the video, clearly.

"Yes, she's fine. A million pinpricks from a million tests, but a clean bill of health."

She's waiting for me to say more, probably about the video, but I will not make Zoey part of the water-cooler gossip circuit. They can have me, but not my daughter.

"How was the funeral?"

Now we've gotten to the real reason she's here.

"It was . . . very sad."

She purses her lips. "I can imagine. Thanks for doing that. Going, I mean. Not something I was looking forward to."

"Right."

"Lot of people there?"

"Of course. Everyone liked Jeff. And Springfield is his hometown."

"Oh? I didn't know."

Am I completely paranoid or is she looking at me like I just confessed to something? But knowing Springfield is his hometown isn't anything. It isn't anything at all.

"Is there something I can do?" Lori asks.

"About?"

"I thought, with Zoey and all, that you might have a lot on your plate."

"I can handle it. We have that meeting at two, right?"

"Sure. See you then. Your day for the Safety Minute, BTW."

Of course it is.

"Thanks for reminding me."

"There's a list of topics on the interweb, if you're at a loss."

"Right."

She lingers for a moment longer, then leaves. I stand up and close the door behind her. I feel weary and like my body's tingling with nerves. I wish I'd saved one of the pills I stole from Brian, something to steel me against today. But today is the first day in a long series of days that might feel exactly like this. I have to learn how to face them, as I am, chemical-free.

I sit at my desk and spend a mindless half hour cleaning up my emails, something I haven't done in a while. Moving ones I need to keep into subfolders. Deleting the endless series of reply-alls, etc., that are the bane of office existence. I leave my sent items folder for last. Scrolling through it, I come to the last emails I sent to Jeff. There are eleven over the course of the weekend, *that* weekend.

I'm surprised there are so many. I thought I had better control of myself than that, but clearly not. My mouse lingers over the first one, but I don't need to open it. *I'm worried. I'm worried. I'm worried* is what they all say in one way or another, and I already know that. The manifestation of the worry is something I don't know how I'll recover from.

So I delete the emails, all of them. Then I put my head down on my desk and try to keep myself from weeping.

At the end of the interminable day, I slog through a heavy rain to my car, pull the soaked-through warning citation off my windshield, and drive home. Everything's starting to take on that bright green spring look, the good part of so much rain.

Brian's in the kitchen, surrounded by the ingredients for a salad. A large piece of fish is on the counter, waiting to be steamed.

I give him a kiss, resting my head against his shoulder.

"You smell like rain," he says. His hand cups my head and holds me there for a moment, then releases me.

"It's brutal out there."

"I heard on the radio that there might be a slide on the backside of Tupper."

"Yikes."

"Hopefully there aren't any hikers caught out."

"I guess you'll be on call tonight, then?"

"Till the danger passes."

"Where's Zoey?"

"She's up in her room. So you really don't think we should ground her?"

He starts to shred a head of lettuce with his hands, tossing it into a large wooden salad bowl. I pull olive oil and balsamic vinegar out of the cupboard.

"I think she feels badly enough already, don't you? And it must be terrible for her at school."

"If she were a normal kid, we could take away her video games or something."

I smile at him. "I think I'll take Zoey as she is."

He smiles back. "Me too."

He picks up a knife and starts dicing tomatoes. He's not a surgeon, but he dices tomatoes like one. Every cube the same. Perfect.

"How was your day?" he asks.

"So-so. Got a parking citation."

"On purpose?"

"Maybe. You?"

"Hectic. And I think a patient of mine might be stealing meds."

My hand freezes on the bottle cap. "Why do you think that?"

"Some pills I keep in my medical bag for emergencies are missing. I usually check regularly, but with everything that's been going on, I can't remember the last time I did."

"What's missing?"

"A mild sedative."

"Any idea who might've taken them?"

"Could be any number of people, unfortunately." He stops chopping. "You don't think that Zoey . . . ?"

"Of course not. No. She'd never."

"You're right. And maybe I miscounted. It was only off by a bit."

Thank God I never went back for more.

"You want me to cook that fish?"

Dinner's a quiet affair. We try to get Zoey to tell us how school went.

"Fine," she says. Some kids in eighth grade got caught drinking after the football game on Friday. They might get suspended or expelled, and that's what people seemed to be talking about mostly. At least, when she was around.

I suspect she's downplaying how it really was. There's a red rim around her eyes, but she must be sick of talking about it, and I can't blame her for that. I'll follow up later. A few hours of dishes and homework and normalcy are due.

Brian's beeper goes as we're clearing the table. He steps away to call in and comes back looking grim.

"The slide?" I ask.

"Two people. Trauma evac."

"I'm sorry."

"Hopefully they'll be all right. I'll be back late."

"Of course."

We kiss quickly as he grabs his coat and medical bag and sprints for his car through the rain. I watch him for a moment. Someone's parked across the street, the smoke from their cigarette trailing out the open window. A red ember glows brighter, fainter, brighter.

I close the door and finish clearing the table. Zoey's in the breakfast nook, a few missed days of assignments spread over the table.

"You need any help with that?"

"Nah."

"Well, how about I try to help anyway? Let your mother feel like she's doing something?"

She laughs, but the doorbell interrupts her answer.

"They make those Mormon guys go out in the worst weather," she says.

"Your brain works in mysterious ways sometimes."

She shrugs. "Why are they always dressed the same? Does God choose their outfits?"

I walk to the front door, laughing. I swing it open, "We're not interested" already forming on my lips.

But it's not two young men in neat black slacks.

It's Claire.

CHAPTER 30

Storm Warning

Did I ever really get over the shock of seeing Claire and my brother kissing? I'd ask myself that after enough time had passed that it wasn't something I thought about every day. I'd forgiven her, I had, but I'd been changed by it. We'd been changed by it. And not in the ways I might've thought. I didn't distrust her. I didn't think she was going to end up in the arms of another man. I didn't think she was going to leave me for Tim.

But did I feel like I had some credit? Some bad deeds stored up, some chips to cash?

I guess I did.

But that doesn't mean that when I cashed them in, I didn't feel guilty at the payout window.

The morning of day two at the retreat was taken up with putting together prize packs for the golf tournament and a couple extremely boring lectures on "who we are" and "what we want to be."

The only good thing about it was knowing I'd be playing golf all afternoon, and the shy, proud look on Tish's face as she inscribed copies of her daughter's poetry book for the prize packs.

I'd been assigned to the prize committee, as had Lori, the woman Tish was replacing at the retreat. As part of the team-building aspect of the weekend, we were supposed to put something personal in the prize packs — a kind of adult show and tell. All I could come up with were prints of pictures I'd taken of people from around the office on my phone at candid moments. Since Tish was late to the party, and Lori hadn't been organized enough to put something together before she got sick, the only thing she had time to bring was her daughter's book.

"You're showing off," I teased Tish as she wrote *I'm a proud mama* in copy after copy of the slim volume. There was a prize pack for everyone, fifty of them in all.

Apparently "winning" meant being there in the first place.

"If you can't live vicariously through your kids once in a while, what's the point?"

"So you have someone to look after you in your old age?"

"There's that too." Her pen paused. "Do you think it's weird, me signing these instead of Zoey?"

"Do you think she'd mind?"

"No. She was kind of embarrassed when Brian ordered so many copies in the first place ... and you should see our garage. We can't even park in there anymore."

I flipped through the deckled pages. "I'd love to meet her someday."

"I'd like that," she said, but there was a hesitation in her voice. I had a flash of her meeting Seth, and I felt weird. Cold.

We finished our task and went to the buffet lunch. At some point, I slipped away to check our golf assignments; Tish and I were playing together, I saw with pleasure. In fact, we were a twosome in a sea of foursomes, presumably because of our low golf handicaps. Tish had listed hers as a four. Halfway into the second hole, I knew she'd lied.

"Why'd you do it?" I asked after she'd landed on the green in eagle position.

"What?"

"Lie about your handicap? You clearly don't have one." She shot me a look over her collared shoulder. Her expression was hidden by the shadow cast by her cap.

"Didn't I tell you I suck at putting?"

"Did you? When?"

"The first time we met."

"I don't remember you saying that."

"Well, I did." She tapped the side of her head. "I have perfect recall of conversations."

"That must come in handy."

"Sure. Especially at three in the morning. You're away."

I was the farthest away from the green, by a long shot. Unlike hers, my third shot wasn't even on the green.

You know how you think you're good at something until you see someone who's really good at it?

I pulled off a tricky chip shot that was more luck than skill, but I took Tish's "nice shot," anyway.

I picked up my ball as a loud horn blasted through the air.

"Storm warning," Tish said. "We should head for cover."

She was looking into the distance at a massive black thunderhead that hadn't been there ten minutes ago.

"I thought it never rained here?"

Her reply was silenced by a zigzagging flash and concomitant boom.

"What'd you say?" I yelled.

"Run!"

She pointed at a decrepit wood structure about five hundred yards away, a rain shelter that had been sorely neglected because it never rains in Palm Springs. Except when it does.

A second burst of thunder clapped us to attention, and we sprinted to the shelter, abandoning our clubs. We reached it as the rain began to fall, fast and loud, thrumming against the sloped metal roof, running off in a curtain.

We stood there listening to it, our breaths escaping rapidly.

"I guess there's going to be flowers this spring," Tish said.

"Too bad we're going to miss it."

"It is." She watched the rain. "I did lie to you before."

"I knew it."

"Not about my golf handicap."

"What then?"

"About why I didn't tell you I was coming."

"Lori Chan wasn't sick?"

"No, she was. She is." Her shoulders rose and fell. "I didn't tell you I was coming because I wasn't sure I was going to. Not till the last minute."

"Why?"

"You know, if we were in a movie, this is when we'd have our first kiss. In the unexpected rain."

She blushed and looked at her muddied golf shoes.

"You're right," I said as my heart sped up. "Tish . . ."

She raised her head. We were inches apart. I could smell her sunscreen and feel the warmth of her body as the air cooled around us. Her eyes were wide, her lips slightly parted. It took an act of will not to pull her to me, put my mouth on hers, and finally taste this person I knew so well in some ways, and so little in others.

She started to raise her hands, then lowered them. "I didn't tell you I was coming because of the possibility of this."

I took her hands in mine. It felt like touching a lightning rod right after it's been struck.

"You don't have to worry."

"I don't?"

"No."

She dropped her arms to her sides. I let her hands slide away.

"So I've been imagining it?" she asked. "There's nothing happening between us?"

"You haven't been imagining it."

"Then I'm worried."

"Why?"

"Because we shouldn't. Because I should say no. But I don't think I can. Not if . . ."

"No, Tish. It's okay. I mean it."

"How? How is it okay?"

I looked at her and I thought about how hard it was to say things, even though it was easy to think them, to feel them.

"Because I'm not going to ask you for anything. I'm going to keep myself from saying and doing what I want to say and do. I'm going to make that effort. So you don't have to worry. You really don't."

She let out a long slow breath that sounded like relief.

"Is that what you want?" I asked.

"It's what I've decided too. Not because . . ."

"No."

Her wide eyes met mine, all at once happy and sad, mirroring the feeling in my heart.

"Did I make a mistake, coming here?" she asked.

"I'm glad you're here. I'll always remember this."

She smiled as the rain stopped, the water still dripping from the roof.

"Me too," she said. "Always."

We sat at different tables at dinner that night. We could easily have fudged with the dinner assignments, but we didn't. Instead, I sat with seven people I didn't know from her office, and she sat with seven people she didn't know from mine. I made polite conversation with the twenty-something sitting next to me. I think she might've been flirting with me — or maybe she was someone who always repeatedly touched the leg of the person she was speaking with — but I was too distracted to decide. My mouth answered her questions when necessary, while my brain was still half on the golf course, in the rain shelter, and what had almost happened. I couldn't decide if the twist in my gut was guilt or regret or a combination of both.

My eyes darted across the room to the back of Tish's head, the white of her neck below where she'd bunched her hair into a knot, the side of her face when she faced the man sitting to the left of her, the right.

I ended up behind her in the food line again, but this time it was no accident.

"How's your table?" she asked.

"Deadly. Yours?"

"A notch below a Safety Minute." Her hand hovered over the chafing dishes. "What do you reckon? Pasta or fish?"

The fish looked dried out, even though it was drowning in a thick white sauce. "I'm thinking pasta."

She nodded and helped herself to a small serving of shaped pasta in an orangey sauce. It looked like something from a can.

I guess the consultants hadn't specified that team building worked better surrounded by creature comforts you couldn't regularly afford.

"The sun and the moon and the stars," she said.

"I . . . what?"

She nodded at the shape of the pasta on her plate.

"Seth would love it," I said.

"Zoey used to make galaxies with hers. Did you know there's a conjunction tonight?"

"What's that?"

"Jupiter and Venus are at their closest point. They'll be lined up in the sky in a row with the moon. It's rare and pretty cool."

"How did I not know you liked astronomy?"

She shrugged. "There're lots of things we don't know about each other, right?" She paused. "Zoey and I usually watch that kind of stuff together."

"Will you watch tonight?"

"I might do."

I waited for her to invite me to come along, to go with her and lie out in the grass somewhere and watch the heavens. But I also didn't want her to ask. On some level, I didn't want to have to face the choice I knew I shouldn't be making.

"Well, I should be getting back," she said.

"Right, me too. How about a drink after dinner?"

She bit the edge of her thumb. "How about . . . breakfast tomorrow? Yes?"

"Yes. Sure. That sounds good."

"Have a good night, Jeff."

"You too."

She started to leave, then turned back quickly, her plate tottering on one hand. She leaned in close to my ear for the briefest moment, her breath a tickle.

"This is hard," she said, her lips touching my skin. Then she walked to her table without looking back.

I would have stood there, frozen, if it wasn't for the person behind me in line knocking into me, propelling me out of whatever dream world those five seconds had sucked me into. As it was, I don't really remember going to my table, starting to eat, knocking back half my glass of wine in two gulps. I came to when my maybe-flirtatious dinner companion took up where she'd left off, touching my arm, saying my name once, twice, to get my attention.

"Pardon?"

"Did you look in your prize pack?" she said, swinging the small party-favor bag.

"No need. We . . . I helped put them together. No surprises there."

She wrinkled her nose. "You're no fun."

I agreed and took another swig of wine, trying to decide if I could take one of the bottles and leave without it being remarked on.

It was only later, in my room, after too many glasses of wine and too many speeches, that I found that my prize pack did contain a surprise, after all. When I upended it onto the bed, looking for the souvenir wine bottle opener we'd included to keep the party going, Zoey's book slid out. It fell open to the inscription page, the page where Tish had written the same thing over and over. Only, somehow, she'd managed to inscribe this copy to me personally and sign it. And though the three extra words — *To, Jeff, Tish* — weren't much, I held them against my chest and thought: *Always.*

CHAPTER 31

I Spy

I awaken at noon feeling disoriented, like I don't know where I've been or even where I am.

Then, I do know.

I'm in our bed.

The book, the texts, all of it, are real.

Jeff and I? Maybe not so much.

I lie there pondering this, staring at the ceiling, until I feel like I'm going crazy. Not bothering to change out of my pajamas, I go downstairs in search of Beth.

She's in the kitchen, but not alone. Tim's here, and they're talking like conspiratorial buddies, though they've never been. Beth's always disliked him, from the first, though she'd never tell me why.

"What are you talking about?" I ask, and in their guilty looks I know.

"Did you have a good rest, honey?" Beth replies.

"I'm kind of hoping I'm still sleeping, to be honest."

She shakes her head and walks to the counter where the coffee machine sits, gurgling slightly, the pot full of the blackest coffee.

"Don't believe it, Claire," Tim says. "Don't you believe it for a second."

"What do you know about it?"

"I know that Jeff would never —"

"What? Betray me? How could you possibly know that?"

"He's my brother. I know him in my bones."

"Like he knew you? Like he knew me?"

"Yes. Exactly like that."

"So if Jeff were here, and I were dead, and he found . . . He found out about us, he wouldn't have been surprised? Devastated?"

"Devastated, yes. Surprised, no."

"If you're saying what I think you are, then fuck you. And get out of my house."

Beth puts her hand on my arm, pressing a warm mug into my hands. "For what it's worth, I think he's right."

"Well, then, fuck you too."

My knees feel weak. I sway away from Beth. She steadies me, and in an instant, Tim's there to help her. They hold me up and sit me down, and neither of them looks like they're going anywhere.

"That's not what I meant," Tim says. "I only meant," he glances at Beth, wishing, maybe, that she wasn't here, then continues, "I meant that he wouldn't have been surprised *I* acted that way."

"We *both* acted that way."

"But we had a history, and . . . do you want to hear this?"

"If you know something about what Jeff thought, then yes."

He runs his hand over his face. "Jeff worried, sometimes, that he was your second choice. And so, what he saw confirmed it, but . . . you already know this, right?"

"How do you know that?"

"Jeff told me, when we started talking again, how you'd worked things out."

I can't help the hurt from creeping into my voice. "He told you?"

"I think he needed to. But you have to listen to me. You have to believe this: When you told him that you really did choose *him,* he believed you."

I absorb this information like a dry sponge.

"But even if that's true, that doesn't explain any of this. It doesn't mean that he didn't —"

Beth's arm is around my shoulders. "Of course it does, honey, and that's why there has to be a rational explanation for all of this."

"There does?"

"Yes," Beth and Tim say together with certainty.

I look back and forth between them until I connect the dots.

They're certain Jeff wouldn't betray me because I'd betrayed him. He knew how it felt, and he was too good a person to ever make someone feel the way I'd made him feel.

But see, I have another theory: If Jeff was going to betray me (*if* he did), it wouldn't have been prevented by my actions, but caused by them. Like a chemical reaction that needs the right condition, my actions, Tim's and mine, created the nitroglycerine, waiting, locked away until the right reagent came along.

Then somehow, somewhere, he met Tish, and the air rushed in, and any resolve he had exploded.

The problem with my theory, though, is that Jeff's not here for me to test it. He's not here for me to ask. He left me clues that point to something, something, but maybe nothing, and I already know in my clouded brain that if I don't solve this puzzle, I will sink, I will go under, I will drown.

So when I get away from Beth and Tim and their little co-conspiracy to make me forget, make me believe, make me dismiss for lack of evidence, I check one last thing on the computer.

Springfield to Springfield.

If I leave right now, I can be there by dinner.

It's after six. I'm in my rental car, driving.

I'm driving. I'm actually driving. For the first time since Jeff died, I'm driving.

The minutes I had between flights were enough time to realize that I literally didn't know where I was going, and that I'd be arriving too late to find Tish at her office. I had no idea where she lived or how to contact her other than through Facebook, and something told me she wouldn't accept my friend request.

Or maybe she would, this woman I met in a moment of crisis, this woman I tried to help, this woman who had the audacity to come into my home, talk to me, talk to my son.

Then it struck me: Maybe there was something Facebook could help me with after all. A quick check on my phone proved me right. Her husband's a doctor, and his number's listed in the phone book. A reverse address search later and I have their address. It's so easy, even in this day of suspicion and privacy, to find someone if they're not careful.

It's so easy to lose someone too.

Her address is loaded into the car's GPS, and the woman's voice emanating from it tells me calmly but firmly to turn right in a hundred and fifty yards, turn right, turn right, your destination is on your left.

I pull over, too close to the curb, and my wheels skim it. Half a cigarette later, a man backs out of their driveway. His car passes mine on his way out. This must be her husband, Brian.

I watch her husband's taillights fade. Does he know the answer to my questions? Does he have his own clues, his own suspicions? Or if I follow him, ask him, would I bring his world crashing down?

I find this option tempting for a moment. There's something about the power in it, but no. Dr. Brian Underhill isn't the answer to the wreck that is my life. He's just another person caught in the jetsam.

When Tish opens the door, half laughing, words of dismissal on her lips, her mouth drops open. She closes it quickly, hiding her surprise. She must be good at hiding things, I think.

"Claire? What on earth are you doing here?"

She's still wearing her work clothes (a black skirt, a pale yellow sweater), and her hair is tied back.

"I came to get some answers."

"You . . . what? I'm sorry, I don't understand."

"I find that hard to believe."

She bites her thumb and glances over her shoulder. "Um, why don't you . . . come in?"

I follow her into the house. It's a typical four-bedroom suburban, not that different from my own. The furniture is nicer, though; a doctor's house.

She takes me into the family room and motions to the couch. "Will you take a seat? I need to check on something in the kitchen. Do you want anything?"

"I'm fine."

She stares at me for a minute, then disappears. I look around the room slowly. School shots of her daughter and family vacations are on the mantelpiece. There's an afghan over the back of a squashy chair holding a half-read book, the spine cracked, and unobtrusive art on the walls hanging over the taupe paint. With a bit of straightening, this house would be for-sale ready.

I track back to a shot of her on the mantelpiece, the same shot as on the company website. *She isn't prettier than me,* I think, then feel a wave of disgust for making the comparison at all.

Tish reappears holding two glasses of white wine.

"In case you changed your mind," she says, putting one of the glasses on the coffee table in front of me.

There's a coaster next to it, and I resist the urge to move the glass onto it. I want to let the glass bleed water onto her nice mahogany, as petty as that is.

She sits across from me, cradling her wineglass in her hand, not drinking from it. She's eyeing me like my therapist used to, waiting for me to say something.

Eventually, she does.

"I guess I'm just . . . really confused about why you're here."

"I have something to ask you."

"Okay."

I hesitate. In court, when you're trying to get information out of someone, trying to get them to admit what you're trying to prove, the better strategy is generally to ask a series of innocuous questions, laying a trap, building up to the final question so carefully that they can't escape. But sometimes another strategy works: Ask what you want to know so directly that the witness will be shocked into telling the truth. And because I haven't had enough time to prepare properly, this is the strategy I use.

"Were you sleeping with my husband?"

"No!"

The vehemence of her denial startles me. Startles her too, I guess, since she nearly drops her wineglass, and as it is, half of its contents spills on her leg.

She looks down at the spreading wet and pats it with her hand, as if it's absorbent. She puts the wineglass on the floor next to her.

"Sorry . . . I . . . that's not what I expected you to say."

"What were you expecting?"

"I really don't —"

"Mom? Are you all right?"

Her daughter's standing in the doorway, looking frightened. She's wearing her school uniform, and she looks innocent, and less confident than in her book jacket photo.

Tish rises quickly. "Didn't I say to stay in the kitchen?"

"I thought you hurt yourself."

"No, I . . . spilled something. See, nothing's the matter." Zoey looks at me with her pale blue eyes. I feel a stab of guilt that I've made this child worried somehow, but that's her mother's fault, not mine.

"Who's that?" she asks.

"This is . . . Claire. She came to . . . visit for a few minutes."

Zoey relaxes and holds out her hand. It's stained with blue ink. "Hi, Claire. I'm Zoey."

My hand reaches out automatically. She takes it and pumps it up and down, once, twice, a grown-up's handshake, though I know from my Internet snooping that she's just a year younger than Seth.

"Nice to meet you," she says. "How do you know my mom?"

"Zoey."

"What? I was just curious."

"Curiosity killed the cat. Why don't you take your homework and go up to your room? I'll be up in a few minutes."

"Aren't you going to change out of your wet clothes?"

"I'll do that after Claire leaves. Room, now, please."

"*Ooookkkaayyy.* Bye, Claire."

"Bye, Zoey."

She leaves and pounds up the stairs, leaving an imprint on the world.

Tish comes back to her seat. "Sorry about that."

"No, I . . . I know how it is. Seth's . . ."

"Seth is . . . ?"

"You know what? I don't want to talk about him with you."

"Because you think that Jeff and I —"

"Were sleeping together. Yes."

"No, Claire. We weren't. We were only friends."

"I find that hard to believe, given everything."

"What everything?"

I rotate through the list that's been cycling through my brain.

"Why did he have that book? Her book?"

"Zoey's book? That Seth read from at the funeral?"

"For starters."

"I gave it to a lot of people. Brian, my husband, ordered so many copies —"

"Did you give it to him at the golf retreat?"

"Yes, that's right. I brought a bunch of them with me. For the prize packs. Everyone who attended got one."

A muscle twitches in my eye. "Why did you text him?"

"I did?"

She looks genuinely puzzled, but I press on. "It was on his phone. A text from you."

"What did it say?"

"I couldn't read it. The phone's busted," I admit.

Her brow creases, concentrating. "I think . . . you know I work in HR, right?"

"No."

"Well, that's how we met. Jeff and I. About a year ago, he had to do HR training, and he was in my group. Afterward, when he had an issue, he'd call me. Anyway, he called me a couple of weeks ago. He had to fire someone in his department, Art somebody, I think, and he was finding it hard to do it. So I gave him some pointers. He said he'd let me know how it went. When I didn't hear from him . . . I thought I sent him an email, but I guess I sent him a text."

"How did you have his cell number?"

"From the golf retreat. We were both on the prize committee, and we had to coordinate, so he gave me his cell number."

"So why was he texting you?"

"I . . . I thought you were talking about me texting him?"

"He texted you too," I say, reaching into my bag for the cell phone bill. "This is your number, right?"

She takes the bill and looks at the three times her number appears that I've highlighted in yellow.

"Yes, that's my number."

"So he *was* texting you."

"To coordinate, like I said. I . . . that's right. His phone wasn't working properly. He could text, but nothing else."

She hands the bill back to me, and I feel my confidence slipping. I didn't have time to go through Jeff's other cell phone bills before I ran off to confront her. I've gone about this the wrong way. I'm asking questions I don't know the answers to, breaking the first rule of cross-examination. And her lies seem to come so easily. Is there any possibility they're the truth?

"Why were you at the funeral? Why were you so upset?"

"Someone from HR had to go. I . . . I volunteered. I was the only one who knew him. I thought it made sense if it was me. And I'm sorry for being such a mess. I genuinely liked Jeff, and I am sad about what happened. But also, my father died a few years ago, and that poem Seth read, Zoey wrote that about him. I have a hard time listening to it."

Her voice catches as she says this, but she holds her tears in check. She watches me, waiting for my next question. She looks sad but in control.

The texts. The book. The funeral. I have one piece of evidence left.

I reach into my purse again and pull out the corkscrew. "What about this?"

She stares at the item in my hand as if she's trying to figure out what it is.

"I've never seen that in my life."

CHAPTER 32

Deny, Deny, Deny

I'm back on my dining room floor, phone clutched in my hand, Julia on the other end of the line. Only this time, my daughter's upstairs and my husband's due back any minute, and I thought that the worst had happened, but now I know better.

As much as it hurt to lose Jeff, I was losing him anyway. I decided, we decided, to lose each other so we could keep this. My daughter upstairs, my husband due back any minute.

I can't lose this. And I can't let Jeff lose it either.

"What should I do?" I ask Julia, speaking low, as calm as can be, so Zoey isn't alarmed again, doesn't come to my rescue.

"Maybe she'll leave it alone now?"

"No, I . . . I don't think I convinced her. I don't think I said enough."

"What's the last thing she said?"

"It's hazy. I was in shock."

I think I still am. And that's what I said to Claire, after her questions had run out. We stared at each other across the room, neither of us blinking, each of us wondering what the next move was, the next thing to say. Then we could hear Zoey banging around upstairs, and I asked, I tried not to beg, Claire to leave. Said that now wasn't a good time, my daughter had just gone through a health scare. Asked her if we could talk about this later as I was inching her up, guiding her to the front door, querying whether she needed a cab.

"You're in shock," I said. "You need to rest. You need to stop wondering about this. Because there's nothing. There's nothing."

Claire looked at my mouth moving. Maybe she heard me, maybe she didn't. But she seemed to have run out of words, or the energy to say them. She was doubting me, herself, Jeff. Her thoughts were a coin tossed in the air, twirling, twinkling, with a fifty-fifty chance of coming down on either side. Belief or doubt. But I couldn't pick which one she'd choose. I only knew that I had to get her away from me, and the butterfly effect I'd had on her life. The sooner she was out of here, the better the odds were of it playing out naturally.

"She didn't say anything. She held on to that corkscrew like it was the only thing holding her together."

"Maybe you did all you could?"

"No. I . . . I have to make sure . . . I have to . . ."

"Make sure of what?"

"That she believes me. That she doesn't leave here thinking that Jeff and I, that . . ."

"Because you didn't?"

I close my eyes. I think of my promise.

"We didn't. We couldn't."

"Don't lie to me, Tish."

"I'm not."

"So tell her that."

"I can't do that. Would you want to hear that?"

Will wails in the background. The phone scrapes against Julia's ear and I can hear her shushing him.

"Hear that my husband almost cheated on me, that he might've been in love with another woman, but he decided to do the honorable thing and stick by me?"

"It sounds so awful when you say it like that."

"Is there any way to say it that doesn't make it awful?"

"But it wasn't like that. That's not why —"

"For Christ's sake, Tish. What do you want me to say?"

"I don't know, okay? I just ... need someone on my side, right now."

She sighs. "I'm on your side. Barely, but I am."

I pace the floor waiting for Brian to get home, trying to formulate a plan, figure out what to do. Sometimes less is more, I remember an English teacher saying in college, in a creative writing class. But this isn't fiction. This is my life. And I'm pretty sure that more is required. More is necessary. Less isn't going to get the job done.

And though I want to be a coward, crawl away, wait to see what the outcome might be, I can't. Claire has enough to live with. She doesn't need me too.

Brian finally gets home looking tired and sad, and smelling like the disinfectant that's supposed to wash the death away but never quite does. After an hour of worrying, I have my plan ready. Julia's not doing so well, I tell him. She's not sleeping and Will has croup and her husband isn't being any kind of help. I said I'd go over there, if I could. Watch Will for a few hours so she can get some sleep, keep her sanity.

Of course, Brian says. Zoey's sleeping. He needs to sleep too. They'll be fine without me.

I hold him close, tell him how sorry I am that things didn't go better, that the climbers didn't make it. I want to take the death away, but I can't do that tonight. It will take weeks before he forgives himself, before he really believes that he did all that he could, that no one could do more.

I will give him those weeks. I will.

But first I have to do one last thing for Jeff.

This time, Claire's the one who's surprised when her door swings open, revealing not the room service she must've ordered but me.

She's wearing one of those white terry-cloth hotel robes, and her hair is damp. The room's nondescript, and a small red suitcase sits on the edge of her bed, a few clothes spilling out of it.

"What are you doing here?" she asks. "How did you even find me?"

"Small town. I called every hotel in the book until I found you."

It didn't take that long. Third time was the charm.

Her bloodshot eyes barely meet mine. "What do you want?"

"Can I come in?"

Maybe she wants to say no, slam the door in my face, but the curiosity I was counting on, the lingering doubt, makes her step back, leaving me enough space to enter the sad little room and sit down in the red fabric chair wedged into the corner.

She sits on the edge of the bed, the farthest away she can get from me in this miserable space.

She holds the top of the robe closed. "I thought we were done."

"I'm sorry I pushed you out of my house like that. I know how it must look."

"Really?"

"I think so. I've been trying to understand things from your perspective since you left. To see why you might think —"

"That you and Jeff were having an affair?"

I try not to flinch. "But we weren't. We really weren't."

"How can I believe that? Of course you're not going to admit it."

"I've been thinking about that. Why would you believe me? Would I believe you if the tables were reversed?"

"Would you?"

"I don't know. I'd want to, though. I'd like to think I know my husband well enough that whatever I found out, there'd be some reasonable explanation. I've been racking my brain, trying to think of a way to convince you, but proving a negative, that's a hard thing to do. Then I thought, maybe that's the explanation."

"I don't follow."

"What I meant was, if it was true, wouldn't it be obvious? Wouldn't there be lots of signs and clues? More than a few tiny connections that I have with lots of people, that we all do?"

"Like?"

"Like . . . the book, for instance. Fifty people have that book, all with the same inscription. And the texts, they were about work."

"That's easy for you to say. I can't read them."

I let my face go slack, then register surprise. I've just thought of something.

"But you can. I have them here."

I pull out my phone and scroll down past the barrage of texts from Zoey and Brian, till I get to the text I sent to Jeff on Saturday.

"Here," I say, holding it out to her.

She takes the phone and reads the words I reread earlier tonight: *How'd it go?* There's no answer from Jeff. Of course, there can't be.

"If you scroll up, you can see the earlier texts you were asking about."

These are trickier, but I'm counting on the fact that if I treat them as innocent, she'll see them that way too.

Jeff to me, 10:53 a.m.: *Where are you?*

Me, a moment later: *Where are *you*?*

Where I said I'd be.

Then, an hour later, me to Jeff: *John Scott is here. Help!*

Jeff's instant reply: *I'll be right there.*

"Do you know John Scott?" I ask.

"Yes," she says.

"Is it just me or is he a total jerk?"

She keeps her head bowed over my phone for a long moment of silence. Then she looks up at me and hands me back my phone.

"He is. Is there anything else?"

"No." I stand. "Only that I'm so terribly sorry if I've done anything to make you feel this way. There wasn't anything between us."

He chose you. Please believe me.

He chose you.

I don't know her, so I can't tell if she's buying this. But what I want to believe, what I want to see, is that she's hoping I'm telling the truth. That what I've said, what she's read, clears away the questions, eases the pain of surprise, of hurt, of doubt.

What I want to see is a coin flying up, flipping over, and coming down on the side that will convince her of Jeff's innocence.

That she's content with that.

That she won't try her luck again.

Or mine.

CHAPTER 33

Home Again, Home Again

When I got home from the golf weekend with Tish, it felt like I'd been away for longer than two days. It felt like I used to feel when I got home from summer camp, or college, the feeling that I'd missed the changing of the season, or something else that happens by inches when it's right in front of you.

It was a feeling that was hard to get rid of, that I tried to ignore, though I knew I couldn't or shouldn't.

But I tried.

I buried myself in work, barely looking up from the moment I sat at my desk.

I made an extra effort to do things with Seth at night and on the weekends. I helped him with his homework. I bought him a new set of golf clubs, the clubs that would see him through till he was fully grown, and we made plans for the summer, discussed the rounds we'd play when school let out.

I made some time for Claire too. We cooked meals together, me acting as sous chef, chopping, tasting, and cleaning up when we were done. I got a sitter for Friday night so we could go to a movie she'd been eager to see for months. Afterward, we made love slowly, quietly, after we'd taken the sitter home and made sure that Seth was actually asleep instead of just pretending.

A weekend full of mending fences, literally — a whole section at the back of our lot was rotting into the ground. It wasn't my sort of thing, I wasn't any good at it, but I drove those fence posts home. I hammered the cross sections into place, so they were there, slightly off plumb, for all to see if anyone was looking, even though I knew I was the only one who was.

I was here. I was staying.

I kept myself busy so my mind wouldn't stray, so it would stay faithful.

I tried, but I couldn't do it.

A week after we got home, I got an email from Tish at 11:04 a.m.

I was sitting at my desk, my muscles aching from the unfamiliar effort I'd put in with the fence posts over the weekend, my mind aching too.

I know the exact time I received the email because I'd been watching the clock on my computer tick over every minute since I sat down at my desk, an email to her open but unstarted.

This was not the first communication we'd had since we said good-bye in L.A. — we'd kept up a light flow of banter since then — when we'd given each other a brief hug at the airport, when we'd wanted to hold on tightly. But I knew from the first and only word that this email was different, that somehow, in the symbiosis that was us on our good days, we were finally going to have the conversation we should've had, maybe a long time ago.

So . . . is all she wrote.

So, I answered back.

We have a problem, yes?

Houston, we have a problem.

Don't joke. Not now.

Sorry, I wrote.

It's okay. What are you thinking?

Honestly?

Of course. Always.

I paused, trying to think of what to write. Trying to put together the words I'd been puzzling out since I'd come home.

But there wasn't any way I was ever going to get this right.

2 + 2 = 4, I typed eventually with cold fingers and the blood rushing in my ears. *We learn this as kids, we teach this to our kids, and unlike so many other things we're told and we tell others, it's always true. So maybe that's why I've been trying to add all of this up. But the thing is, the awful thing is, whatever I do, it doesn't. No matter how I work it, no matter what formula I use, nothing works. Because what I can't take out of the equation are Claire and Seth, but — and this is harder to say than you could possibly know — if I take you out of the equation, it works. It adds up. At least, I think it does. I'll never know unless I do it, as much as I don't want to. Does any of this make sense? Can you possibly not hate me right now?*

I hit Send before I had time to stop myself. Then I sat staring at the screen, wondering what I had done.

I had to wait a long time for a response. Several hours. Hours with my door shut, my fingers pressed against my eyelids, trying to blot out the worst headache I'd ever had.

Then, finally:

Will you believe me if I say that your email is one I've known has been coming since the beginning? she wrote. *It's one I've known I should be writing. It's one I've written a million times in my head. For all the reasons you've said. For all the reasons we talked about. Of course I understand. Of course I agree. Of course you're right. Only, one thing, okay? I need a soft landing before we rip the Band-Aid off.*

I felt like I'd been punched in the stomach, but what other outcome was I hoping for? That she'd beg me to reconsider? That she'd have the missing piece to the formula I couldn't figure out?

Soft landing? I wrote back. *Band-Aid?*

Haven't you ever done that with Seth? When he's been hurt but then he's healed, and there's only the Band-Aid as evidence? So you say, I'm going to rip it off quickly at three, because doing it slowly is worse in the end. I'm thinking that if we do it on a count we agree on, it will hurt like hell for a moment, but not as much as a slow peel.

Okay, I get that, but not the soft landing part.

What I meant is that I need some time to heal before I get injured again.

How much time?

A long pause, then: *April 30.*

A month away.

Why that date?

I don't know. Jesus. It's not like there's a rule book here.

What do we do from now until then?

Act normal. Be friends.

And then what?

We rip off the Band-Aid.

We say good-bye?

We say good-bye. Yes?

One last moment of doubt, then I typed the last word. The hardest word.

Yes.

CHAPTER 34

Rondo

When Tish leaves my room, I realize I can't stay in this town any longer. Coming here in the first place was probably a massive mistake. Before, I had questions. Now, I have answers, but can I believe them? Can they possibly be true? If only there was a way to verify them, to not have to rely on the word of someone I don't know and, instinctively, don't trust.

I check online, and if I don't care about arriving in the middle of the night, I can get home. I throw on my clothes, zip up my suitcase, and drive the car back to the rental place.

I have half an hour to wait at the airport, and those minutes of being alone in a crowd give me an idea. Maybe there is a way I can check some of the things she said. Maybe there's some certainty I can seek from a third party.

It's late, but it isn't too late for that.

I use my phone to find a number on the company website and call.

"John Scott," he says, his voice rough and slightly slurred.

"Hi, John, this is Claire Manning."

A pause. Ice clicks in a glass. "Claire. My goodness. We didn't get a chance to speak . . . the other day. I'm so sorry for your loss."

"Thank you."

"I . . . did you need something?"

I can't think of any way to say this that won't make him think I'm crazy, but I have to go ahead anyway, and at least I have recent widowhood to fall back on if I ever need to explain myself.

"You were at that retreat, right? The one in Palm Springs?"

"Sure. It was a great time. Jeff won the men's golf tournament."

"He was excited. He . . . had fun. Look, this is going to sound nuts, but do you remember getting a prize pack there? A kind of gift bag?"

His ice clinks again, a deep swallow. "Um, oh, yes. That's right. Something with pictures, and a book."

"That's right. Would you still happen to have it, by any chance?"

"What's all this about?"

I almost hang up, but I have to know more than I care what he thinks of me.

"Could you check? It's important. And hard to explain."

"Yes, all right. Let me ask Cindy."

He clunks the phone down and I hunch over in my seat, a cramp of nervousness attacking my stomach. I take a few deep breaths and straighten myself up, looking out the black windows at the silhouette of the mountains that surround this Springfield.

A thud. A scrape. "Claire. You still there?"

"Still here."

"Cindy had it. She's such a pack rat." He chuckles. A bag crinkles. "You want the inventory?"

"You still have the whole thing?"

"It was in her processing area. She has this kind of staging area where she keeps stuff before she makes it into crafts."

"Right. Anyway, what's in the bag?"

"Give me a sec. Okay, one mini-album of photos from the office, courtesy of Jeff. He used one of those programs, like a computer thing—"

"Yes, I remember."

"Of course. Ha! Tom's going to die when I show him this one."

"Was there anything else?"

"Oh, yes. Sorry. There's a macramé picture frame. That must be from that crone from the other Springfield, and a book of . . . poetry it looks like. Ah, yes, the golf girl's daughter."

"Would you mind . . . is there an inscription in there?"

"Let me check." The pages flip. "Here we go. 'I'm a proud mama.' Huh. What an odd thing to write."

"Kind of, yeah. Anything else?"

"A corkscrew from the hotel, but that's it. Did you need anything else?"

"What? Oh, no. Only . . . did you notice if Jeff was . . . spending any time with anyone in particular over the weekend?"

He chuckles again. "You mean his dinner companion? I wouldn't worry about that. He rebuffed her pretty hard. Though I couldn't see why. Flirting never hurt anyone, am I right?"

I hear a voice squeak near him in protest. His wife, presumably, reminding him who he's talking to.

"Sorry, I —"

"No, it's all right." I force a laugh. "Flirting's fine. Did Tish . . . flirt with a lot of people?"

"Tish? Oh, you mean Golf Girl? No, it was that girl Tiffany, or Brittany, can't remember, anyway, that new girl from the secretarial pool. But don't you worry, like I said, Jeff shut her down." He lowers his voice. "I think she ended up hooking up with one of the bartenders. She was hot to trot, that one."

I force another laugh. "Don't you go spreading rumors about her."

"Who, me?"

The loudspeaker crackles to life and echoes through the nearly empty airport. My plane is starting to board.

"Where are you?" John asks.

"Nowhere. Could you do me a favor and not tell anyone about this call?"

"All right, if it's important."

"It is. I've got to go. Thanks for your time."

"Anytime. And again, we're so sorry for your loss. Jeff was —"

I end the call and look at the phone in my hand.

Is what he said enough?

Will anything ever be enough?

· · ·

Beth shakes me awake the next morning. An angry face greets me.

"Where have you been?"

I open my eyes. She's looming above me, her hair wild, shadows under her eyes.

"I left you a note. I wasn't even gone for twenty-four hours."

"I was worried sick about you."

I sit up and hug her to me. For once, it's not a touch I want to shrink away from.

"I'm sorry, Bethie. There was something I had to take care of."

She holds me away from her, giving me a hard stare. "You went to see her, didn't you? Tish?"

"Yes."

"What did you do that for?"

"I had to. I was going nuts trying to figure out what had happened, if anything had happened."

"And now you know?"

"No."

"Did you actually talk to her?"

"Twice."

"What did she say?"

"She denied it. She had explanations for everything."

"What kind of explanations?"

I fill her in. She sits on the edge of the bed, listening, pushing her bottom lip in and out, in and out.

"Do you believe her?"

"I want to. I really want to. But mostly, I wish . . ."

"That you never knew any of this?"

"Yes."

"I told you so."

There's a bark of excitement from down the hall. "Eureka!" Seth yells.

Beth and I run to the study. Seth's sitting at the computer wearing a pair of board shorts and a ratty T-shirt. Tim's standing over him, a big grin on his face.

"Hey, what's going on?" I ask. "Shouldn't you be in school?"

Seth shoots me a guilty look. "Uncle Tim said I could stay home, since he's leaving today."

"Oh, he did, did he?"

Tim gives me a slow smile. "I hope that's okay."

"It's all right. What was all the shouting about?"

"It's supposed to be a secret."

"Seth."

"Okay, okay. Jeez. We got into Dad's email account."

My heart skips a beat. I look at the screen more carefully. They really are in Jeff's email.

"Why were you trying to get in there?" I ask.

"It was supposed to be a surprise."

"What kind of surprise?"

"I wanted to get all of his friends' email addresses, to ask them to send photos, to make this kind of collage for you. Like that AIDS quilt thing. It's probably stupid."

"No, that's incredibly sweet."

He ducks the hand that's trying to pet the top of his messy head. "Mom."

"Well, it is, but how did you do it?"

I look to Tim. I can't remember if, in my panic yesterday, I told him I'd been trying to do the same thing. And if I did, how could he have let my son, maybe helped my son, get into a place that could hold something devastating?

"I didn't," he says, looking innocent. "Seth figured it out. Tell them."

"I remembered how he used that word *abacus* for everything, but that wasn't working. Then I realized that this email provider makes you add a number or a character or something to your password for better security or whatever, so I tried *abacus1* and that worked! See?"

He angles the screen so I can see it. My eyes devour the long list of emails. Ones from me, from Seth, from Tim, his mother, his college friends. I look and I look but I don't see her name anywhere, or even any name I don't recognize. She's not there.

She's not there.

"Claire, you okay?" Beth asks.

I lean my back against the wall.

"I'm okay," I say to Beth. "I think I might be okay."

An hour later, I'm driving Tim to the airport.

"You didn't have to take me," Tim says, his fingers drumming out a pattern on his knee.

"No. I wanted to."

"Well . . . thanks."

"Sure."

"Is it okay that I'm heading out? I could stay longer, if you'd like."

"It's fine. You have your life to lead, you should get back to it. We'll be okay."

I exit the highway onto the road that leads to the airport. It's so weird to think that yesterday I was on this same road, in a panic, heading toward I didn't know what.

"What about you?" I ask.

"Me? I'll be fine, but I'd like . . ."

"Yes?"

"I'd really like to stay in touch with you and Seth. I'm going to try to come home more. Be a man in his life."

"I'm sure he'd like that."

I pull into the drop-off area and cut the engine. It cycles down, knocking in a way I probably shouldn't ignore for too much longer.

"What about you?" he asks. "What do you want?"

I look at him. I used to think that he and Jeff looked so much alike, like brothers, of course, but something more than that. But now he's just Tim, and Jeff is . . . I'm not sure yet, but he's separate.

"I want you to be happy, Tim. I really do."

"Thank you."

He opens his door and climbs out. I pop the trunk. He removes his suitcase as I come up next to him.

"You know we can't . . ." I say.

"I didn't mean that. I wasn't trying to replace Jeff."

"That's the past, Tim. Us. It's what we used to be, and whatever happens, however I figure out how to be now, I've got to put all that behind me."

"For Jeff?"

"For all of us. Do you understand?"

"Of course."

He fiddles with his suitcase, trying to unlock the rolling handle. I click the plastic button that will release it and it springs to attention.

"Thanks," he says, but he won't look me in the eye.

"Hey, come here."

I put my arms over his shoulders. He straightens up and stands immobile for a moment, then puts his arms around my waist, pulling me in.

My face is in the front of his shirt. Citrusy laundry detergent fills my nostrils. I hug him tight, counting to ten in my head, because on ten I'm going to let him go.

"I never stopped, you know," Tim says. "Loving you."

I step back. It's been ten seconds.

"You don't have to say that."

He shakes his head. "And I wanted to tell you that, despite everything, how angry I was, how I took it out on you and Jeff, the crappy things I did, it was because I loved you. It was because I didn't know how to be without you."

"But you were always okay without me, Tim."

"I wasn't. Not really. But that doesn't mean I didn't understand why you wouldn't come with me, or why you chose Jeff. I never thought he was the consolation prize. I knew he wasn't. And I told him that."

"Did Jeff believe you?"

"Yeah, I think so."

I kiss him on the cheek. "Thank you."

"What for?"

"Telling me. It . . . it helps, knowing that Jeff believed it. It helps a lot."

"I'm glad I did something right."

"More than one thing."

He smiles and grabs the handle of his bag.

"Keep in touch," he says.

"You too. Have a safe flight."

He nods and walks away. I watch him until he's in the building, then climb back into the car and start the engine.

And when I look back, he's gone.

It's a strange next couple of days, and given how my life's been going recently, that's saying something.

But maybe it's more that it's strange inside my head, rather than outside, in my life, because as I go to work, and care for Seth, and half listen to Beth's (I can only call them) lectures, my mind is striving for forgiveness. No, that's not even the right word. My mind is striving for . . . *doubt,* and giving its benefit to Jeff. It's leaning toward acquittal, and eventually, toward innocence.

It's hard to say what tips the scales. I replay the conversation with Tish over and over and over, and a line from *Pride and Prejudice* keeps coming into my mind: "There was truth in his looks." But that thought is confusing because the person Elizabeth Bennet is talking about (the charming but dastardly Wickham) is anything but truthful. Regardless, Tish looked innocent, she sounded innocent, and everything she said, everything I could verify, has been borne out.

I spend more hours in Jeff's email, find and check his cell phone bills, and those bear them out too. There's nothing in his inbox, his sent messages, his deleted files, his calls or texts. If they communicated on a regular basis, then nothing she wrote was worth keeping, and that means something, doesn't it?

Doesn't it?

Jeff stayed. When I strayed, when I let him down, when I acted the fool with Tim, Jeff had every reason to pack up and leave. But he didn't. I stayed in Springfield for him, and he stayed for me.

This I know. Of this I am certain.

"What do you think you're going to find in there?" Beth asks when she finds me in front of the computer for the second morning in a row, still investigating, still searching, still trying to make sure before I decide.

I quickly close Jeff's email. "I don't know."

She's in her running clothes, sweat stained and smelling like salt. She sits on the floor, stretching her legs out in front of her.

"Remember what I told you about Rick?"

"About the cheating?"

She lunges at her toes. "About me wishing I didn't know."

"Is that really true?"

She sits back up, bringing her feet together in a yoga pose, centering her back. "Damned if I know."

"But that would've been a lie. He betrayed you."

"Everyone says that, but we all lie about things. Little things, big things. We all keep stuff hidden. And the longer you're with someone, the more stuff there is like that, I think. That doesn't mean he didn't love me, or wasn't good to me in other ways. So it made me think. Maybe honesty isn't always the best policy. Because him telling me about it was selfish. The only person it was going to make feel any better was him. So maybe if you make a mistake, you have to live with it by yourself, and that's how you fix it."

I twist Jeff's chair back and forth, back and forth, watching Beth trying to calm herself, trying to let her mind be.

"But what if you found out? Then wouldn't all the time you'd spent together between when he did it and when it came out, wouldn't that all be a lie?"

"People always say that too, but what does it really mean? Like, if you'd been on some great trip, say, and had an amazing time together, would that mean that it wasn't really amazing?"

"I've been trying to figure that out."

"Precisely, because it's not obvious. I've spent a lot of time thinking about this, too much probably, and I don't think that bad actions erase good ones. Not really."

"So if you could change the past?"

"I'd tell Rick to keep his goddamn mouth shut, and maybe we'd both be happy right now, instead of neither of us being happy."

"Are you really unhappy, Bethie?"

She opens her eyes, looks at me for a moment. "Sometimes. Yes. It's hard. It's hard to find someone you'd rather spend time with than not."

"I know."

"I know you do, honey. I'm sorry. I'm not trying to bring you down. I'm . . . I think you should let this go. I think you should focus on the good times you had together, the good life. Getting hung up on this, it's a way of not moving on, of keeping happiness at bay."

"Jeff only died a couple of weeks ago. I wouldn't be happy, anyway."

"Of course not, but you're going to be someday, and sooner if you focus on what used to make you happy." She comes up on her knees and rests her chin on my lap. "Don't let this define you, even if it happened. Jeff didn't tell you. He didn't leave. He chose to stay."

Beth's right, of course. Maybe not about all of it. Maybe not the part about knowing and wishing you didn't. Or maybe she is. She's the one who really knows. I only have suspicions, doubts, and circumstantial evidence. I can still decide. I can acquit Jeff. I can choose. Like I did all those years ago. I can choose him, and that's probably the right thing.

"Mom?"

"We're in here."

Seth pops his head in the door. "Can you give me a ride to school? I missed the bus."

I drive Seth to school, drop him off, watch him walk into the building, greet his friends, act normal.

When he's safely inside, I cue in the latest piece that Connie wants me to learn on my iPod, Mozart's Rondo in A Minor, a tricky piece I don't know. As it starts playing through the car's mediocre sound system, I think about what Connie told me about it. How the principal theme, or refrain, alternates with contrasting themes, called episodes, or digressions. There's always a pattern: theme, episode, theme, episode 2, and so on. The number of themes can vary, and the recurring part is sometimes embellished or shortened to provide variation. But when you listen to it, it's reassuring, because no matter how far off it goes, it will always come back to the theme. It always ends where it starts, telling a story, then folding in on itself, its end in its beginning.

When I get to my office at the daycare, I find Mandy Holden waiting for me, her foot tapping her impossibly high heel on the tiled floor.

"Claire, finally. I need to talk to you about something."

I sit down at my desk. My message light is blinking angrily once again. Maybe I'll return some calls today.

"What's up?"

"I've been thinking. Have you ever considered being open on the weekends?"

"Pardon?"

"The week's so hectic, and that's the only time I can really get things done, and it's hard to find reliable babysitters, so I was thinking, if you had Saturday and Sunday hours, maybe even half days, you could make a killing, right?"

I sit there watching her, speechless, no idea even where to begin.

"What do you think?"

"I think that's the craziest idea I've heard in a while."

"Come on, you won't even consider it?"

"That's when the staff is off. We need the weekend. I need the weekend. Surely you can understand that?"

"Oh, well, when you put it that way . . ."

I can tell she's thinking that if she sits here long enough, I might cave in to her insane idea. I start moving things around my desk, adjusting a pile of paper, opening my email, giving all the social cues that a normal person would know meant "We're done."

But not Mandy. "What if you hired additional staff?"

I shake my head as I notice a small card-sized box sitting on the edge of my desk. I'm pretty sure it wasn't there the last time I was in the office, but it looks vaguely familiar. I put my hand on it as Mandy watches.

"What's that?"

"Not sure." I pull off the lid. There's a sticky note inside with my sister's handwriting on it. It reads: *Found this at Mom and Dad's. I'll do it if you will.*

I pull the sticky off and underneath it is a yellowing pile of business cards. *James & James — Attorneys at Law.*

"Are you going to be a lawyer again?" Mandy's voice has a note of panic. "Are you closing Playthings?"

I close the box, smiling, which I'm sure was Beth's intention. "No, Mandy. Relax."

"But no weekend services?"

"No."

She sighs. "I kind of expected you'd say that."

"Good of you to ask, though. If you don't ask, you don't get."

"That's totally what I think!"

I smile at her, my eyes drifting away, and she finally gets it. She leaves, muttering something about checking on LT one last time. I reach for the box again, lifting the lid, taking out a card, wondering if this is something I should consider, if maybe Beth was being serious.

I connect my iPod to the speakers on my desk and cue up the Mozart again. I close my eyes and listen to the pattern, the little bits of the theme scattered through the different episodes, letting the music fill me, crowd out the lingering doubts and uncertainties, smoothing out the vast rocky unhappiness that fills me.

The main theme comes around again, tweaked, revised, but still close enough to the beginning to know that the journey hasn't been so far. There's a map back to where it all began.

It's an ordinary day at the daycare.

CHAPTER 35

Promises to Keep

I spend the days following my confrontations with Claire nervous, worried, waiting for the axe to fall.

But it doesn't.

I go to work expecting the phone to ring, an email to arrive, Brian to text me angrily that we need to talk, but none of that transpires.

Work is as it always is. People are hired, reprimanded, fired. They might be bringing a new round of consultants in. There's a rumor that they're thinking of eliminating the Safety Minute. I get two more citations for parking "illegally" in the parking lot. My pay will be docked next time, but I don't care.

Zoey returns to normal. Back to hiding behind her curtain of hair, scribbling on pieces of paper. Brian sticks to his word, the doctor's advice, and doesn't bring up next month's competition, one she's already registered and paid for. She does. She wants to go. She wants to show Ethan and the others that Nationals was an aberration. That she's stronger than that. Stronger than me.

And since she is, I'm all for it. Brian protests, but I talk him into it. We'll all go together, I say, and we'll see. If she can't handle it, then we'll leave. But if she wants to do it, if she feels like she has something to prove, let's help her do it.

Brian puts up a good fight, but his opponents are the two women in the world he loves most. We win.

By Friday, three weeks to the day that Jeff died, I'm starting to relax. Not entirely, but enough to have moments where I'm not feeling like some prisoner on death row, eating her last meal, spending her last hours with her family. And while Jeff's face, things he said and wrote, the way his hands felt on mine that day on the golf course, are a constant companion, they feel more like a scrapbook than a threat. I know why I took the risks I took, but I'm relieved too. That I can keep all this as a memory. That I seem to have contained the collateral damage.

I try not to ask myself if I would do it all again. What we were thinking. Why we were willing to get so close to risking everything, other people. I tell myself I got sucked into the happiness, the surge of the drug we seemed to make together. But was it real? Would it have survived in real life? Would it even have happened if we didn't have other lives to lead but had met each other first?

I guess everyone asks themselves that, about one thing or another. Jeff must've too. But we chose to give in to it. Each time we spoke or wrote or thought, we chose. The line we drew, the deadline, we chose that too. And it's because of this one thing, this one right thing that we were going to have to live with even if the worst hadn't happened, that makes me feel like, in some small way, I deserve this reprieve.

I probably don't. I probably don't deserve any of this. But I'm not perfect. Nobody is. And maybe I'm kidding myself, but it feels like I paid for my mistakes, that I'm paying still.

And Jeff? Jeff has paid in full.

It's Friday night. Brian's out on a call and Zoey's downstairs, waiting for me to watch *The Notebook,* a movie she's chosen because she knows it will be "so bad, it's good."

The popcorn's in the microwave, popping furiously, suffusing the house with its buttery smell.

"Mmooomm! Let's go!"

"I'll be down in a sec. Fast-forward through the previews."

I go to my bedroom, open a drawer, and feel for the back of it until my hand closes on the USB key. I pull it out by the lanyard, letting it dangle in front of me like a hypnotist's watch.

I cross to the bed where my laptop is sitting. I insert the USB key, click it open, and highlight the emails, my hand hovering over the Delete key. Erasing these will be like erasing part of myself, but I count to three quickly and do it. I pull the Band-Aid off. It stings, I'll have moments of regret, but everyone has regrets.

Then I open my email, go to the draft section, find the email I wrote weeks ago, right after we imposed the deadline. It's entitled, simply, *Good-bye*.

It contains the only poem I wrote about us, the one I read to myself on the plane ride to his funeral. It's not any good. It's not anything I would've published in any circumstances. But when the words come, and they come rarely now, I write them down. And when it came time to write this email, something I felt like I had to do in advance as part of my preparation, I thought of it and typed it out.

They're the words I wanted to try to leave with Jeff at his funeral. The words no one but the two of us should see.

My hand hesitates. Shifting between wanting to send the email and erasing it. But I know what I have to do.

I hit Delete.

I have promises to keep.

And I will keep them, always.

Epilogue

Turns out that Tish's room wasn't just on the same floor as mine, it was next to mine. We shared a wall, and that Saturday night, after the maybe-okay-she-probably-was-flirting-with-me dinner partner, and too many glasses of wine, I lay on my back in bed listening to her move around her room: the TV turning on; her smashing into something and swearing loudly; running the water for a bath.

I turned on my own TV then. I had willpower, and I was exercising it, but every man has his limits.

When I was about to drift off into a wine-fueled sleep, I heard her door open. I sprang from my bed and pressed my eye against the peephole, fast enough to catch her walking past, her hair wet, wearing the kind of loose cotton clothing one might wear as pajamas, hugging a blanket to her chest.

I pulled on my jeans and a sweatshirt, grabbed the bottle of wine I stole and the corkscrew from the prize pack. I almost forgot my room key, but remembered it right before my door clanged shut. Key in my pocket, I walked in my bare feet down the hall to the elevator.

Tish was nowhere to be found.

I waited thirty seconds for the elevator, and then I was in the empty bright lobby with one person behind the desk. Was I imagining it, or were the front doors still rattling in their hinges?

Outside, my eyes adjusted to the night, searching for movement. There. Something white in the dark, moving away quickly, a determined destination.

I followed her. I tried to walk casually, to make sure I didn't spook her like a deer in the woods. She was heading toward the golf course. The sky was clear and full of stars, the air damp from the irrigation system, the grass wet and slick against my tender feet. The moon was rising in a sliver.

She walked through the first tee-box. She seemed to be almost running away, or maybe I imagined that because in this moment it felt like we were running away together.

She stopped on the other side of the ladies' tee on the second hole and spread her blanket along the slope.

Then she whirled around and spoke into the night. "Why are you following me?"

I thought she sounded afraid.

"It's me," I tried to reassure her. "It's Jeff."

"I know who it is."

"Oh, sorry, I —"

"No, it's okay. You're here now."

She sat on the blanket. I hesitated for a moment, then followed her, setting the wine bottle down next to me. The corkscrew dug into my thigh, but I left it there.

"What are you doing out here?" I asked.

"Told you. Conjunction." She pointed to the sky. "See that bright star near the crescent? That's Venus." I nodded. "Now look left. That fainter star's Jupiter."

"Neat."

"Don't make fun of me."

"I'm not. Truly."

She turned toward me. In the darkness I couldn't tell if her face was registering annoyance or if she was trying to gauge my seriousness.

"I mean it," I said. "Tell me more."

She lay down, her legs straight below her, her arms at her sides. "If we had a telescope or binoculars, we could see Mercury too. And in a couple of months, Venus is going to traverse the sun, like an eclipse, and that's really rare. It only happens twice every hundred years or so. Not again in our lifetime."

I chuckled.

"What?"

"Nothing. You're cute."

"Gee, thanks."

"I don't mean it in a bad way. I like how enthusiastic you are about things."

"I talk too much."

"I like listening to you talk."

"Okay," she said, but then she fell silent while we watched the black sky and the bright stars.

I lay there, listening to her breathing, feeling the world spin underneath us, tilting as all the wine I'd drunk refused to release its grip.

After a while, I heard her shifting. I looked over. She was on her side, facing me, her hands tucked under the side of her face, her knees pulled up.

"This is . . . nice," she said.

I moved so my position mirrored her own. "It is. It really is."

"I'm glad I came."

"Me too."

I reached out and stroked the side of her face. She made a small noise — a gasp — but didn't pull away. Her skin was soft and my brain was fuzzy, and the only thing I could think of was how her lips would taste.

I kissed her. Hungrily. Slowly. Her lips. Her face. Her neck.

I kissed her.

And she kissed me back.

Afterward, we lay wrapped in the blanket, our clothes scattered around us, loose limbed, our tastes mixed together, mixing with the night, mixing with the stars. Our foreheads were touching, our mouths inches apart, then together again, small kisses, resting against each other. My thumb rubbed little circles into the small of her back, and her hands rested on my waist, holding me inside her. She was warm, so warm, and the small beat of her pulse kept me hard enough to stay in place.

"Someone may have heard that," she said eventually, smiling against my lips.

I kissed her again. "Shh. Don't worry. No one heard."

"The birds did. And the stars." She let out a sob, then caught it. I felt a few tears fall against my cheek.

"I'm so sorry, Tish. This is my fault."

"That's not why I'm crying."

"Why then?"

"Because I feel so happy. And I know I'm never going to feel this way again, and that makes me sad."

"Do you want to? Feel this way again?"

She pulled my hips closer and it was my turn to gasp. "Of course I do. But, we said . . . we said we wouldn't. We shouldn't have done this. We can't."

"We can't," I agreed, though maybe she'd been asking a question. "A one-time thing."

"Yes."

Her hands moved to my face, forcing me to look her in the eyes I was already lost in.

"We can't tell, okay? We have to . . . this has to be our thing. Ours."

"Yes."

"Promise?" she asked.

"Promise," I agreed.

Acknowledgments

Once again, thank you to my constant earliest reader, Katie, for giving me the courage to go on when it would've been easier to stop.

To my agent and friend, Abby Koons, for telling me this book wasn't good enough until it was. I am always listening, even when you think I'm not. And to the whole team at Park Literary for making it possible for me to keep writing books.

To my editors at HarperCollins Canada, Jennifer Lambert and Jane Warren, for being there from the beginning of this one and encouraging me to continue. And for that great lunch in Toronto, where we worked the last third out. And to my U.S. editors, Liz Egan and Katie Salisbury, for their valuable input.

To the writers in my life, particularly the members of the Fiction Writers Co-op, for being a source of information, a circle of trust, and a constant support system. And to Shawn Klomparens, whose own words made me want to do better this time around.

To Nancy Tan for copyediting this book with a fine hand. Any mistakes that remain are mine. To the whole team at Amazon/New Harvest for giving this book a chance at an American life.

To my friends Tasha, Phyllis, Janet, Tanya, Eric, Presseau, Candice, Kevin, Lindsay, Marty, Annie, Phil, Christie Brown, Patrick,

Sara, Dan, Katie, Stephanie, Thierry, Amy, and Olivier, what would I do without you?

To the many readers who've taken the time to write me or connect with me on Facebook and Twitter, your kind words mean more than I can say. And to all my readers, for making this fourth (!) book possible.

And to my family: Mom, Dad, Cam, Scott, Owen, Liam, Mike, Katherine, Alex, William, Jennifer, Michael, my amazing grandparents Dorothy and Roy, and David. Your love and support help get me through.

Book Club Questions for **Hidden**

1. Claire and Seth must cope with Jeff's sudden disappearance from their lives, and they are obviously in shock at the news of his death. Do you think it is more difficult to cope with a loved one's death if it's sudden than if you have had the chance to prepare yourself for their passing, as in the case of a prolonged illness?

2. Although Jeff is one of the narrators of the novel, he cannot answer any of the questions Claire is left with after he passes. How do you cope with unreconciled questions about someone you love after they are gone? Do you think Claire finds any amount of peace after visiting Tish?

3. Claire's family takes an active role during her bereavement — her parents, her in-laws, her sister, and even her brother-in-law surround and support her — while Tish must face the true extent of her grief alone. Have you ever had to hide the extent of your feelings from the closest people around you? Did you end up confiding in someone?

4. Is Jeff's pre-funeral a grim foreshadowing of his future, or just a cruelly ironic coincidence? Do you agree with Claire that "if you [are] prepared for the worst, you might make it come true"?

5. Throughout the novel, it appears that Jeff and Tish's affair begins

as an emotional attachment rather than anything physical. Is having an emotional affair as damaging to a relationship as a physical one? Is it possible to be in love with more than one person?

6. Jeff and Tish agreed to put a deadline on their relationship, after which they would no longer contact each other for the sake of their respective families. Have you ever had to end a relationship you really wanted to continue?

7. In the end, Tish holds true to her pact with Jeff to keep what happened between them a secret. Do you think it is selfish of her not to tell grieving Claire the truth? Do you think it is better for Claire not to know?

8. Do you think Claire is justified in going through Jeff's emails once she becomes suspicious of his relationship with Tish? Would you feel comfortable if someone close to you had access to your cell phone or computer?

9. Do you think Claire's past relationship with her husband's brother provides Jeff with some amount of justification for his affair with Tish, or contributes to its development? Do you think Jeff is truly reconciled to the idea of Tim and Claire's relationship?

10. Tish and her daughter, Zoey, are both intellectually gifted individuals, and they also end up sharing anxiety about performing in front of an unseen audience. Does this factor in to larger issues in the novel surrounding the idea of being observed and judged by others? How important are other people's opinions of you, and of your relationships?